Everything Started in the Bathtub

Conrad Smyth

Riot Electric Publishing

Published by Riot Electric Publishing, in 2024.

Library and Archives Canada Cataloguing in Publication Smyth, Conrad 1988-, author
Everything Started in the Bathtub / Conrad Smyth.

ISBN: 9781738106868 (hardcover) ISBN: 9781738106837 (paperback) ISBN: 9781738106844 (ebook)

Cover design by: Laura Boyle

RE001

www.conradsmyth.com

www.riotelectric.com

Everything Started in the Bathtub

CHAPTER 1

SEPTEMBER 2012

THE LAST YEAR HAS been the most distressing of my life. I have endured periods of paralyzing darkness, of anxiety so acute I could not draw a breath, and of the horrible sinking feeling brought on by absolute defeat. Everything is over and done with now, and there is finally peace to be had.

I left Stanford three years into an astronautics PhD. My work was a mess by the end. Lingering problems of combustion and propulsive efficiency destroyed what could have been a revelatory thesis on matters crucial to deep space exploration. All surviving research fragments and half-baked journal drafts are unfit for publication. The West Coast years represent an enormous failure—my biggest yet.

The decision to drop out came during a brief period of psychiatric hospitalization and much painful soul-searching. My early doctoral studies were marked by great promise and academic gusto, as is so often the case with an undertaking as mammoth as a PhD. Year two in Dr. Kaminsky's lab was the apex of potential, after which time output faltered and patience expired. In the end, the mind-exploding physics necessary for serious examination of propulsion efficiency in long-haul interplanetary space travel proved too convoluted for even me to process. I, Lesley Chang, have reached the extreme edge of my intellectual capabilities. I am twenty-five years old.

A cool breeze passes my face and rolls across deep green hills. Leaves float and sway overhead. I work to recapture feelings that are morphed by time and distance but still feel urgent, pointing to some serious revelation hanging just out of reach. For now, I am in a self-imposed quarantine from the headiness of the aerospace community. Work will materialize when I need it to. NASA, Boeing, Lockheed Martin, or some such organization, though the role will be removed from true cutting-edge science.

I have been back home in Woodbury, New York for the better part of a month. My mother, the indomitable Mary Anthony, is long divorced from my father and shows no outward desire to downsize or remarry. Last spring she accepted early retirement and is presently taking a dark-horse run for town council. It is as an official representative of my mother's campaign that I walk north up Dunderberg Road.

Tucked under my arm is a clipboard and novella-length voter list. Names and addresses are laid out in tight rows of Calibri text, the origin and accuracy of which are indeterminate. I make pitches that are precise and robotic: a smile and a handshake followed by a foldout pamphlet with campaign bullet points and candidate headshot, then the question of whether the resident would consider voting for Mary Anthony. Each front-door interaction is scored on a scale of 1 to 5, 1 representing adamant opposition to Mary Anthony, 3 being neutral or apathetic, and 5 indicating fervent and enthusiastic backing. The information will be used to target undecided voters via strategically timed phone calls and house visits, and as assurance that all categorical supporters are assembled on election day, no matter how infirm or otherwise immobile. Anyone assigned a 4 or 5 is asked if they will display a *Mary Anthony for Town Council* election sign on their property. So far, few are willing.

I step onto the front lawn of a modest split-level. A woman in her sixties holds a garden hose above bunches of manicured shrubbery. Mist sprays from the nozzle head and clings to the bush's wide foliage. The woman has a noticeable slouch and moves with the deliberate motions of a body resigned to chronic pain. She catches sight of me and loosens her grip on the nozzle's spring-loaded handle.

"Good morning. I'm campaigning on behalf of Mary Anthony for Town Council." I extend an arm and offer a pamphlet. "Would you consider supporting Mary this fall?"

The woman scrunches up her face. Her skin is yellow-hued and leathery. She has a vague and unplaceable familiarity, like she once spent time on local television or as a background accessory to an otherwise forgotten part of my childhood. The woman holds the pamphlet at arm's length. She squints. "I'd consider it, sure."

"Mary's platform highlights are listed in front of you."

"Hmm, you say she's running for town council?"

"That's right."

"Of Woodbury?"

"Correct." I take a breath. Words exit my mouth with a smooth and methodical cadence. "Mary has a wealth of professional and volunteer experience. She's a strong woman of extraordinary integrity and is committed to serving the people of this town. Can we count on your vote?"

The woman scratches her left ear. "You're saying Woodbury elects councillors?"

"We sure do."

"This is a new thing?"

"No, ma'am. Old as the town itself."

"And what do they do, these councillors?"

"Four councillors and the mayor oversee all important municipal matters: budgets, passage of bills, maintenance of common space…"

"What about the Hasidim?"

"What about them?"

"Over in Kiryas Joel." The woman shakes her head. "Personally, I have a lot of concerns with what's happening over there."

"That's Monroe's jurisdiction. Woodbury doesn't have anything to do with that."

"Well, we certainly live in strange times, don't we?"

"You could say that."

"Hmm." The woman turns the pamphlet over in her hands. "Mary's new to politics?"

"Officially, yes. She's a long-time public servant and community volunteer."

"A bureaucrat?"

"She worked in nursing for twenty years."

"Is that so? I spent a few nights at Orange Regional myself—heart trouble."

"I believe support for healthcare is integral to Woodbury's continued well-being."

"You don't say." The woman crosses her arms, left over right. "Now why is it that you're here and not Mary herself?"

"She's canvassing the north end of town."

"And you have nothing better to be doing?"

"I'm donating my time. I believe Mary will make an extraordinary trustee."

"What do you do for work?"

"Right now the election is my commitment."

The woman's expression turns maternal, and she rests a hand on my shoulder. "Unemployment happens to the best of us, dear. My nephew runs a placement agency in Syracuse. He says there's plenty of jobs out there if you're willing to work."

"Your nephew sounds like a sensible man." I run a thumb along my quarter-inch-thick voter list. "I should be getting on my way."

"We've all got things to be doing, don't we?" The woman tilts her head sideways. "Good luck next door. A renter. Just moved in and seems to associate in peculiar circles.

Something about this town feels off lately." She leans toward me and lowers her voice. "A man ran out from the backyard not even ten minutes ago." She traces a finger across her lawn. "He came right this way and hurdled clear over the hedge—soaking wet with hair down past his shoulders."

"That's very unusual."

"Did you see a naked man coming your way?"

"He was naked?"

"Naked as the day he was born. You tell Mary Anthony that nude men running our streets pose a risk to public safety." The woman brandishes the pamphlet at me. "Now, I couldn't care less about my neighbours' personal lives. If they want to hang out with long-haired nudists, that's their right—I'm a Democrat, for goodness sakes. The whole spectacle is just a little much for an old gal like me. Did I mention he was wearing running shoes? Why would a naked man wear running shoes?" She shakes her head. "I have no interest in seeing such flagrant flaunting of the human form. We have laws against that sort of thing! There are laws, aren't there?"

"There certainly must be."

"Thank God for that." The woman goes silent. I offer an outstretched hand and thank her for her time. She brushes it aside, saying she could use a walk and is overdue for a round of neighbourly visits. The woman is, in my estimation, a burgeoning Mary Anthony supporter. I choose not to rebuff.

We move together toward a red brick house set against a sloping lawn of yellow brush. Eyeball-rattling thuds sound from inside, as though something of enormous weight is being dragged across an uneven surface. I steal a curious glance at the woman—her appearance is unaffected.

The front porch creaks when weight is applied. Clumps of dead bugs hang from the awning's upper interior. I peer through the door's square window and see a foyer with cardboard boxes stacked two and three high. A staircase leads to the second floor. I raise my hand, and the house goes quiet, leaving a dull silence hanging in the late-morning air.

I knock three times on the extreme edge of the door—a canvassing trick of my mother's designed to resonate into all corners of a home. I hear loud crashing and a man's shrill scream. My chest tightens. I watch a white porcelain bathtub slide down the staircase and smash into the foyer's far wall, a mangle of human limbs squished between tub, floor, and plaster.

The woman manoeuvres past me with surprising agility and extends onto her tiptoes. "What on earth is going on in there?"

Adrenaline pumps. I rattle the lock and heave my body against the door.

"Is that a bathtub?" says the woman. Her tone is one of smug affirmation. "Highly irregular." She shakes her head. "I'll call the ambulance."

Chapter 2

October 2003

Light inside the Monroe-Woodbury High School weight room was artificial and low, filling the space with flat shadows and a palpable dinginess. Murray Buchanan stood with feet shoulder-width apart and a dumbbell clenched tightly in each hand. He pulled in a breath and lowered his hips until his buttocks was parallel to the floor, then exhaled and pushed up to a standing position. His quadriceps and calves strained. He repeated the motion a half-dozen more times and released his grip. The barbells landed on the rubberized flooring with a reverberating slam, causing a handful of junior varsity baseball players to look up in interest. "Woo-wee!" Murray grinned. "Everyone awake?"

A few players grunted unintelligibly. Murray pointed at a diminutive utility infielder named Irwin Bullwright, notorious for ducking line drives and plate performances best suited to the over-forty softball circuit. "Hold your back steady, would you? Don't let momentum do the work."

Irwin grimaced as he curled a weighted bar toward his chest. "I'm trying."

"That's right, baby. Target the muscles you're supposed to target!"

"Right. Got it."

"Coach Sanderson letting us in here unsupervised is a big deal—pretty sure it's a violation of school policy if we're going by the book." Murray held his hand palm up and guided Irwin's arms to the completed curl position. "I had to vouch that no one would mess around. We're here to get better and crack varsity."

Irwin lowered the bar to the floor and crossed his arms. "Team is going to be good this year."

"That's what I'm expecting."

"And playing with your brother will be great."

"Looking forward to that."

"I hear he's been pitching real fast."

"And much better control too. He's becoming an exceptional student of the game." Murray started up a slow throwing motion. "Most batters prefer hitting inside, so lefty pitchers like Don need to have an off-speed ball that breaks away from right-handed hitters—better odds for an out that way. Tom Glavine had it down to a science."

Irwin bobbed his head up and down. "The goal for me is to put on ten pounds before next season. All muscle."

"I like that," said Murray. "Remember that we lift to get stronger, but we also lift to prevent injury. You can have the biggest arms in the school, but they're not worth a damn if your shoulder is torn up."

"Right." Irwin moved toward the leg extension machine.

"And don't waste your time there. When are you going to make a move like that in the game of baseball? It's a knee injury waiting to happen, with negligible strength benefits. Do squats. Deadlifts. Anything but leg extensions."

Irwin squinted. "I saw your brother doing leg extensions last spring."

"On that thing?"

"Uh-huh."

"Must have been a joke."

"No, he was doing sets and everything."

"Doesn't seem right. Remind me to ask him about that." Murray grinned. "Fun fact, Bullwright. Did you know there have only been twelve unassisted triple plays in Major League history?"

Irwin shook his head.

"It's rarer than a perfect game."

"Wow."

"What do you think the most commonly executed configuration is?"

"Uh, not sure."

"Runners on first and second. Offence calls a hit and run. Shortstop catches the line drive, touches second base, and tags the runner from first. It happens in an instant, and it's a beautiful thing."

"That makes sense, I guess."

"Imagine if you pulled one off this season?" Murray tilted his head back. "Man, oh man, what a day that would be. You'd be a hero!"

"Probably not going to happen."

"Probably not, but you never know. Think positively!"

"I guess."

"How about this one: did you know LASER is an acronym?"

Irwin shook his head.

"Do you know what it stands for?"

"No idea."

"Anyone? Anyone at all?" Murray looked around the room. "That's light amplification by stimulated emission of radiation."

"Interesting."

"And did you know there were four twentieth century Olympic host cities that start with the letter 'M'?"

"Where do you get this stuff?"

"Name the two that aren't capital cities."

"I couldn't tell you."

"Munich and Montreal."

"Huh. And the two that were capit—"

"Moscow and Mexico City."

"I guess that makes sense."

Murray slapped his hand on the squat rack. "I'm done! Great morning, everyone!"

A few junior varsity players grunted in Murray's direction. He crossed the threshold into the changing room, stripping out of his gym clothes and putting on jeans and a t-shirt through which his unusually developed pectorals and biceps popped. Murray ran water over his face and adjusted his hair in the mirror. He emerged in the school's rear hallway and cruised through morning traffic toward the main office.

Large glass windows looked out into the lobby. The office was neutral-toned and sterile. Murray grinned at Ms. Uppendahl, Monroe-Woodbury's skeletally slim principal. "How are you, ma'am?"

Ms. Uppendahl wore her hair in a tight bun and did not smile. "Just fine, Mr. Buchanan. How are you?"

"No complaints." Murray scanned a paper pinned to the office bulletin board. "Hmm."

"Is there a problem?"

"Do I really need to say this stuff about the janitors?"

"Afraid so."

"Because if we're trying to fill time, there's plenty of other stuff I can talk about."

Principal Uppendahl narrowed her eyes. "You'll need to read what's on the page, or we'll find someone who will."

"Are you sure?"

"I am painfully sure, Mr. Buchanan."

"Right," said Murray. "Whatever you say."

"The Star-Spangled Banner" crackled through the school's intercom at exactly 9:05 a.m. Murray stood with his hand on his heart. His limbs pulsed from his morning's workout. He closed his eyes and swayed on the spot. There was calm. He thought of baseball and leaned into the office microphone. The anthem's last note faded into quiet static. "Good morning, Monroe-Woodbury High School. Today is Friday, October 10th, 2003." Murray sucked in a breath. "In football action, the Crusaders senior boys team plays tonight against the Warwick Wildcats in a game that has serious playoff implications. Kickoff is 8:00 p.m. sharp under the lights. Be there and cheer our boys on!" He paused. "In other news, the cross-country team travelled to Albany yesterday for a state-wide meet. Top finisher on the boys' side was Daryl Bok in twentieth place. On the girls' side, our very own Melissa Gorski put together a blistering fast run good enough for the silver medal. Great job to the whole team and much luck as the season continues!" Murray paused again. "A reminder to the entire student body that Art Guild Club meets after school in the second-floor studio. As always, all are welcome. On the science and technology front, the Monroe-Woodbury Robotics Club is seeking new members with an interest in software, hardware, design, and engineering. Please see Mr. Baker or Lesley Chang for more information." Murray took his hand off the microphone—FM radio static advertising a deferred payment mattress sale pushed through the speaker. He cursed under his breath and leaned forward. "Lunch special today is fajitas with salsa and sour cream for five bucks. The janitorial staff requests all students remember to clean up after themselves in the cafeteria, hallway, classroom, and anywhere else you may be inclined to leave a mess. Got that?" Murray let his words hang. "That's all for me, ladies and gentlemen. Have an extraordinary day and a safe weekend. See you tonight at the game." Murray stepped away from the microphone and turned to Principal Uppendahl. "Can we get someone in here to fix the static? It's killing me."

"You're trying my patience."

Murray raised a hand. "Enjoy the weekend, ma'am."

Chapter 3

April 2004

S TEAM FLOATED THROUGH THE hotel bathroom and covered all available surfaces with a thin layer of moisture. Byron Somerfield raised his left knee. Little bits of soapy residue funnelled to the heel of his foot, dropping into a brief free fall before breaking the water's surface with an almost imperceptible plop. He extended his leg straight out and held the position until his hamstring began to shake and quiver. He let the leg fall limp. It crashed against the bathwater with a smack, churning up a great mess of bubbles and accumulated body filth. Dissatisfaction had taken hold in the deepest recesses of Byron's consciousness. The intensity and frustrating vagueness of the feeling was unusual even for him, a boy of sixteen who spent extraordinary stretches of time lost in contemplation, routinely forgoing sleep in favour of overnight radio broadcasts from fuzzy-voiced hosts working through matters of human sentience and global extinction cycles and the sun's eventual destruction into a great dead mass of whatever yet-to-be-discovered matter might possibly be present at the time of catastrophic solar burnout. The tub settled around him. He gazed at the complimentary offering of travel-sized shampoo bottles and let his vision go blurry.

A quiet knock sounded at the door. Byron said nothing.

"Are you okay in there, dear?" His mother's voice was patient and soft.

"Getting out soon."

"It's just that I have to use the toilet."

"Out soon."

Byron emptied a tiny shampoo bottle onto his head. He lifted his feet and slid down the smooth enamel finish until he was parallel to the floor. The water created a distortion of auditory space as his heart beat in slow, rhythmic pumps. He farted. A short burst of bubbles trickled to the surface.

Byron brought his hands to his head and massaged his scalp. His hair felt creamy. He listened for the sound of his heartbeat again. His neck, tensed forward in an unconscious act of self-preservation, loosened slightly, bringing the back of his head to rest against the bottom of the tub and pointing his nose toward the ceiling. A stream of water rushed both nostrils. Byron flailed and righted himself. He pulled his head above water and blew through his nose, discharging a messy mix of bathwater and mucous. There was another knock. "Dear?"

"Getting out now." Byron stretched forward and pushed down on the drain plug. He lifted his hand, and the plug sprang open with a spring-loaded pop. He wrapped a towel around his waist and opened the bathroom door. A wave of cool air hit his bony chest. He shivered involuntarily.

Joy Somerfield patted her son's head. She stood five-foot-one, with spindly arms and legs. Her chin was pointed and severe from a radical underbite she said she never had the money to correct. She reminded Byron they would be leaving any minute and eased the bathroom door shut.

Manhattan was cold for April. Byron stood on the sidewalk, overdressed in an old down-filled jacket and gloves still damp from the previous evening's outing. He and his mother walked west as car exhaust circled around them. Byron took in a testing breath. Gasoline fumes tickled the back of his throat. He stuck out his tongue and coughed. A homeless woman began yelling obscenities and prophesying end-times. Joy quickened her strides. Little bits of perspiration clung to Byron's lower back and shoulders, weighing down his bought-specially-for-this-trip collared polo shirt with a wetness that made him wiggle and squirm.

Byron spotted his father at 89th Street and 5th Avenue. James Somerfield was round and balding. He wore a shabby windbreaker and faded Converse sneakers. The streetlight changed from green to yellow, and traffic disintegrated into a panicked series of accelerations and merges. Byron moved between gawking tourists and seasoned New Yorkers projecting stoic self-absorption. His father's face broke into a grin. Joy held a thin smile and stared expectantly at her husband. He waved his hand dismissively and gestured toward the white-spiralled building in front of them. His nose crinkled in a mock expression of olfactory disgust. "We come to the greatest city in the world and bring the kid to the Guggenwhatchamacallit?"

"The Guggenheim."

"All I'm saying is there's culture everywhere—no need to buy a ticket for it."

"We talked about this."

"We did?"

Joy ran her tongue over her teeth, like she always did when loading up for a verbal sparring match. "Yes, we did."

James Somerfield shrugged. "Whatever you say." He laid a hand on the back of Byron's neck and guided him through the museum entrance's tinted double doors. Voices and footsteps echoed through the airy expanse of space as visitors milled around the atrium. A white walkway twisted gradually upward, passing over itself a half-dozen times before plateauing below an intricate glass-panelled dome. The Somerfields lined up along a rope strung between metal barrier posts and bought tickets from a vest-wearing man at the box office. Byron crossed the floor and homed in on a yellow canvas depicting a flask and goblet amongst pieces of fresh fruit. Joy touched her son's shoulder. "This is a good one. Classic post-impressionist still life."

Byron stared.

His father pointed to the canvas. "Cezanne, right? His portraits are astonishing. I can leave everything else."

"Don't be a prick," said Joy.

James Somerfield snorted and shuffled up the ramp. Byron continued to stare, taking in the slightly oblong shape of the flask and the messy, ambiguous background, making it unclear if its design was careful intent or an afterthought disguised as infallible artistic license. He ascended the floor slowly, dragging his right hand along the outside wall and keeping a lookout for employees, since the act of touching gallery space, while not explicitly forbidden as far as he knew, did not seem right considering the carefully curated surroundings.

Byron stopped at a rectangular painting the size of a dinner table. Thin bits of black paint started up on either end of the canvas and met in a crescendo near its middle. Byron titled his head. He squeezed his eyes closed and opened them slowly. The colours and shapes gave the faint suggestion of a soaring pterodactyl. He stared ahead as murky voices pushed through the back of his consciousness. His heart rate kicked up. He unfocused and refocused his eyes, going so far as to turn around, spread his legs, and peer at the piece upside down until he inadvertently tripped up an elderly man, then went scampering to his father.

"Had enough?"

"I don't know what to say."

"Say whatever you want, kiddo."

"This place is amazing!"

James Somerfield frowned. There were deep wrinkles around his mouth and cheeks. Light brown bags lined the undersides of his eyes. He gestured to an enormous canvas covered with teal brush strokes. "You like this?"

Byron shrugged. His father chuckled and shook his head in faux condescension. Joy Somerfield, her face tight and severe, stepped toward her husband and began a low-toned discussion on the subjective quality of work they were exposing their son to, expressing conviction that Byron deserved a well-rounded appreciation for the arts, while James rolled his eyes and wrote off the whole abstract expressionist movement as asinine and not worthy of serious attention.

Byron slunk away as his parents' exchange devolved into less and less eloquent points of contention. It was his mother who deployed the guaranteed argument-ender, citing the now-vacant basement art studio a younger James Somerfield had spent much of his non-work time holed away in, never outwardly admitting though undoubtedly hopeful he could one day make a go of it as a professional painter. His production during that time had been—Joy shouted—unfit for any gallery of repute, and his best bet for artistic legacy was to paint over every last work and hope to God the next person to touch a brush to one of his canvases had talent superior to his own, which, as a matter of probability, was nearly certain.

Joy and James Somerfield were hysterical. Gallery-goers pointed and whispered. Byron zoned in on a painting with singular focus, mesmerized by the textured greens that bunched together and produced a beautifully complex third dimension. He tingled. Something had changed. He moved closer and noticed subtle strokes in the dark background, dividing the canvas into perfect quadrants. He felt dizzy and weak. The room swayed and went fish-eyed. His thoughts were disjointed. The work in front of him was art—well within the grasp of anyone desirous of meaning and purpose. Byron's consciousness burst with expression and desire. Everything was taken care of. He would need to start immediately.

***

The walls of Monroe-Woodbury High School were painted concrete the colour of weak porridge. Halogen lights dotted the ceiling and produced low-frequency humming only detectable after long stretches away from the building. The smell of cafeteria cooking oil hung heavily in the air.

Murray Buchanan was scheduled to write an honours accounting test first period after lunch. His performance had been strong all semester—an untarnished 100% grade over a half-dozen homework assignments completed between ball practice, Yankees games, and vigorous masturbatory sessions. Under normal circumstances, he would retreat to the library for depreciation and amortization cramming. On this day, he bee-lined toward the gym with the singular focus of a young man overcome by desire. Murray knew monstrously difficult challenges lay ahead. To lose focus risked everything imploding. He refused to entertain the thought.

A small collection of baseball players huddled in a semicircle just off the Phys Ed office door. Murray had performed well on the junior varsity squad his freshman and sophomore years. The next two seasons would decide his feasibility as a prospect in both MLB draft and NCAA scholarship circles. Now was the beginning of serious high school baseball, when scouts sat in the bleachers and postseason games aired on local television. Life-changing decisions would be made. Murray's upperclassman seasons meant everything.

The assembled group skewed heavily athletic, with a handful of team shoo-ins sporting the enormous traps and ox-like glutes of serious weight room devotees. Murray settled behind a senior wearing scuffed jeans and a backward Mets cap. He smirked at Irwin Bullwright.

"Going to be a good team this year, don't you think?" said Irwin.

"You know it, baby." Murray spoke without making eye contact.

"You and your brother both. That's a one-two punch—some serious Buchanan muscle power."

"Don topped 90 MPH the other day."

"And you behind the plate catching heat?" Bullwright shook his head and whistled.

The Phys Ed office door rattled and burst open. Coach Sanderson, a beefy and bespectacled man, nodded at the boys. He pinned a printed piece of letter-sized paper to the Athletics Department bulletin board and muttered his congratulations. The mass of bodies shifted. Murray waved Bullwright off as a visceral surge of excitement ignited. He stared. The paper glowed amongst outdated winter sport schedules and faded photographs of long-graduated student-athletes. Murray extended his right index finger and ran down the printed names. He blinked and then read the list a second time. Then a third.

He, Murray Buchanan, a two-year JV starting catcher and steadfast home run threat, did not make the final cut.

"Hey, Buchanan!"

Murray turned and saw his brother ambling forward. Don's body was lean and muscular—noticeably taller than Murray's six-foot-one. Murray looked to the floor. "Can't talk now."

Don put a hand on Murray's shoulder and steered him around a hallway corner. "It's a tough break, Mur."

"A tough break? Come on, Don. This is terrible."

"Lots of returning seniors and not many roster spots."

"Fourteen fielders, five pitchers, two catchers, and I can't make the team? What am I supposed to do now?"

"Play league ball this summe—"

"What good is league ball if I can't even make varsity?"

"Listen to me: you get better this summer and make varsity next year."

"What about all the camps and extra coaching Dad paid fo—"

"Don't worry about Dad."

"How could I not worry? He's a menace."

"It comes from love."

"Remember how he said the money spent on baseball was just a loan until we went professional?"

"He was joking, Murray."

"What if he wasn't?" Murray moved closer to Don and lowered his voice. "Did you see some of the names up there? I understand Jenkins, senior year and all that stuff, but Bullwright? Irwin fucking Bullwright surviving two rounds of cuts? I outplayed him. No question in my mind."

Don's face looked strained.

"Why did your forehead just wrinkle like that?"

"It doesn't matter."

"Your nose went all tight, like you just smelled something real bad."

"Don't worry about it."

"Worry about what?"

"It's tough to say."

"What does that mean?"

Don's cheeks stretched, and he sucked in a breath. "It means you missed a play here or there that might have cost you a spot on the team."

"Missed a play? I thought I was great. Next to you, I thought I was the best player out there."

Don shrugged. "Like I said, a lot of good talent."

"This isn't some behind-the-scenes manoeuvre, is it? Was Bullwright a sympathy case? Did your dominance last year create unrealistic expectations for me? Was I too flashy? Not flashy enough?"

"I don't have any answers for you."

"Did one of the seniors complain? Were my dugout games alienating?"

"I don't k—"

"Etymology of the periodic table? US presidents in alphabetical order forward, then back, then forward again? That stuff played great in JV. I was killing time!"

"Coaches want focus."

"*I'm focused!*" Murray's voice cracked. "I want this more than anything."

"Then shut up and play baseball—forget all the other shit."

"But it's an inherently boring game. Energy was low. I was rallying the guys!"

"Learn from this, work hard, and make the team next year."

"So I can sit on the bench with a bunch of stoned jocks? Forget about it. I need to start getting looks now. I've been playing high-level ball for five years. This is th—"

"Wait, what do you mean 'looks'?"

"Looks like you're getting—a mediocre senior year and you'll have tons of Division I offers and some MLB interest. Overperforming will send you into the stratosphere." Murray paused. "Why does your face look all scrunched again? Why are you shaking your head?"

"Come on, Murray."

"What are you talking about?"

"I wouldn't count on that."

"Wouldn't coun—why not?"

"There are a whole bunch of really great ball players out there."

"So? You're doing fine. You're a bona fide stud—a blue-chipper. Why not me too?"

Don was silent.

"Are you saying I'm not good enough?"

"I'm saying you might not be good enough."

Murray ran both hands through his hair. He stood, fingers tightly gripping his scalp, pivoting at the waist from side to side. "Well, shit, Don. Thanks for telling me."

"Or maybe you *are* good enough. These things are hard to project. Just be prepared for a whole lot of disappointment."

"What am I supposed to do with that?"

Don craned his neck as a rumble of commotion started up down the hall. Sounds of rambunctious chatter and many pairs of clomping feet grew louder. A batch of newly confirmed varsity team members rounded the corner. The group's tone was upbeat, full of anticipatory excitement and promise for the season ahead. Don looked back at Murray. "You've got plenty of talent outside baseball—much more than me."

"Who cares? I'd rather be a better ball player."

"Remember what Dad said the other day? 'If you want to make it in this world, you damn well better be good at something.'"

"Yeah."

"With your smarts, there's plenty you can accomplish."

"I don't find that comforting."

"You should." Don moved toward the group. "We'll get you where you need to be."

Murray's arms dropped from his head and hung limply at his waist. He watched his brother slip into the mob of ball players and march toward the school's rear exit. Don's strides were smooth and effortless. His kinesics radiated innate social intelligence and irrefutable cool.

Honours accounting began in less than an hour. The day's test would cover cash flow, profit and loss, and accruals. Murray would ace the questions, even now, when the idea of committing attention to last-minute study was an impossibility. He considered the idea that coaches were brushing him off. He thought of the team's tight contingent of mind-altering substance enthusiasts, showing up to tryouts high, and in the case of the odds-on starting shortstop Evan Friedman, seriously hopped up on nasally ingested junk.

Murray's eyeballs panned from one side of the hall to the other. His skin felt hot and clammy. He evened his expression as Irwin Bullwright approached him. "Hey! Are you okay?"

"What do you mean?" Murray spoke slowly and deliberately.

"It was just, you looked sort of off."

"Nothing you need to worry about."

"Sorry about not making the team."

"It's not your problem."

"A few plays didn't go your way. You'll make it next year. You have to!"

"What plays? What are you talking about?"

Bullwright looked to the ceiling. "Oh, there was that one pitch you let through. Jansen sent it right down the middle. Coach probably didn't like you losing that. There was also the pickoff attempt." Bullwright raised a hand above his head. "The one you threw up here—can't make a tag with that. There was al—"

"You saw that?"

"Well, sure. But don't let it bother you. We're always getting better, right?"

"Until we start regressing."

"But that won't happen for years. No, you've got lots of promise, Murray. Don't worry about that."

"Maybe."

Bullwright smiled weakly and said he had to be off, mumbling something about an unfinished essay on constitutional amendments. Murray stood in stasis. He thought of the time spent fixated on obsessive athletic development and how superfluous it might all be to whatever happened next. His mind veered toward convoluted thoughts of school, his father, and Don's runaway successes. Murray lifted a foot and stepped forward. He would spend the rest of lunch in the library. There was nowhere else he cared to go.

***

I sit in a hard plastic chair and wait for some indication of what will happen next. The walls are lined with oblong bookshelves jammed with textbooks and stuffed binders. There is a strong smell of industrial cleaner. In front of me is Ms. Uppendahl, wearing a wool turtleneck and black-rimmed glasses. Her face hints at requisite levels of professional educator kindness, but also the serious no-nonsense edge that earned her the nickname "Principal Sarge" among much of the Monroe-Woodbury student body. I rest my hands on my lower belly and look to my mother, Mary Anthony. She stares at Ms. Uppendahl in tense silence. Her round face is curious and alert.

To Sarge's immediate right is my functions teacher. Mr. Marcotte's forehead is creased with intense concentration. He wears a white button-down shirt against which the outline of a soft midriff is visible. He sits, back straight and head tilted forward, looking intently at Ms. Uppendahl.

"It seems Ms. Chang has been involved in an incident of sorts." A subtle sneer creeps across my principal's face as she turns to Marcotte. "Is that correct?"

Mr. Marcotte dips his head in a slow nod.

Sarge's expression tightens. "Your class is wrapping up its unit on trigonometric functions?"

"Yes."

"And you employed a system of reward to encourage competent demonstration of the material?"

Mr. Marcotte's head rocks back and forth.

"In this case the reward was…?"

"Candy," says Mr. Marcotte. "There's a jar of candy in the classroom. Fruit chews, specifically."

"Of course."

The insides of my palms begin to perspire. I say nothing. There is a rustling to my left as my mother readjusts her weight. "And?"

"And what, Ms. Anthony?"

"And what happened next? You've called me here in the middle of the workday." My mother's tone is sharp, her childhood East Texas accent pointed and accusatory.

I watch Sarge make the smallest of glances toward a metallic desk clock embossed with a phrase I know to be Latin but cannot make sense of. The time is almost 4:00 p.m. She smiles again. "It seems Mr. Marcotte's incentivization runs in direct contrast to your daughter's, shall we say, ideological belief system."

Sarge turns and faces me directly. She lets her words hang. The ends of her lips curl upward.

Mr. Marcotte exhales. "A handful of pupils were lagging behind the rest of the class. This is not unusual, of course. I've known many intelligent students who simply cannot grasp this particular element of the curriculum."

"And the candy jar?"

"We do a quiz every Friday—a series of problems on the blackboard. Each student providing a correct answer earns a candy."

"And the evaluation is designed to get markedly easier, so that all students have opportunity for success?"

I raise a finger and open my mouth. Sarge holds up her right hand. Mr. Marcotte nods with the thinnest of smiles. "That's correct. Lesley recently expressed concern about the quality of candy, especially toward the end of the exercise."

Sarge locks her gaze on me. Her eyes are sharp and war-like. I keep myself steady and worry that a pronounced facial reddening will betray my manufactured appearance of calm.

"Is that correct, Ms. Chang?"

The gaze of everybody in the room are on me now. I poke at an eraser head-sized mole just below my hairline and resettle my weight against the plastic chair. "Well, it—"

"Yes, but is that correct?"

"I guess so."

"The candy Mr. Marcotte buys—on his own free time with an extremely modest stipend the union nearly lost in its last round of collective bargaining, I might add—is packaged in a mixed assortment of flavours. If I understand correctly, there is a firmly established flavour hierarchy among you students?"

"Sort of."

Sarge counts on extended fingers. "Strawberry, orange, cherry, lemon, and banana—in that order." She turns her whole body toward Mr. Marcotte. "It was last Friday that Lesley first became disruptive?"

"It's a matter of how you define disruptive, really."

"What did she say?"

"She sai—"

"Excuse me." My mother leans forward. "Let's let my daughter tell the story, shall we?"

Sarge's eyes are saucer-like. Her face is livid. "That sounds like a marvellous idea, Ms. Anthony."

I swallow. "Uh, I guess it just doesn't seem fair." My voice echoes and distorts as unpleasant sensations kick around my chest cavity. "Mi—"

"No names, please."

"Some kids are struggling. It's not right that they have to settle for banana candy."

"There are people who like banana candy. Mr. Marcotte is offering choice."

"No one likes banana candy. It tastes like medicine."

Sarge narrows her eyes. "Perhaps this will provide motivation for students to improve their standing. A little bit of remedial work could bump them up to a more palatable flavour, say, lemon?"

"They do get extra help. I just don't see why they should be penalized!"

There is a long pause. I hear an engine start up in the parking lot. Sarge checks the time again. "Tell me something, Lesley."

"Okay."

"Do you perform well in functions?"

"Sure."

"You're being modest. The board's standardized testing indicates you're an exceptional student—prodigal, even. Mr. Marcotte says you're the best he's ever taught."

"What does that matter? Why are you penalizing kids who aren't excelling?"

Sarge looks thoughtful. She leans her chair onto two legs. "Classroom spending allowances are extremely small. What do you propose we do?"

"Well, we cou—"

"I am all for a secondary market in which candies are swapped after they've been awarded. What do you think about that?"

"Someone will still be stuck with banana."

"What about two banana for, say, a single lemon? Would that be fair?"

"I don't think so."

"How about sponsorship of some kind? Private funding? Do you have a part-time job, Ms. Chang?"

I nod to indicate the affirmative.

"Would you consider shoring up the difference?"

"Maybe. I hadn't really thought of that."

"And tell me, would you willingly give up your preferred candy to someone else, knowing you had earned it and they had gotten a free ride?"

"I might."

"But would you, really?"

"It's possible."

Sarge stares at me silently. My innards feel as though they are squeezing themselves dry. My mother clears phlegm from her throat and swallows. "I'm still not sure why we're all here. I left work early for this."

Sarge is unflinching. "Remind me what you said when the candy jar came around last week?"

"Well, I, uh, asked Mr. Marcotte for more strawberry candies—enough for everyone in the class."

"And Mr. Marcotte explained that there was no budgetary justification to buy up extra bags of candy so students could cherry-pick what they wanted and discard the rest?" Sarge pauses. "No pun intended."

"He said something like that."

"It sounds awfully wasteful and inefficient, doesn't it?"

"It doesn't have to be."

"But it is! We simply don't have the money for what you're suggesting." Sarge looks quickly to my mother and back to me. "That was last week. I've heard differing accounts of what transpired over lunch today. Would you tell me your version of events?"

I readjust my buttocks against the chair. The seat is rigid, perhaps even purposefully uncomfortable. "Nothing, really. I got to talking with some of the other students."

Sarge gestures for me to continue.

"We agreed that this whole candy business seemed a little unfair."

"And then what?"

"Not much happened after that, really."

Sarge brings her hand down on the desk with a dictatorial slam. "You organized the student body in direct opposition to Mr. Marcotte!" Little bits of spittle fly from her mouth. "You corralled the entire class onto the football field and forced them to refuse all further functions evaluation unless strawberry chews were made available to every last student, no matter how daft or mathematically incompetent!"

"Wait." My mother holds up a hand. "You led the class in a coordinated act of rebellion?"

I poke at the mole below my hairline again and say nothing.

"Well, that's marvellous!"

Sarge's face bulges. "I hardly need to tell you that I, as a public educator, am unequivocally pro-solidarity. This is something else entirely."

"As it stands right now, Lesley has done nothing wrong."

Sarge's voice settles back to socially acceptable indoor levels. "Unity disintegrated as soon as that first strawberry chew was made available to the class-at-large. A student was offered the jar and took an opportunity for individual short-term gain. Lesley confronted the scab."

"And?"

"There was a verbal exchange. Then all hell broke loose. Pardon my language."

"Can you be more specific?"

Mr. Marcotte raises his hand to shoulder level. "If I ma—"

"Go ahead, please."

"Lesley and the boy got into a shoving match. I moved in to separate them. An elbow accidentally connected with the jar and knocked it to the floor."

"How do you know it was an accident?"

Mr. Marcotte shrugs. "It didn't seem intentional."

"And then what happened?"

"The jar shattered."

"And?"

"The class swarmed."

"I was privy to the height of the mayhem," said Sarge. "The situation was bordering on anarchical—the worst I've seen in all my time as an educator."

My mother's expression is apologetic. "Everything I'm hearing sounds like a problem with control of the student body. With all due respect, that falls to the staff."

Tendons tighten on Sarge's neck. "Your daughter's actions led to one instance of broken glass causing lacerations to a boy's palms, two minor tramplings, and one Heimlich manoeuvre performed admirably by Mr. Marcotte on a student who managed to stuff a full dozen fruit chews into his mouth and nearly paid the ultimate price." Sarge takes in a breath. "Certain preventative measures must be taken. Lesley is being suspended three days, effective immediately."

Involuntary tears burst from the sides of my eyes. My mother begins a heavy verbal deluge. Sarge deflects words like *cowardice, incompetence,* and *thuggery* with seasoned prowess. My mother shifts so that her weight moves onto her hands and her rear goes airborne. I watch the two argue for a full three minutes before my mother throws up her hands in a some-people-are-beyond-help sort of way and falls back into her chair, breathing heavily, and her face a dark plum colour. Sarge keeps her expression steady. Mr. Marcotte is silent.

"Excuse me," I say. The gaze of everyone in the room are on me again. "What about the candy jar? It's still not fair, is it?"

Sarge squares her face to my own and assumes a thin smile. "How are things at home, Lesley?"

"Fine."

"Forgive my asking, but I understand your parents separated recently?"

I nod.

"And your father now lives in Buffalo? Thomas Chang, is it?"

"That's right."

"What the hell does that have to do with anything?" says my mother.

"Do you see your father much these days?"

I shake my head. "Not as much now."

"He's quite successful, isn't he? A doctor of some kind?"

"He does ear, nose, and throat."

"I just worry what it all means for a young woman like yourself." Sarge pauses. "Your motivation. Your drive. Your ambition. Where does that come from?"

"Not sure."

"Any idea at all?"

I shrug. "I like doing good work, I guess."

"Great work."

"Sure. Great work."

"And you like being told you've done great work? By your teachers like Mr. Marcotte? And your parents? Your father?"

"I guess I like that too."

"Because it's important your talent be properly guided."

"Lesley's well-being is my top priority," says my mother. "Whatever you're implying here, I don't like it."

"Ms. Chang, I expect you'll do great things one day."

I say nothing.

"Our job at Monroe-Woodbury is to offer an education that positions you for a lifetime of success." Sarge's posture loosens for the first time. "How old are you, Lesley?"

"Sixteen."

"And how can you even begin to think you know your way around this world?"

My mother snorts. "Lesley is extremely mature for her ag—"

"From what Mr. Marcotte says, you have nearly limitless potential." Sarge looks grim again. "You also have a severe lack of appreciation for respect and order. It will serve you well to reflect on how your actions have failed your goals. I expect a little tact next time you deem something objectionable." Sarge stands up. Her chair makes a shrill squeak against the public education-grade linoleum. She extends a hand to my mother and nods—an acknowledgement that we will all meet again soon.

Chapter 4

November 1995

The classroom's desks are lined up in rows. My teacher, Ms. Samson, walks the aisles with a parent volunteer. I grip my pencil and lean toward the test booklet's last page. My stomach cramps. Breakfast was eggs, peanut butter, and, without my mom's permission, two cups of instant coffee. My hands shake badly.

Today is reading comprehension. Questions are multiple choice and short answer. Earlier this morning Mitchell Matthews started crying when Ms. Samson explained that several answers could be right, and it was our job to choose the answer that was most right. He was taken into the hall and did not return.

The air here is warm. I watch Ms. Samson play with the blue shawl wrapped around her shoulders. I know nothing about her personal life but know the parent volunteer is the mom of a kid two grades above me. I tap my pencil on the desk and think about giving up everything to be a mom. The trade-off makes no sense. I hope to never do it.

Three days of standardized tests are happening across the state. Us students will be awarded a grade of "Excellent", "Good", "Satisfactory", or "Needs Improvement" in reading, writing, and mathematics. According to Ms. Samson, we should not worry about individual performance. She says results will act as a report card for teachers, with serious adult stuff like jobs and money at stake. Still, I want to be the best and think I can accurately rank each of Woodbury Public School's sixty third-grade students by smarts. Everyone except the boy sitting to my right.

Byron Somerfield has pale lips and strange eyes. He spent most of the morning writing quickly and is still now. His body is thin and shakes a little bit. He is famous around the school for breaking his arm playing touch football three different times. I have never heard him speak unless called on. Anything he does say is odd, like he's in a world that is entirely his own.

I blink and look down at the page in front of me. *What do paragraphs 2-3 tell us about how Tom is feeling?*; *Explain why Sammy was scared in paragraph 4?*; *How did Jessica solve her problem in paragraph 5?* I scan the reading package. Paragraphs are numbered down the left side. The story is boring. I write a series of short sentences and put down my pencil, then begin to worry I have messed up a trick question somewhere. I turn to the front of the booklet and recheck all my work, which takes twenty minutes. There are no changes.

Strong test scores would please my parents greatly. Both are extremely smart. My mom is the star from a big rural Texan family and my father is the only child of Chinese immigrants. It is my mother people say I most take after. She tells me all the time about the greatness she knows I will achieve.

I like math the most. Sometimes I fantasize about becoming an astronaut like Sally Ride but worry about how physically tough space travel is. So much of being an adult seems miserable—stressful stuff necessary for survival but no fun at all. I think of the blank looks on Mom and Dad's faces when they come home from work and worry about my own future. I wonder how Sally Ride felt after a hard day at NASA. I hope, at least, that she was happy.

There is noise from across the room. Murray Buchanan, the tallest boy in the class by at least an inch, has his left hand raised. His right hand drums on his desk. The parent volunteer rushes toward him. She points to the wall clock and raises a finger to her mouth. Murray shrugs. He pushes back from his desk and moves down the aisle toward the exit. We make eye contact, and he puts on a show of dusting off his hands. His face is cheeky and entitled. He disappears into the hallway as Ms. Samson hurries after him. I believe he is the only third-grader to beat my raw intelligence. He's also an asshole. I grimace. My stomach feels like it is churning through itself.

The room settles into full silence. The parent volunteer's jaw is clenched. Students write quickly. My intestines gurgle. The powerful urge to fart hits me in waves. I clench. A groan escapes my mouth. I relax. The smell is immediate and unusually bad. I look around the room for signs of acknowledgement and keep my face quiet. Byron glares toward me and covers his booklet with his hand.

I sit in silence. The smell has gotten worse. I watch the parent volunteer's face. Students are looking around at one another. No one is saying anything.

There is a commotion as Murray runs back into the room holding a bag of Smarties from the vending machine. Ms. Samson is behind him. Murray sits down at his desk then jumps up and waves his hands back and forth in front of his nose. "Does anyone else smell that?" He leans over and pushes open a window. "Pee-yew!"

Ms. Samson tells him to be quiet. He shrugs and sits back in his chair. Ms. Samson looks angry, and she tells Murray to put the candy away. Murray grins. He shoves a handful of Smarties into his mouth. Ms. Samson stomps her foot on the ground and points to the door. Murray does not move. I watch the parent volunteer leave the room and return with Mr. Vogel, the janitor. He pins Murray's arms behind his back and carries him into the hallway. Murray raises his chin and shouts, "Victory, baby!"

The class sits in silence. Byron is staring at me. I let my mind go blank and think of the future.

CHAPTER 5

JULY 2004

BYRON SOMERFIELD STRODE QUICKLY up Harriman Heights Road toward home. The trip from the National Academy School of Fine Arts in Manhattan was long—almost two hours by train when perfectly executed without track delays or missed transfers. He usually took the time alone on the Port Jervis Line to sketch. Sometimes he closed his eyes and fantasized about a future rubbing elbows in the galleries of New York City.

The academy was housed in an upscale limestone building on the Upper East Side and run by Frances Zaiontz, a frizzy-haired woman partial to large glasses and billowy pants pulled up to her belly button. Programs were held through the summer months and designed to foster a love of artistic expression but also stress rigour and hard-ass discipline as part of a proper creative experience. Byron was presently enrolled in a class of sixteen- to eighteen-year-olds, with abilities ranging from god-awful to prodigal. For his part, he took to poring over any student canvas the administration deemed exceptional, seeking out little flaws and irregularities that might bring the work back down to the level of adolescent mortal.

The last year had been a whirlwind of creative experimentation. It was in recent weeks that Byron had voided all abstract expressionism Pollock and Newman-like aspirations from his system, instead moving toward the comparatively refined American realist movement. Works by George Bellows, William Glackens, and Edward Hopper were particularly enthralling, though the current talent gap between them and him was considerable. One day, he would paint as they painted. Anything less would be a colossal disappointment.

The Somerfield house was a rented grey-siding bungalow in the south end of Woodbury that teetered on the edge of neglect. Byron heard rustling and sounds of heavy exertion as he pushed open the front door. His mother stood alone in the kitchen, her face pomegranate-red and locked in concentration as she systematically scrubbed through the full contents of their small appliance cupboard. Joy Somerfield looked up and smiled, dropping a rag and wiping rogue hairs from her face. "Oh, I'm home a little early today. There was some restructuring at work." She sat down in a chair, her face straining to maintain indifference. "I'm now reporting to a man ten years my junior. A child. Imagine that."

Byron stood still. There was a wine bottle, still mostly full, on the counter next to the refrigerator. "I thought you were going to Albany tonight?"

"They didn't need me after all—cutting operating expenses. I won't bore you with the details."

"Do you still have a job?"

"Sure, sure." His mother's gaze was distant. "Freakishly good-looking people have life a whole lot easier than regular folks, don't you think?"

"I guess."

"They just instantly present a favourable impression."

"I've never really thought about that."

"Take the Boy Wonder—flawless skin, bulging arms—the man has the intelligence of a tree stump. Daft. A nonperson. You want something taken care of properly? Find the conventionally unattractive person in a position of power. They're the ones who worked to get where they are."

"You might be right."

"I've been the family's breadwinner for twenty years. Did you know that? A meandering career with the State of New York, and I'm the one making the money."

Byron looked toward the front hall. "When's Dad coming home?"

"Your father and I are very different people. He has big ideas. Unfortunately, he struggles with confidence. It's sad, really. Of all his moneymaking schemes, not one has been profitable. Ever! We eat because of me."

"Is everything okay? I mean, with you and everything?"

Joy waved her hands. "This shouldn't be causing you anxiety. Focus on happiness, why don't you? You're sixteen years old and have so much life in front of you. You need to chase your happiness. Chase it! You must do what makes you happy. Otherwise, what's the point in being alive?"

"Can you be more specific?"

"Is the academy bringing you joy? I mean, real, sincere, earth-shattering joy?"

Byron nodded.

"Really?"

"Sure."

"Sensational! There's a certain integrity to youth that is thrilling. You're doing your work, whatever it is, and you're expressing yourself honestly. You have creative fulfillment without fear of financial responsibility. I'm not projecting, am I?"

"What do you mean by projectin—"

"Because I'm completely floored by the energy you're putting into your painting. You're undertaking work for the love of just doing it. Like, the pleasure gained from the task is the motivating reward. It sounds so simple, doesn't it? A simple concept that is simple to live. Forever. Indefinitely. Imagine that?"

"Well, sure," said Byron. "I want to be a professional painter—a professional artist of some kind. It's my calling. It's all that's ever spoken to me! If I can't do it, if I don't do it, my life will be a waste."

Byron's mother sniffled. "Generating revenue. Making profit. Getting people to part with money they've earned doing something they probably don't even like doing is some of the most unglamorous work I can imagine—a real humbling, eye-opening, dream-destroying experience. It's disguised for some of us. Complex. The lucky ones are a few degrees removed from the profit centres. The lucky ones get to distance themselves from the hustle and the stress and the demeaning existence of begging for a living. In that sense, I'm a lucky one." She stopped and shook her head. "Your father is living it. He's on the front lines. Of course, it's challenging for a man of his current reputation to be taken seriously, but his persistence is extraordinary." Joy paused. "Would it be a problem for you, Byron? If your wife out-earned you?"

"I don't care about th—"

"I should say, if you choose to have a wife and she out-earned you. Feel no pressure on account of me. Heck, marry a man if you want. I support you unequivocally. You can do whatever you want with whomever you want, so long as it's consensual. Really, Byron. It has to be consensual."

"Right."

"Just know that life tends to get extraordinarily expensive. People think they need to live by a certain standard. Keeping a house is not cheap. A week of art education in the city sure as hell is not cheap. But don't let it weigh on you. You don't have to worry about that. Not yet. Keep doing what you're doing." Joy paused and smiled. "I remember all those years ago in elementary school when we found out you were gifted. The day those test scores came back was extraordinary. We knew then, for certain, that you were special. Keep up your curiosity about the world. Don't stop if something scares you. Don't let the world crush you. Don't give in to the brown-nosing and the apple-polishing and the bootlicking. It will leave you dead."

Byron squeezed his lips together. "Understood."

"All anyone really wants to know is that their life is going to be okay. That's it! A measure of safety. Of control. Of promise that what we have won't be unceremoniously ripped away from us. We want to be safe, and it can't be that way for everyone. Know that any success you have will be tainted. If life is manageable for you, someone else is eating shit. That's just the way it works, Byron. There's nothing you can do to change it. So persevere. Push through. Working for love will be revelatory. It's the best shot you've got."

Byron pointed to the open bottle of wine. "Have you had anything else to drink?"

"Don't be ridiculous."

"Just the top off that bottle?"

"And a whole bottle before."

"So you're, like, blotto right now?"

"That's irrelevant."

"W—"

"This is an important conversation to have. Do you know why? Everything I just said comes with an important caveat..." Byron's mother let her voice trail off. Her lips teased a smile.

"What?"

"Wanting success is not enough. You need more. Your father is extraordinarily desirous of success. That doesn't mean he'll find it."

"Do you get blotto a lot? Does Dad know about this?"

"We've had issues for a long time, your father and me. You must have known. Bad marriages give off a sickly aura. They get into your bones." Joy's voice lowered. "We bought books. We did exercises. We went to therapy! Can you imagine? Paying $135 an hour for a divorced therapist to tell us how relationships work." She shook her head. "No, splitting up would be unfair to you—to force you to choose between the two of us. Just imagine the harm and the serious damage that sort of environment would cause. We know you struggle to relate to kids your own age. We know that we, your parents, are the closest friends you've got. We couldn't do it. We love you too much."

"I think I'm going to go sketch."

"This conversation has been too negative, hasn't it? I can see it on your face. Some people will say negativity keeps you realistic and grounded, but I don't buy it. Strive for happiness! There have been moments of great happiness in my life. Of jubilation. Of real, honest-to-goodness, can't control my faculties, unadulterated joy. It's like nothing else."

"When have you ever felt like that?"

Byron's mother let out a long exhale. "Memory tends to distort emotions, doesn't it? There were carefree times. Times when I knew less and was a whole lot happier. At least, I think I was. Admittedly, I used to be a nervous wreck. I was afraid of dying and disappearing forever—never to exist again. Now I have no fear. I experience my life, and then one day I won't experience it anymore—it or anything else. Not caring whether you live or die is freeing. It's almost enough to make you happy. People spend their whole lives trying to rationalize death and still don't get anywhere. Think about it this way: I am enlightened."

Byron nodded. His mother swayed. She looked old. Withered. Tired of everything.

There was an unmistakable groaning as James Somerfield's four-cylinder Buick pulled into the driveway. The engine strained and coughed. Brakes squeaked. A car door opened and slammed. Byron's mother popped up to her full height. Her face remained distant and murky. "I'm going to bed now. If your father asks, say that I'm sick." She fluttered her hands in the air. "Or tell him the truth. Whatever floats your boat."

Byron watched his mother disappear down the hallway. He lifted the uncorked bottle of wine and inverted it over the sink. The front door creaked open as cheap Merlot spiralled down the drain.

***

I lie wrapped in a sheet of white Egyptian cotton with my back turned to the near wall. A streetlight casts an orange hue over the room, illuminating shelves of carefully sorted books and a pinned Voyager 1 poster. My double mattress is extraordinarily hard—a preference since childhood with deviation in firmness causing days-long back and neck discomfort so unpalatable I have considered, though never executed, a plan to bring cut plywood on overnight travel for use as a makeshift bed-stiffener. Sleep will not come. It is 11:37 p.m. I was kept up past my normal bedtime by a curious round of extra-credit homework questions for AP Physics B involving gravitational force law between two objects of enormous mass. The problems focused on matters of energy and momentum, with digressions of auxiliary research occupying my focus for the bulk of the evening. I only emerged from my room for dinner. The freshly wiped counters and absence of foyer clutter suggested something unusual was happening.

Mom had smiled as I entered the kitchen. Her cheeks glowed red with blush. An ironed blouse betrayed her manufactured casualness as she explained a friend would be joining us for dinner, a banker named Daryl whom she had, apparently, been seeing romantically for several months. I made a throaty indication of acknowledgment and kept otherwise silent.

The evening's preparations were meticulous. My mother, a high-ranking healthcare administrator at Orange Regional Medical Centre, wore a floral-patterned apron and fussed over colour-coordinated place settings. Her mood was bubbly as she pulled a Le Creuset braiser from the oven. The logistics of working a ten-hour day steeped in patient workflow planning and budget battles, while still producing a chuck roast finished with greens and glazed root vegetables, entirely escapes me.

Daryl arrived on our front porch around 7:00 p.m. He was tall, with the build of an aged athlete resigned to physical decline and a receding hairline that exposed a wrinkled forehead. We shook hands like two participants in a meet-and-greet precursor to a business transaction. He smiled politely. I did the same.

My mother had baited us with conversational prompts, citing a NASA-sponsored human space exploration conference I attended in Boston last spring, and twice bringing up Daryl's evening work as a mathematics instructor at Rockland College. Talk failed to ignite. The conversational void carried on through dinner, during which time I ate silently, mulling over my mother's choice to complicate her life with romantic pursuits, and retreated to my room as soon as I was excused.

Schoolwork dominated the rest of the night. A strong AP mark would set the foundation for a competitive university application to the school of my choosing. I desperately want to get out of Woodbury and away from Uppendahl, but the institution needs to be top-notch. My father lived with his parents and attended San Francisco State for his undergraduate degree. I know I can one-up the old man.

There is an aching in my hip and shoulder now. I kick the bed sheet loose and flop onto my right side, my face six inches from the wall. There are faint notes of wind and central heating. Structural creaks discharge from unidentifiable areas of the house. Something catches my attention. I hear noises I've never heard outside of schoolyard mockery and brief encounters with Internet pornography—noises that are immediately disturbing. Sounds of human pleasure are coming from the master bedroom.

I am frozen as horrified comprehension dawns: copulation, coition, bona fide hanky-panky. My mother's moans are loud and uninhibited. I press my palms into my ears. Feelings of personal violation course through me, as though a burglar has entered the house and riffled through treasured possessions. I am overwhelmed. It is too much to consider. The ramifications are too far-reaching. All this, on a school night.

I lift a hand from my ear. The sounds are louder now. I begin mentally counting prime numbers as a distraction exercise, drawing out the end of each with a slow "Mississippi." I reach 997 and test the room. My mother is still audible.

This current horror was set in motion by my parents' divorce three years earlier. Their dissolution featured little outward conflict and was a by-product of emotional distance and indifference aggravated by my father's fanatical career focus. The marriage's deathblow came when he was offered a job as acting head of Otolaryngology at Buffalo General. I see my father once a month or so now. Dad has never introduced a girlfriend or subjected me to an experience comparable to the one presently taking place. Still, our relationship aches.

The noises of bodily pleasure have quieted, replaced by a rhythmic thumping of bed against floor and wall. Anger usurps repulsion. I consider Daryl spending the night to be a wholly unfair double standard. Requesting similar privilege for a romantic interest of mine, hypothetical or otherwise, would send my mother into an arm-waving frenzy. I am furious with her for so blatantly disregarding my emotional well-being.

The thumping is speeding up. I feel trapped. Distractions—television, radio, the shower—are impossibilities. It is imperative I do not draw attention to myself. I look to my second-floor window and consider exit scenarios: jumping, hanging and dropping, rappelling via bed sheet. Nothing is realistic. Everything is rapidly deteriorating. Above all else, my knowledge of the situation cannot become known. A frank conversation between mother and daughter on the matter of human sexuality is too uncomfortable to bear.

I rise slowly from my bed and cross the floor. My movements are vigilant in their noiselessness. I flip the room's light switch. Sharp incandescence fills the space. I squint and scan the vicinity for headphones—a big over-ear pair of noise-cancelling Sennheisers my father bought me two Christmases ago. My efforts are unproductive. I remember now that they are downstairs in the living room, last used to aid the study of an intermediate Schubert piano piece and useless to me in this most critical of moments. Coital sounds reach an apex and abruptly let up. The house and its inhabitants settle into unadulterated silence. I am fearful of movement and stand frozen. The silence draws on, growing louder and approaching a shrill, screaming pitch, as long silences sometimes do. There is the sound of a body—Daryl's, judging by a mental weight-to-floor creak calculation—moving toward the bathroom. I listen as he relieves himself, washes his hands, and moves back into bed. I hear all of it. There is a moment of absolute and total dead air. My feet feel cement-like. I do not move.

The groan of a door's hinge breaks the quiet. My chest and torso tighten as footsteps move from the master bedroom down the hallway and toward my room. Light bleeds out from under my door. My arms and chest are vibrating. I will be discovered. I hear my mother's footsteps stop. There is the subtle repositioning of weight as she turns toward my bedroom door. We are no more than ten feet apart, separated by an inch and a half of painted fibreboard. I will her to keep moving. She must not know that I know of her and Daryl's bedroom activities. There is more quiet, and then a slow lurch as she descends the stairs. I turn off the light and slide back into bed.

I am still. The kitchen faucet is running. The refrigerator door opens and closes. My mother climbs the stairs and enters her bedroom. The house sinks into a final silence. I squint up at little bits of white ceiling stucco and turn over the night's events. I decide my mother and Daryl's relationship is built on mutual longing for companionship and that this common desire could be sufficient foundation for sustained romance. Both are incomplete humans lacking emotional union and longing for shared experiences. They are, in a word, lonely. I will never let my romantic choices be affected by loneliness. It's simply not worth the trouble.

I close my eyes. The house is silent. Sleep will be impossible now.

***

"Wa-wa-watch the release! You're leaving speed on the table!" Murray's father, the thick-limbed and squared-jawed Donald Buchanan Sr., paced in tight circles. Little bits of discoloration dotted his shirt's underarms. A loose half-Windsor knot was pulled to one side of his collar. His words stuttered like they always had. "We-we-we're shutting you down at fifty. Make 'em count. Let's go. Let's go!"

Don Jr. faced Murray from forty-six feet away. Their mother, April Buchanan, was framed in the kitchen doorway. Don held a glove out in front of his face and assumed an unblinking gaze. Both hands rose over his head, his body twisted. He stepped forward and brought his left arm whipping over the top of his shoulder. A scuffed baseball exploded from his hand, spinning furiously, and slammed into Murray's mitt with a deep thump.

"Your release is early! Come on!" said Don Sr.

Murray threw back to his brother. Don caught the ball without acknowledgment and raised his glove. Another pitch released. Murray sprang left and caught the ball on a one-hop. Don Sr. gestured madly and smacked his chest. April Buchanan straightened her posture and crossed her arms, a lingering habit from her time as a state prosecutor two decades previous.

The day was inhumanely hot. Don Jr. threw two dozen more pitches before his father called for the ball and had both boys run wind sprints. Murray's legs pumped. The backs of his knees stung as sweat trickled over skin chafed raw from prolonged crouching. Only as vomit was imminent did his father wave them off. He clapped his hands lazily and kicked the grass. "Don, you threw we-we-well. Not extraordinarily, but well enough. What did you think, Murray?"

"Oh." Murray took long breaths. "Good."

"Just good?"

"I mean, didn't you say it was just good?"

"Don't be a smart ass. How do you think your brother pitched?"

"He was throwing fast. Can't argue with speed."

"And your performance?"

Murray raised both shoulders. "Good?"

"Call it passable." Don Sr. clapped his hands again. "Remember to stretch." He turned 180 degrees and disappeared into the house. April smiled at her sons and followed Don Sr.

Murray moved to a patch of shade below the Buchanans' old treehouse and lay on his back, studying the underside of the faded pine planks. His breathing was rapid. He closed his eyes and focused on the rise and fall of his chest. "Hey, Don?"

"Uh-huh?"

"Dad comes to your games, right?"

"Of course."

"What about a few years back, before you started getting attention?"

"Back then it was mostly Mom."

"So he only took an interest when you started getting good?"

"I've always been good."

"I mean, really good."

"You could say Dad became a baseball expert around the time I started to excel."

Murray opened his eyes. "And that doesn't bother you?"

"I don't let it."

"He's never been to one of my games. Did you know that? Not one!"

Don put a hand on the treehouse's rung ladder and heaved himself onto the landing. He lay stomach-down, his face pressed against the slatted floor. "Don't worry about that."

"I'm batting .480 this summer!"

"Hits mean nothing without converting, Mur."

"I'm leading the team in runs!"

"Then keep performing well, and everything will work out."

Murray groaned.

"You know my situation isn't all great," said Don. "Dad wants excellence in whatever we choose to do. He's extremely opinionated—extremely hands-on."

"But you said he's coming from a place of love. That's what you told me!"

"Doesn't mean he's not fanatical. Did you know he's against me going to Vanderbilt?"

"Vanderbilt's got the most guys in the show of any NCAA school. I looked it up."

"He wants me closer to home: Syracuse or St. John's. He thinks he'll have more influence that way. Or Yale. He obviously wants me to go to Yale."

"Shows what he knows."

"That's just the way he is, Mur. Sometimes love can be misguided. He had a lot to say about the draft too—said the MLB has its head up its ass, and they'll be sorry for letting me slide as far as they did." He paused. "Playing at Vanderbilt is the best thing for me right now. Signing after going in the fortieth round would be nuts—at least we agree on that."

"Do you think you're going to make it?"

"You mean, like, the Major Leagues?"

"Not 'like' the Major Leagues. I mean the Major Leagues!"

"They draft 1,500 players a year. It's a crapshoot."

"But someone's going to make it, right?"

"Sure."

"So why not you, baby?"

"It's a meritocracy, Mur. I continue to improve, and the MLB keeps me on the board. Starting now, my job is to dominate in the NCAA."

"What happens if you don't?"

Don exhaled. His mouth made flapping noises against the slatted pine floor. "I guess I keep on living like a regular person."

Murray kicked his heel into the ground. "How do you think my game's coming along?"

"Don't be insecure, Murray."

"I've been working hard: weights and technique."

"And this spring you'll make varsity for it."

"What about after high school?"

"What'd I say? Crapshoot."

"How about a scholarship?"

"Don't worry about that."

"Dad thinks I should apply to West Point."

"Don't discount the army. West Point is an extraordinarily prestigious school. It'll open doors."

"They also play D1 ball."

"That's true, but I'm talking about opening doors outside of baseball."

"Fuck that. Too many rules in the army—not for me."

"Did he say anything about Yale?"

"Course," said Murray. "He wants me to apply there too. Says I'll have a good shot because I'm legacy."

"And you're smart," said Don.

"But I want my focus to be baseball. Can't lose sight of that."

"Stay right there, would you?" Don puckered his lips and let out a thin string of spit. Murray squawked involuntarily and rolled aside. Saliva swayed a foot above the ground. Don made a great sucking noise, and the spit shot back up into his mouth.

"Why would you do that?"

"You should be asking, 'How did you do that?'"

"What's the answer?"

"Dumb luck. Strange, isn't it?"

"Is 'strange' the word you're looking for?"

Don loaded up another loogie and let it drop from his mouth. He sucked intermittently, causing the spit to fall, bounce to a stop, then fall again. Murray's head was tilted skyward. He watched his brother's saliva come within an inch of his face. Don sucked with enormous force, and the loogie disappeared back through the floor. "That's trust, Murray. Trust will take you far."

"Trust in what? Take you far where? What are you even talking about?"

"Relax, would yo—"

"Donald Buchanan Jr.!" Lillian Monk's voice sounded from the neighbouring yard.

Don lifted his face from the treehouse's floor. Vertical red marks lined his face. "I've got a big hork ready to go!"

"That's disgusting." Lillian climbed her backyard's chain link fence and jumped, landing in a tight tuck and roll between two forsythia bushes. She stood up, revealing the six-foot frame that afforded her several years of highly competitive play in New York State Little League boys' baseball circles.

"I just had a workout with the old man."

"How's the arm?" said Lillian.

Don leaned his entire upper body out the treehouse window. "It's real fast."

"And control?"

"Good enough for Vanderbilt."

"Good enough like it's no longer a liability, or good enough like it's become an asset?"

"Like, I can put the ball where it needs to be, when it needs to be there."

"I heard otherwise, Buchanan."

"You want proof?" Don swung his legs out the window and dropped to the ground. "How about a little target practice, Mur?"

"What do you mean? I just caught you!"

"Was he throwing strikes?" said Lillian.

Murray shrugged. "Mostly."

"Little Buchanan's not convinced."

Don bounced on the spot, his neck twisting incredulously from his brother to Lillian. "See that bucket by the garage? I'll knock it right off his head. One pitch. All or nothing."

Murray held out both hands. "Let's just wait a moment. This hasn't been discussed in an—"

"You can't do it," said Lillian.

"Distance?"

"Major League?"

"Sixty-feet-six-inches. Count it out."

"What do you need me for? Just put the bucket on the ground and stop showing off for your girlfriend."

"She's not my girlfriend, and no one's showing off. Your involvement simply raises the stakes." Don smirked. "Be a man, would you?"

Murray's shoulders dropped. "What do I stand to gain?"

"Anything you want."

"Can you clarify that, please?"

"Any reasonable thing you want."

"I stand with the bucket on my head for one pitch..."

"Go on."

"...and you come to my game tonight."

"That's it?"

"No excuses."

"None."

"And you have to stay until the last pitch. No ducking out early!"

"It's done."

"And hang out for a bit after."

"Of course."

"And you have to get Dad to come."

"I can do that."

"You can?"

"Why are you doubting me? It's all taken care of."

Don extended a hand, and the brothers shook. This was how Murray came to be standing with a yellow bucket balanced on his head and Don's t-shirt wrapped tightly over his eyes. The penetrating odour of uncontained armpit sweat tingled Murray's nostrils.

"Keep moving back," said Lillian.

"Here?"

"Further."

"This ought to do it."

"Looks good to me."

"Done." Don punched his glove.

A quiet settled over the backyard. Murray felt a light breeze across his body. He sensed movement in front of him and tensed up. Silence. He loosened, then more movement, then the head-splitting blow of a baseball contacting his temple. Murray's knees buckled, his body sank, and his head smacked uselessly against the corner of a rock poking out from the hard earth.

Panicked shouting echoed from all directions. Murray opened his eyes. Don Jr.'s face had an expression of primal horror. Lillian was nowhere to be seen. Murray's thoughts went to baseball, and he tried to sit up. His father pushed him down as nausea bubbled up his throat. April spoke frantically into her phone. Murray felt distant and curiously removed, like the events of the present moment were playing out in a movie of which he was both the subject and audience. Strong arms helped him into the back of an ambulance, the interior of which was utilitarian and bland. A moustached paramedic wearing shiny blue gloves examined the growing welt on Murray's temple and the bloodied mess on the back of his head. Don Sr. crouched beside his son. "Can you hear me?" Murray opened his mouth. He produced no words.

The paramedic placed a rubber oxygen mask on Murray's face and pushed white gauze against his head. "Do you know where you are?"

Murray opened his mouth again. "That's sort of an open-ended question. I mean, does anyone really know where they are?"

The paramedic's moustache wiggled. "How old are you?"

"Sixteen."

"When's your birthday?"

"August 8th."

"How are you feeling?"

"Oh, I don't really know about that. I couldn't say."

The paramedic adjusted the valve on a portable oxygen tank. Don Sr.'s face was clenched. "Wh–wh–what do you think?"

"I think he's taken a considerable blow to the head."

"Of course he has. How severe is it?"

"The doctor will give a diagnosis."

"But wh–wh–what do you think?"

"The doctor will be better equipped to p—"

"Yes, but wh–wh–what is your opinion?" Don Sr.'s tone was that of a man used to unchecked command over entire floors of business subordinates.

The paramedic exhaled slowly. The underside of his chin flopped loosely. "He's conscious, with strong vital signs. That's a good start when dealing with head trauma.

"What about long-term issues?"

"It's possible."

"And what does that mean?"

The paramedic spoke slowly, enunciating each word. "Injury to the head, depending on severity, can cause certain cognitive impairments—either temporary or permanent."

"Because you must understand he's an academic star. Test scores off the charts. Have been since the third grade."

The paramedic's left eyebrow rose.

Don Sr. looked down to Murray. "How do you feel, son?"

"He already asked me."

"*I'm* asking you."

Murray squeezed his eyes open and shut. "My head hurts."

Don Sr. looked back to the paramedic. "His brother has one of the strongest high school arms in the state."

"Is that so?"

"Sure is. I want every precaution taken."

Murray stared at the paramedic's moustache. The sensation of facing sideways in a moving vehicle was odd and disorienting. An overwhelming wave of exhaustion hit without warning. Murray closed his eyes and let rest come.

CHAPTER 6

SEPTEMBER 2004

I SIT AT A rectangular laminate table. Thin rays of dawn light peek through beige track blinds that sway slightly, pushed into motion by a stream of recirculated air. The room is small, perhaps a third of the size of a regular classroom. First period will not begin for another hour, and the school is bare. My early-morning presence here is voluntary.

Mr. Marcotte stands at the room's rear. His hands are interlocked behind his back, and he rocks from the heels to the balls of his feet, sending hair bouncing rhythmically off his scalp as he wraps up a lecture on chess theory. Much of the talk is focused on openings and how study of underlying principles is critical to board control and serious competitive advantage. I take in his words and feel my face burning. Mr. Marcotte makes my mind reel in a way that cannot be quantified.

Murray Buchanan and Byron Somerfield sit to my right and left respectively. Murray wears a rep tracksuit that scrunches whenever he adjusts his limbs. Byron is silent and holds a straight posture. He grins at me, his face partially obscured by strands of deep black hair.

I watch Mr. Marcotte lift a manila folder from his desk and remove a single printed page. "I've received official communication from the Orange County Chess Bowl's organizing committee." His expression is serious as he wets his lips with his tongue. "The event is being held at Mount Saint Mary College on March 25." He looks up. "Competition will be stiff. Continued focus and dedication is essential to maximizing our odds of a good performance." Mr. Marcotte chuckles. "Is something the matter, Murray?"

I look to my left. Murray's expression is dour. His chair creaks, and he blinks slowly. He yawns and rubs his eyes. "Nothing."

"You look off."

"You know I get made fun of for coming here?"

"That's the inherent risk of attending gifted and enriched extracurriculars, especially this early in the morning."

He shrugs. "It still pisses me off."

"What are you being told?"

Murray's cheeks and nose wrinkle. "That Chess Bowl's a dumb waste of time."

"Says who?"

"Guys on the baseball team, mostly."

Mr. Marcotte nods again. I watch the subtle movements of his frame. He is no older than thirty, wedged somewhere between my parents' generation and my own. "What do you think about that?"

Murray shrugs again.

"The three of you have a demonstrated history of academic excellence. Test scores. Grades. Class participation. Your inclusion in Chess Bowl is something to be proud of." He raises a finger. "You are proud, aren't you?"

Murray exhales and says nothing.

"The best Chess Bowl competitors will challenge themselves past their perceived intellectual limitations. The thrill of achieving what was previously thought unachievable is extraordinary." Mr. Marcotte crouches. His hamstrings hover parallel to the floor. "Has anyone ever experienced this before?"

Murray shrugs and mumbles something about batting practice.

Mr. Marcotte frowns and points to Byron. "What about you?"

Byron shakes his head.

"Come on, give me something."

Byron's nostrils squeak as he inhales. "I believe, like, nothing is unachievable. Especially if you're Lesley Chang."

"An eternal optimist!" Mr. Marcotte extends back to his full height and paces. His steps are slow and methodical. "When we talk about Chess Bowl, we're really talking about math-based decision-making. Mathematics, when executed with knowledge and consistency, is capable of perfection in a way like nothing else: not painting, not sculpture, not poetry. A strategic equation, rock-solid and without flaw, is something entirely its own. Strip away all the glitz from a game of chess, and what do you have left? A series of decisions. Your job is to make the best decision given the circumstances." He smiles and looks right at me. "A decision made in life can never be absolute. Confined to a game of strategy, the perfect decision is waiting to be found."

Mr. Marcotte reaches behind his desk. He produces two boxed chessboards and lays them on the table. "Lesley, match up with Murray. Byron, play the winner." Mr. Marcotte steps to the window and pulls open the track blinds, revealing a great burst of light.

I squint as Murray grunts and pulls the box toward himself. He arranges the 8×8 board and offers me first play. I lift my hand and move my king pawn two spaces forward to E4. Murray holds me in his gaze for a long moment and then plays his king-side bishop to C5. I bring my queen-side knight forward to F3. Murray scratches the tip of his nose and plays his king-side knight to C6. I move my king pawn two spaces forward to D4.

Mr. Marcotte pops a strawberry chew into his mouth and watches with rapt attention. I picture him at home, all assumed formalities and professionalism dropped in favour of sweatpants and unadulterated comfort. I wonder if he has a girlfriend or a wife. I wonder if he loves his job or if teaching is a dreary struggle he would rather do without. Mr. Marcotte is more mature, more astute, and more complex than any of the boys in my grade. Mostly, I wonder if he thinks of me.

Murray's hand is on his pawn. He looks to the board and back at me, then slides the piece diagonally forward and makes the capture at D4. I take my castle and remove the pawn. Murray's eyes pan slowly over the board. He moves his queen-side knight's pawn to G6. I move my second knight off the back line to C3. Murray's king-side bishop moves diagonally forward one space to G7. My king-side bishop moves two spaces to E3, sheltered behind a pawn. Murray moves his knight forward to F6. I move my bishop off the back line forward to C4. Murray castles. I move my bishop to B3. I wait. My breaths shorten. Murray squints at the board. He moves his knight forward to A5. I smile. The advantage is mine, and I quickly lock Murray into checkmate. His jaw tightens, and he pushes over his king with a dismissive flick of a finger. "Stupid game."

Mr. Marcotte crosses his arms. "As in, the game is stupid, or you played stupidly?"

"All of it."

"You're going to dismiss a game that's been played for hundreds of years because you lost a match?" Mr. Marcotte's stare is piercing now.

"No."

"Then what?"

Murray shook his head. "I guess I'm competitive."

"Is that it?"

Murray looks in my direction, approximately level with the table. "Sorry. I guess I just like to win."

***

"This case is another classic in Common Law study—one of my own personal favourites. The verdict remains controversial to this day and demonstrates the importance of concurrence in securing a conviction."

Ms. Wilson pointed at the blackboard as she spoke, her face etched and sagging from sixty-five years of life. "Concurrence. Can someone please refresh the class's memory?"

Evan Friedman let out a long whistle, emptying his lungs and lowering his pitch to simulate the sound of a bomb dropping. Scattered laughter sounded.

"Okay. Yes. Very good. That would be Mens Rea and Actus Rea. Okay. Did everyone get that?"

There was silence.

"Okay. Good. Let's continue then."

Murray rested both elbows on his desk. An odour radiated from his underarms, smelling of onions left to rot in the sun. He wrinkled his nose and stole a look around the classroom. Murray tried to recall the moment he applied deodorant that morning.

A hand smacked Murray upside the head. "You reek, Buchanan!" Evan's voice was boisterous, even when whispered.

"Huh?"

Evan plugged his nose and waved his hand back and forth. "What's the matter with you?"

Murray shrugged. "Forgot deodorant." He looked to the front of the room. The lesson fluttered in and out of focus. Ms. Wilson mispronounced "bona fide" as "bon-a-feed-eh" and the class erupted into laughter. She chuckled, unaware of or unwilling to acknowledge her own students' mockery. Murray tried to concentrate. Ms. Wilson's words dissolved as soon as they entered his consciousness. His fingers went to the scar on the back of his head, now two months old and still not normalized. At his worst, he had considered calling a doctor. The parental fallout would be horrific.

Murray's gaze drifted two desks to his left onto Sally Anway. Her lips were deep red and her eyes set far apart on her face, partially obscured by strands of luminescent hair. He watched Sally take diligent notes. His mind flickered.

"You know all this shit is a waste of time, right?"

"Huh?"

Evan Friedman leaned toward Murray. His voice was low. "I mean it's all a waste of time. What good is studying law?"

"It's important for some things—working as a lawyer, for example."

"You think our country needs more lawyers?"

Murray shrugged. "They make a lot of money."

"The bad ones do."

"You mean the good ones?"

"I mean the good ones who do bad things—the scum lawyers." Evan smirked. "Me, I'm going to college, having the time of my life, and becoming a general contractor."

"Really?"

"Excuse me!" Ms. Wilson pointed at Evan. "Can we stop the conversation, gentlemen?"

Evan waved and nodded. "Sorry." He looked at Murray. "Contracting is good honest work." He lowered his voice further. "You ever considered it?"

"I'm trying to listen."

"Fuck law. Think about the future."

Sally Anway turned toward Evan. "Hi. Can you be quiet, please? This is important."

Evan grinned and saluted. "Will do." Sally narrowed her eyes. She looked quickly at Murray, and her nose crinkled.

"Excuse me. Once more and you're out. Got that? Thank you very much."

"Sorry, ma'am." Evan grinned at Murray. "Whatever you do, don't piss off the authority figure."

Murray was silent.

"I said don't piss off the authority figure."

"Shut up."

"Calm down, Buchanan."

"I want to learn this."

"Save it for something important."

"How is it that you've smoked pot every day for the last four years and still pull a B average?"

Evan's grin exposed his rearmost molars. He ran his hand over his shaved head. "God-given talent." He pointed to his notebook. "I like to keep expectations reasonable. If SUNY is happy to take me, I am happy to accept."

Murray rolled his eyes and settled into silence. Ms. Wilson's voice hummed at its usual clip and cadence as she wrote the day's assignment in loopy cursive on the blackboard: fifteen pages of reading and a half-dozen short answer questions. Murray scrounged for his textbook and stared down at its pages. Important concepts were highlighted in boxes on the page's margins, most of which Murray did not know and worried he never would. Immediate boredom, mixed with fear, took hold.

Murray looked back toward Sally. There were unsubstantiated rumours she had slept with a varsity ball player at least twice during last spring's playoff run. Murray's chest tingled. He had hooked up with a small collection of girls—mostly from Monroe-Woodbury and one from a neighbouring school he met during a house party—though none with the self-assurance of Sally. He imagined the sensation of holding her body, pressing his lips against hers, running his hand across her stomach and down her pants, and having her reciprocate in kind.

"Hey."

Murray's breath caught. His heart pounded uncomfortably fast.

Sally turned and made direct eye contact. Her mouth was flat. "Is that you?"

"Sorry?"

"Is that you?" Sally's voice was just above a whisper. "That smell."

Murray's body tightened. "What are you talking about?"

"That *is* you, isn't it?" Sally turned around in her chair so that she faced Murray. "How long has that smell been going on?"

"Uh, I don't know."

"My dad had the same problem."

"It's no—"

"He smelled like boiled cabbage for over a year."

"I—"

"It followed him everywhere. Family dinners were ruined. My mom forced him to sleep on the couch. The dog howled whenever he walked into a room." Sally took in a long breath. "Finally, his boss said he needed to get his hygiene sorted out or find other work. He went to the doctor and was diagnosed with a life-threatening liver infection. He made a full recovery."

Murray opened and closed his mouth. "I'll think about tha—"

"That's it!" Ms. Wilson's expression was incredulous. "You've been warned. You'll have to go!"

"What? Come on!"

"That's right, you. Get out."

Murray muttered under his breath.

"What's that?"

Murray was silent.

"What did you say?"

"Nothing."

"Nothing? You said something."

Evan Friedman looked ecstatic. "Tell the nice lady, would you?"

Murray's face shook. "I didn't say anything."

"The whole class is listening," said Ms. Wilson. "What do you have to say?"

Murray closed his textbook. "I said, 'Who are you to teach law when you're not even a lawyer, and if you had any talent whatsoever, you'd work in real litigation instead of this shitty place.'"

Evan Friedman applauded. Sally put a hand to her mouth. Ms. Wilson's jaw dropped. "Please leave now, Murray."

"Fine." Murray shook as he gathered his belongings and walked up the row of desks. Ms. Wilson pursed her lips. "We can't all be your father, Murray. That includes you."

***

Byron's back and head rested against painted concrete as cold air goose-bumped his forearms. Water-stained tiles lined the foyer's ceiling. The school's physical structure was still, a stark contrast to an hour previous, when clumps of students jostled for favourable hallway position. Now the surroundings felt barren. Eerie. A place where one could be and do and think as one wished. Byron clutched a black Bic pen in his left hand and sketched hurriedly. An idea had taken firm hold: extreme authenticity by drawing without conscious forethought. Byron would embrace wild spontaneity to document real human experience. Every lived moment waited to become a masterpiece. The challenge was to have the discipline and the rigour and the innate talent to capture it. His gaze danced between Monroe-Woodbury's darkened front hallway and his spiral-bound notebook. He teetered on the edge of elevated truth.

The summer had been spent assembling a college art portfolio. Byron's parents funded the exploits—some twenty canvases pared down to six presentation pieces—with only mild grumblings about money. Bachelor of Fine Arts enrolment applications were presently in consideration at Boston College, NYU, Rhode Island, and, at the gentle suggestion of Byron's mother, two state schools. Monroe-Woodbury's guidance counsellor was of little support, offering business school and teacher's college as practical alternatives to a life of near-certain financial struggle. The lack of administrative confidence was invigorating. He would succeed.

A rolling baseball hit Byron's shoe. He jerked his neck around. Murray Buchanan stood at the far end of the foyer holding a bat like a putter. He yelled, "Birdie on 18!" and made a big show of pumping his fist. Byron kicked at the ball and sent it rolling lamely into the corner. His sketch, a low-angle wide view of the school's hallway, was ruined. Murray ambled forward. Body odour clung to his cut-off t-shirt and polyester mesh shorts. He lifted the bat to eye level and wiggled it in front of Byron's face. "Oh, bbooyy. Careful, Somerfield."

Byron's eyes followed the barrel of the bat. He produced no noise.

"Well, what do you have to say for yourself?"

Byron was silent.

"Anything at all?" Murray held the bat still, an inch from the space just above the bridge of Byron's nose.

"Why are you doing that?"

"Oh wweee! He speaks."

"I don't understand what you're doing."

"Think about it." Byron leaned left. The bat followed. "Is it a problem that there's a bat in your face?"

"It's unusual, mostly."

Murray loosened his wrist, and the bat swung perpendicular to the floor. "You think you're smart, kiddo?"

Byron paused. "It's possible."

"Because I'm detecting a smugness I don't much care for."

"I don't know what you're talking about."

"Do you think you're entitled to special treatment? Sulking around the school, not saying anything, except to, like, Lesley Chang and a few other weirdos."

"Certainly not."

Murray kicked at the notebook. "What's in there?"

"Drawings."

"Can you be more specific?"

"Drawings of the hallway."

Murray spun his head and squinted. "*That* hallway?"

"That one right over there."

"I don't understand."

"Don't understand what?"

"It's an hour after last period. Go home!"

Byron fiddled with the spine of his notebook. "What about you?" His timbre was even. "What are you doing here?"

Murray puffed out his chest. "Practising ball, Byro. Athletic excellence. Something you'll never understand."

"Worried about getting cut again?"

"Practice or get left behind. Baseball's a complicated sport—competition is stiff."

"So you'll take whatever advantage you can get?"

"Precisely."

"Like how you're only doing Chess Bowl because Marcotte happens to be the varsity team's third-base coach?"

"Oohh weeeee." Murray's face lit up. "What else do you think you know about me?"

Byron shrugged. "I dunno."

"Don't hold out."

Byron shook his head.

"Now is not the time for modesty. Let's hear it."

"Well, I know your brother's a great ball player."

"Sure is."

"Almost certainly better than you'll ever be." Byron paused. "And I know it drives you crazy."

"I'll be starting catcher this spring. No question."

Byron nodded. "Maybe."

"Come on. What else do you have?"

"Why are you asking me this?"

"We're having a conversation, Byro. This is what people do. They have conversations."

"I know your dad makes a lot of money."

"You say it like it's a bad thing."

"It's not, necessarily."

Murray smirked. "He's also got a lot to say about your old man."

Byron nodded slowly. "I know about your grades."

"What about my grades?"

"I know you've been getting bad marks all year, and I know you're scared about it." Byron paused. "At least, I think I know."

"And how do you think you know that?"

"I see you in class. It's obvious, at least to me."

"What are you doing, watching me all day? Don't you have anything else to worry about?"

Byron shrugged and looked at the floor. Murray took in a nasally pull of air and pushed out his upper lip. "Let me see your drawings."

"Then I was right about your grades?"

"I said let me see."

"It's just the hallway, like we discussed."

Murray's hand shot forward and snatched the notebook. He began flipping pages. "This is all yours?"

"Yes."

"All of it?"

"That's right."

Murray's expression was incredulous. "What is this?"

"Can you be more specific?"

"It's just the same hallway over and over again."

"So?"

"Doesn't that seem odd to you?"

"It's development through rapid repetition."

Murray's brow crinkled. "Have you ever been diagnosed with anything?"

"I want to create work that's as honest and authentic as humanly possible."

Murray rubbed the underside of his chin.

"What?"

"This is honesty?"

"It will be if I keep developing myself."

"Because it's really bad—no offence."

"You're an authority of some kind?"

Murray shrugged and began flipping pages again. "See there? And there? The perspectives are all fucked up. This is amateur."

"Can I have my book back, please?"

"And don't give me some artistic license bullshit. I don't buy it." Murray flung the notebook into Byron's stomach. "I thought you were a prodigy or something. This is a letdown." He pointed his bat down the hall. "I'm outta here. Go home."

Chapter 7

January 2005

T HE WALK HOME FROM school can be made exclusively through sidewalks and park trails, taking no more and no fewer than six minutes one way. Getting from class to the school's back foyer adds, on average, two additional minutes, though varies depending on my state of readiness at the bell's moment of ringing and which classroom I happen to be located in. This is an irrelevant consideration for the return trip and leaves me approximately forty-six minutes with which to prepare lunch, eat, and clean up before leaving for afternoon classes. Noon trips home have occurred every day this week due to unconfirmed rumours of early university acceptances being sent out. To my knowledge, no one from Monroe-Woodbury has received an offer. I want to be the first.

Trees are sprawling and leafless against the January air. My house is two stories of white siding covered by a brown shingle roof. Mail delivery concludes by 11:30 a.m. each day, according to a USPS call centre representative who wanted to remain anonymous due to her uncertainty as to whether specific scheduling information was public domain. Our mailbox, nailed to the left of the front door, is full. I pull out a small bundle of envelopes. The most prominent is off-white and thick, feeling like a stapled booklet and loose sheets of paper. I turn the envelope and see my name in black typeface. The return address is the Massachusetts Institute of Technology Admissions Office. My chest begins to quiver, spreading out to my extremities until my whole body is shaking. My high school transcript is glowing. My extracurriculars are rock-solid. My statement of interest was read, and edited, and reread until my eyeballs felt like they were bleeding. I tear at the envelope's corner and run my finger along the sealed flap. MIT's renowned Bachelor of Science program, more than CalTech, more than Berkeley, more than the mighty Harvard, is my top choice for undergraduate study.

I extract the first sheet of paper. The letterhead is clean and official-looking. I scan the opening paragraph and feel a jolt of adrenaline. A squeal escapes my mouth. I have received early acceptance. Classes start in September.

I pull out and read through the entirety of the envelope's contents, covering all conceivable bases for how my acceptance might be a cruel prank or administrative error. My mother will be thrilled, though she will warn that work and learning must never stop lest I be lulled into a false sense of academic or career security. My father will send the news back to his parents in San Francisco, where it will be greeted as a wonderful but expected development, and the prestige of a top-shelf university will be discussed and bragged about at great length. Lunch is a blur of bread and sandwich meat. I return to school well before the afternoon bell.

Students roam the halls of Monroe-Woodbury in small packs, chatting and occasionally nodding in my direction. I keep my movements and facial features neutral and head toward Mr. Marcotte's afternoon classroom. He sits behind his desk, door ajar, eating a banana. I knock, and he waves me inside. My cheeks stretch and curl upward. I step toward him and start blabbing: MIT, a BSc, early acceptance. My words are breathless and rapid-fire. Mr. Marcotte's smile is wide. He holds out his hand and drops the banana peel into the trash. "Well, this is wonderful."

"It's the best I could have hoped for. There's so much I want to learn—so much I need to learn."

"Sounds to me like this is your biggest accomplishment yet."

"I'll need to work hard. Harder than I've ever worked, probably."

"You've always been a hard worker."

"MIT is a world-class institution. I'll be competing against the smartest kids in the country."

"Working with."

"Huh?"

"I said you'll be 'working with' the smartest kids in the country. Not competing against them."

"Let's be real here."

Mr. Marcotte frowned. "Do you expect to enjoy the experience? It will bring you some measure of fulfillment and satisfaction?"

"Of course. This is everything I've wanted!"

"Well, we as teachers are doing our best work when students achieve greatness. Your next ten years will be extraordinary."

I lean closer to Mr. Marcotte. His cheeks display early signs of wrinkling. "To be honest, I'm excited to get out of here. I've done everything I can do—everything I want to do in this place. No more small-time nonsense. No more shitty cafeteria food. No more Uppendahl."

Mr. Marcotte nodded. "It's important to set realistic expectations for yourself. As Voltaire said, 'Perfect is the enemy of good.'"

"I heard Voltaire lifted that from an Italian proverb."

"He may have, and in a way that proves my point."

"But striving for perfection is important."

"I don't want you putting undue pressure on yourself."

"Pressure drives achievement."

The ends of Mr. Marcotte's mouth twitch. "Just know that everyone has a breaking point."

"I'm going to give it everything I've got." I lower my voice. "I need to get out of here. I have plans. I have ambitions. I'm done with Woodbury."

Mr. Marcotte crosses his legs and leans back in his chair. "Just be willing to accept a little bit of defeat."

"Right."

"And understand that greatness takes time, even for those who are really special."

I nod politely. The bell rings, and Mr. Marcotte shoos me out of the room. I walk down the hall toward physics class and high-five a confused-looking Byron Somerfield, my mind bubbling with promises of the future. For now, I'm stuck in educational purgatory. My last semester at Monroe-Woodbury will be an exercise in overcoming apathy. I will maintain my grades and make it to graduation. After that, everything will happen.

***

Byron sat at the old desk just off the kitchen and stared into the gentle curve of his family's computer monitor on which Boston College's Perspective Students page was presently open. He scrolled through pictures of gothic-inspired buildings dotted with fall colours and stock photographs of smiling students holding textbooks. Images were slow to load.

He had recently pitched a high-bandwidth home Internet upgrade to his mother, without success.

Byron could hear the tense tones of James and Joy Somerfield from the master bedroom upstairs. They had been fighting for over an hour. Discussions that morning were varied and included matters of rent, Byron's 529 plan, car financing, and work.

Byron stopped scrolling and focused in on a photograph. One student, blond, lean, and with a subtly square jaw, was stunningly beautiful. Byron stared at the young man's pink lips and perfectly arranged hair. He took in a breath through his nose. He exhaled. He felt a deep, visceral lust he had suspected for some time though never acted on.

Byron paused. His right ear tilted upward to his parents' bedroom. He opened a new browser window. His hands held still over the keyboard. He could feel his heart pumping and skin warming. He brought his fingers down and carefully typed "naked men" into the search bar. Thousands of hits loaded, and Byron's body exploded. Lean abdominals. Smooth faces. Tight buttocks. Erect penises. His heart jackhammered. Blood rushed and pumped. It was all settled. He would scroll through all of them. Every last image. Every single picture of a naked man he could possibly consume. He slipped his pants down around his ankles. It was on.

***

The Buchanans' white Lincoln Continental pushed east through Sunday morning traffic. Don Buchanan Sr.'s posture was stiff and well-practised. He wore black slacks and a tailored dress shirt with *D.B.* monogrammed on the right cuff. Tinted lenses were clipped to his wireframe glasses. His voice was jovial. "New Haven is an extraordinary town. There's nowhere else quite like it." He smacked his lips and turned to his son, his enormous face glowing with boyish excitement. "A Yale acceptance will change your life."

Murray nodded and made no noise. Sounds of ESPN Radio 1300 floated through the car's interior. His nostrils flared. The upholstery and dashboard smelled of Lemon Pledge.

"Yale students are some of the brightest in the country. It's an institution you'll forever be associated with. Of course, there's that whole Harvard rivalry—fun for a time but of little importance past graduation. Know that a Yale man with his wits about him can take on anything."

Murray grunted. He leaned his forehead against the passenger-side window and looked out over the quiet landscape. He had been passed over for early acceptance at all five colleges he applied to and feared the ramifications of outright rejection. He kept all concerns private. It was imperative his father remain ignorant.

"You should know that attending an Ivy League school brings certain, shall we say, societal baggage. Tuition is enormous—prohibitively expensive for most. Expect resentment once you enter the workforce. Some folks will feel you've been given an unfair leg up and be happy to see you fail. I recommend not giving them the satisfaction." Don Sr. pulled his gaze off the road and looked right at Murray. "Do you understand what I'm saying?"

Murray lifted his forehead from the window, leaving an apple-sized smudge where his skin had been. He nodded.

"Your mother and I feel the cost of admittance, hefty as it may be, is a worthwhile investment."

Murray muttered something indistinguishable.

"Wh–wh–what's that?"

"I haven't even gotten in yet."

"You will if you're qualified."

"What if I'm not?"

"Then you'll know soon enough. For now, a campus visit shows you're serious about attending."

"Yale probably gets thousands of visitors every year."

"We–we–we'll talk to John." Don Sr. smiled priggishly. "You'll see."

Murray slumped against the window and watched billboards and off-ramps blur together. AM radio chattered.

Yale was an elegant mix of gothic revival, brutalist, and contemporary architecture that made the campus feel simultaneously cutting-edge and grounded in enormous legacy. Don Sr. drove slowly down Trumbull Street, mentioning at least twice that his four years at Yale was unequivocally the best time of his life and pointing out landmarks of personal significance while rehashing aged memories forever tied to the physical space. They pulled into a lot off Prospect Street and walked east. Undergraduate Admissions was located inside a whitewashed brick building with protruding bay windows and a view onto Hillhouse Avenue. Murray and his father entered through rear doors.

The foyer was oak-floored, with light green walls that held oil portraits of distinguished-looking university administrators. Don Sr. ascended a maroon-carpeted staircase to the building's second-floor landing. His movements were casual and projected utmost confidence with his present location. Murray followed, watching as his father got halfway down the hallway then stopped abruptly, parted his arms, and turned his body toward an open office door. "John!"

Murray cocked his head and looked past Don Sr. Light shone through a rectangular stained-glass window cut into the upper third of the street-facing wall. Plants and hard-cover books occupied much of the space. An unfamiliar man with a mop of brown hair and thick-rimmed glasses stood up from behind a mahogany desk. He had a stumpy build. Patriarch and stranger hugged. The sight was disarming.

"This is my good friend, Mr. Phillips," said Don Sr.

The man batted the air and scoffed, deflecting any intention of formality. "Please, it's John. John Phillips."

"Mr. Phillips and I went to Yale together—class of 1978."

"Model UN, Investment Club, Intramural basketball champions two years in a row." John produced an involuntary snort. "That was before the three-point line, mind you. Can you imagine that?" He pointed at Murray. "That was also before your father became a feared litigator and an investor extraordinaire across real estate, media, tech, finance..."

"I was always a savvy investor." Don Sr. grinned and turned to Murray. "Mr. Phillips works in undergraduate admissions. He's very graciously agreed to speak with you."

John pawed at the air again and pointed to two empty leather club chairs. He produced a stack of glossy stapled pamphlets, placing them on his desk and leaning back onto his own chair's rear legs. "Yale was established over three hundred years ago. Our students are famous for achieving all-around excellence: Supreme Court justices, business magnates, Oscar winners, Olympic gold medallists, two American presidents..." He stopped, look-ing put off, and gestured to the literature in front of him. "Please, these are for you."

Murray took a pamphlet between thumb and index finger. He glanced through photos of smiling students looking ambitious and life-affirming. He felt profoundly inferior.

"We have graduates in all areas of industry: healthcare, media, banking, computer sci-ence." Mr. Phillips shifted slightly in his chair. "Tell me, have you given any consideration to a career?"

"Oh, sure."

Mr. Phillips smiled and indicated Murray should continue.

"Well, I'm a baseball player."

"Like your brother?"

"That's right."

"And you possess a similar gift for the sport?"

"I'm starting catcher on my regional select team."

Don Sr. crossed his arms and exhaled.

"And I plan on giving baseball a serious run," said Murray. "There's still the possibility I could get a scholarship and maybe play professionally, at least in the minor leagues."

Mr. Phillips let his chair fall back onto four legs. He interlocked his fingers and smiled.

"I know catchers have reduced offensive output and shorter careers."

"Is that so?" said Mr. Phillips.

"But a reliable catcher is hard to come by!" said Murray. "Everyone's saying Don could play pro. Why not me too?"

Mr. Phillip's smile was patient and well practiced. "Professional athletics is a wonderful career to aspire to. Fleeting, but wonderful. Yale has sent several athletes of note to careers in the NFL, NHL, and MLB." He chuckled. "The NBA is proving a tough nut to crack, but we're nonetheless honoured to play in the NCAA's premier division of competition—one of thirty-five varsity teams supported by our institution."

"And there's always coaching or scouting when my playing career is over. Major League teams employ hundreds of people."

"A strong Yale candidate is well-suited to take on any number of challenges. Tell me, what are your plans outside of baseball?"

"You mean if I'm not successful?"

"That's one way to look at it."

"Then there's no question."

"Please continue."

"I want to go to law school like my father."

Mr. Phillips nodded vigorously, sending his glasses bouncing up and down against the bridge of his nose. "The study of law requires exceptional critical thinking skills and enormous discipline. High Yale undergraduate marks, coupled with a strong LSAT score, will set you on the path to a successful career in litigation. Of course, you must understand that competition for admittance is fierce." Mr. Phillips pushed his glasses up to the very top of his nose and raised a finger. "There's no doubt the public university system is capable of great things. Many of our applicants simply feel the Ivy Leagues offer something more. Call it something—"

"Intangible?"

"Quite the opposite, in fact. The Yale difference is felt across every corner of the campus: smaller class sizes, superior instructors, cutting-edge facilities." Mr. Phillips's chin dipped. "It doesn't hurt that your father has done extraordinarily well for himself—a man who many model their careers after but few can hope to equal."

Don Sr. coughed. "You mentioned the fierce competition, John?"

"I did."

"How is it, exactly, that admissions are finalized, er, decided upon?

"Acceptances are based on a combination of high school grades—"

"Murray's been a shining star since elementary school."

"—extracurricular involvement, SAT results, and the applicant's entrance essay." Mr. Phillips opened his hands. "Murray will be competitive, provided his performance in these areas is consistent with what you were telling me over the phone." Mr. Phillips tilted his glasses to his forehead and gazed at his computer screen. "I'd been meaning to review his application before you arrived." He made little clicking noises with his tongue. His fingers worked quickly over the mouse and keyboard. "Department meetings and all that. Time tends to disappear. Here it is. Oh, oh yes. I see his information." Mr. Phillips took quiet breaths. His gaze moved methodically through the application. He stopped, and his face crinkled. "Now this is interesting here."

"What's that, John?"

"I do see a marked decline in performance this past semester—very out of line with Murray's eleventh grade marks."

"Is that so?"

"Certainly is. Very unusual."

Don Sr. looked sideways at Murray as he spoke. "How severe is it exactly, the drop in performance?"

"Enough to raise red flags." Mr. Phillips swivelled the monitor.

"You're confident these numbers are accurate?"

"Yale Admissions prides itself on top-notch data integrity."

Don Sr.'s eyes thinned. Murray looked to the ground. He felt as though his body had turned in on itself.

"How have your marks been this year, Murray?"

Murray's voice was almost inaudible. "There's a drop in performance, yes."

"As bad as Mr. Phillips says?"

Murray nodded.

"And I was not made aware of this?"

"You were not."

Don Sr. paused. "This is disappointing news."

Mr. Phillips held up a hand. "Let's not jump to conclusions. Is there anything that might account for the decline? Yale has procedures in place to accommodate exceptional circumstances."

Murray was silent.

"Are you not being challenged?" said Mr. Phillips. "Are your peers holding you back?"

"No."

"We're interested in hearing more. You'll understand my concerns, how not addressing this sort of thing while still offering admittance could be perceived as nepotism. We don't want to be seen as providing unfair advantage to the son of an alumnus, not to mention a personal friend of an admissions officer."

"It's just..."

"Yes?"

"I'm getting over a bit of a rough patch."

"Can you elaborate?"

Murray shook his head. "I'm going to do better."

"Is there anything you'd like to officially document? Anything admissions should know about?"

"No."

"And your marks this semester? How do you expect they'll turn out?"

"It's just, uh, I need to do better."

Mr. Phillips thumbed his glasses. "I see. And is there anything else you'd like to raise at this time? Any context at all? About anything?"

Murray's head dipped.

"Because looking at your application in its current state—I don't know that Yale is the right fit. It's one of those difficult situations. I struggle to see how we wouldn't be accused of playing favourites."

Don Sr. shook his head. "Well, this is embarrassing."

"Oh, no. There's no need to be embarrassed."

"I'm sorry for wasting your time, John."

"Not a waste at all."

"It's disappointing."

"Still always good to see you! Maybe under better circumstances next tim—"

"I'm going to get it figured out," said Murray.

"No—"

"Between academics and baseball, I'll get it figured out."

"You're not the player your brother is," said Don Sr.

"B—"

"You'll never be the player Don is. You need to prepare for the worst."

"What's the worst?"

"Being a has-been at eighteen. That's the worst."

CHAPTER 8

MAY 2005

BYRON SAT IN THE back seat of Ms. Anthony's Toyota Corolla, behind Lesley Chang and across from Murray Buchanan, from whom he was separated by matching grey banker's boxes and a folded pair of hospital scrubs. He pushed hair out to the side of his forehead and studied the side of Ms. Anthony's face. She had exclusively Caucasian features, in contrast to Lesley's epicanthic eyes. Familial resemblance was most apparent in the pair's identically shaped nose and cheekbones.

Byron folded his hands onto his lap. Mr. Marcotte's yellow Ford Escape followed in the rearview mirror. Banal hints of his teacher's personal life—a hanging spearmint air freshener, rust above the car's left wheel well, a fast food wrapper crushed between the dashboard and windshield—were unsettling in a way he could not quantify.

Ms. Anthony looked over her shoulder and smiled as her gaze settled on Byron. "Chess Bowl is an extraordinary event." She drummed her fingers on the steering wheel. "Frankly, it's surprising the school board pulls it off, given their incompetence in so many other areas of responsibility. Nonetheless, I'll give credit where credit is due."

Byron muttered an acknowledgement and shifted in his seat. He could smell Murray's deodorant across the car. The brand, he believed, was Old Spice Original. Byron did not dare make eye contact.

Hendrick Hudson High School's parking lot was a cluster of vehicular chaos. Children and parents moved between idling cars jammed into perpendicular gridlock. Ms. Anthony clicked her tongue and accelerated past a car turning left, then slammed her brakes, coming front to front with a Volkswagen Jetta nosing blindly onto the street. The driver, a fair-haired man with freckles, thrashed his hands and cursed as a boy sat stone-faced in the passenger seat. Ms. Anthony depressed the Corolla's horn. The man slammed the steering wheel with his palm and accelerated left, pulling up onto the sidewalk and grazing a bystander putting out a cigarette. Ms. Anthony clucked her tongue again. She spoke evenly. "You kids can get out here. Mr. Marcotte and I will park across the street."

The school's foyer projected a consistent familiarity in the way that all public schools do. Erected banners announced the 2005 Orange County Chess Bowl. Students hovered in small clusters. Byron followed Lesley and Murray toward a pair of smiling women seated behind a card table. The older of the two thumbed through laminated ID badges tied with lanyards as the younger read bullet points from a welcome package: Chess Bowl ran five rounds, game clocks received thirty minutes of playing time, win-loss-draw records determined standings, tiebreaks for trophy positions occurred via five-minute blitz matches, spectatorship was encouraged, and respect—at all times—was mandatory. The woman looked up from the page, saying that failure to comply could result in disqualification and, depending on the infraction, removal from the premises at the expense of the offending student's school. The older woman smiled and offered badges. Above all else, she said, everyone was to have fun.

Byron moved tentatively down the hallway. He kept his stare mostly toward the floor, looking up at irregular intervals and inadvertently making eye contact with unknown students. Voices echoed as he approached the gymnasium. A grey tarp lay lengthwise across the hardwood floor, on top of which were desks and orange plastic chairs arranged in long rows. Wooden bleachers extended out from one side of the wall. Volunteers tweaked configurations and nervously checked the time. A collection of focused-looking adults gathered around an enormous computer monitor, pointing at the screen and speaking in quiet tones. Students mingled along the outskirts of the gym. Byron watched Lesley lean her back against the wall and turn to Murray. "This seems a bit silly, don't you think?"

Murray snorted. "Are you serious?"

"What do you mean?"

"This is your chance to show the whole school district how smart you think you are."

"You're being sarcastic."

"I'm right, aren't I?"

"I think it's all a bit showy."

"We're talking about driving twenty miles to play chess—it better be showy."

Lesley poked at the mole on her forehead. "Do you think these kids are smarter than us?"

"It's chess, so all bets are off." Murray pointed to a hefty boy with buck teeth and a bowl haircut. "That guy could be your winner." He slapped Byron on the shoulder. "It could even be ol' Byron."

Byron's stomach turned. "Sure."

"Words of a champion."

"Anything is possible."

"Byron's astute," said Lesley. "When he wants to be."

Murray smirked. "Whatever you say."

Byron smiled lamely. He looked over Murray's biceps and forearms, then down his torso to his quadriceps and bulging calves. He tingled. His simmering attraction was now properly understood as both long-standing and undeniable. Murray was a bully and a jerk, but he was also beautiful. Byron longed to know if there was any chance, however unlikely, that Murray would reciprocate an advance.

Amplified feedback screeched through the auditorium. Byron swivelled his head toward a bespectacled man in a knit sweater and watched as he lifted a microphone to his mouth. "Attention, all Chess Bowl participants." He paused. His voice echoed. "First round action begins in fifteen minutes. That's 9:00 a.m. sharp." There was a smattering of whistling and applause. "Schedules are listed on the monitor at the front of the gymnasium. Each matchup has a grid number corresponding to a desk on the competition floor. Given the calibre of students here today, I don't expect there will be any confusion." The man chuckled. He took in a wheezy breath and continued. "Please report results to the scoring tables at the completion of the round. A reminder that all games are self-officiated, and the highest standards of integrity apply." A grin stretched across the man's face. "Most of all, remember to have fun!" His expression hung, as if expecting thunderous applause. More microphone feedback filled the room.

Participants began to assemble. Byron spotted Mr. Marcotte and Ms. Anthony hovering outside the gymnasium entrance. Ms. Anthony's gaze panned the room. Her face registered recognition as she located Lesley. She slid through the crowd and spread her arms. Mr. Marcotte followed.

"How is everyone feeling?" said Ms. Anthony.

"Couldn't be better," said Murray.

"This is exciting, isn't it?"

"Sure is."

Mr. Marcotte put a hand on Byron's shoulder. "Everyone's development over the year has been tremendous." His hand dropped. His voice was deep and smooth. "You'll be competing against some of the smartest students in the district. The day may be triumphant. It may also be humbling. Take the experience and enjoy it." Mr. Marcotte paused. "How does that sound to everyone?"

"The point is to put our hard work into practice." Lesley spoke delicately, as if to herself. "Control what we can control and forget the rest."

Ms. Anthony extended onto her tiptoes and whooped. "Go Crusaders!"

The gymnasium hummed as students wandered up and down rows, cross-referencing laminate badges against the floor's grid pattern. Byron located his desk and was joined by a brown-haired girl with a visible tic on her right cheek. The girl took a pawn in each hand and held her fists forward—Byron tapped her left hand and drew white. He arranged his pieces slowly. The girl did the same.

At exactly 9:00 a.m. the bespectacled man raised the microphone and spoke again. "Chess Bowl 2005 is officially underway." His words were monotone. "You may begin." Byron moved his queen pawn forward two places to D4, starting and stopping the speed clock with definitive drops of his outstretched hand. The girl matched him. Byron pushed his king pawn a single space. The girl sent out a knight. Byron bit down onto the inside of his lower lip. He looked forward. Kids sat, heads tilted and faces locked in deep concentration. He spotted Murray across the gymnasium, then looked back to the board and pushed a pawn two spots forward. The girl's bishop slid diagonally, sitting benignly at F5. Byron pushed his king-side knight to C3. The girl's pawn moved a single space ahead. Byron pushed a pawn to A3. The girl nudged her bishop to E7. Byron moved his rook two spaces. The girl inhaled noisily through her nostrils, bringing her bishop swiftly across the board and sweeping the rook out of play. Byron grimaced at his unacceptable mental gaffe. The rest of the game fell quickly.

The girl smiled and offered her hand. Byron shook. Her flesh was cold. They moved together toward the scoring table and reported the result to a woman wearing round glasses and typing into a laptop. A short, balding man checked her work.

Byron's subsequent matches were similarly unsuccessful. His final competition line showed four defeats and a draw, settling him near the bottom of Chess Bowl's standings. The day had been a gargantuan waste of time. Worse still, he was twenty miles from home and reliant on Ms. Anthony for a ride. Tiebreak matches, award presentations, and requisite mingling would make it well into the evening before he returned to Woodbury.

The bleachers shook as Murray jumped up from the floor and sat down next to Byron. "Four losses and a W. Tough day at the office." He made a show of dusting off his hands. "Heard you didn't do so well either."

"You heard correctly." Byron's voice was flat.

Murray slapped Byron's back. "Fuck these chess nerds." He nodded to Lesley, her body tight as she sped through a tiebreak blitz chess matchup against a well-dressed Korean boy. "She's an animal, huh?"

Byron nodded. He watched Lesley's opponent stare at the board with unflinching focus. The boy's lips moved silently, as if mentally cataloguing all possible victory scenarios and deciding which should be deployed. Hands shot back and forth between the board and clock. Clicking noises were rhythmic. Lesley's arm grazed a captured rook and sent it clattering to the floor. She bent down and bumped the desk—the board jostled and pieces tipped. The boy's neck snapped up, and he jumped to his feet, screaming for the technical director. The man in the knit sweater rushed over and put a hand on the boy's shoulder. The boy burst into uncontrolled sobbing that echoed off the gym's cement walls. Spectators muttered amongst themselves, and Ms. Anthony looked rabid. The pieces were rearranged, but the boy's focus was lost. Soon, Lesley had checkmate.

Byron kept Murray in the periphery of his vision. The gym moved around them. He desperately longed for affection.

***

This May day, just past noon, on the bleachers at Monroe-Woodbury is warm. There was rain late in the morning, but the sky cleared quickly and brought bright sunlight. The outside space has a rich feeling—not damp but also not quite dried-out. I enjoy fresh air on my forearms and the bustle of bodies around me.

A chemistry textbook is propped open on my knees, and I read about Le Châtelier's principle as it relates to light's effect on photoreceptors and retinene molecules within the human eye. Byron Somerfield sits beside me. He has a canvas in his lap and is painting deliberate black strokes.

In front of us, a junior with blond hair delicately places a football against a kicking tee, then steps back and left. He raises an arm in the air and bursts forward. There's a leathery smack as he connects with the football, sending it tomahawking through the uprights and landing in the grass past the end zone inside a pink Hula-Hoop. Evan Friedman has a cigarette dangling from his mouth and jumps up and down. The junior twirls around, pumping the air with his fist.

"That's something, isn't it?" said Byron. He remains focused on his canvas.

"What exactly is happening out there?"

"Kicking challenge."

"I see that. But why?"

"I overheard some of the baseball guys talking about it this morning." Byron points to the field. "The blond guy is a soccer player. He was hyping up his power and accuracy—said he'd be better cold than the varsity placekicker on his best day."

"And?"

"So Evan Friedman got all excited and asked him to prove it. They came up with this thing where he has to make the field goal and land it inside the Hula-Hoop. They're forty yards out right now, and his accuracy is dialled in. I'm not sure, but I think that's a pretty big deal."

"Weird."

"Sports are weird and arbitrary, but so is life."

I tilt toward Byron. "What are you painting?"

"Like, just fucking around. Trying some stuff out with found materials. I took some scrap plywood from the wood shop and scored some old paint the art room was going to throw out. For now, I'm just seeing what happens."

"That's interesting."

Byron shrugs. "Maybe. Tough to know for sure. What are you doing out here anyway?"

"What do you mean?"

"We usually only ever hang out in the library."

I shrug. "I want to take it easy while I can. Turns out I like being out here. It's a nice change of pace."

"I don't know you as someone who is capable of relaxing."

"I'm trying it out."

"Going to MIT is a big deal."

"For me it is."

"And you'll be great."

I look out onto the field. The blond kicker has his right foot in his hand and is stretching his hamstring. Evan Friedman pushes the Hula-Hoop toward the back of the end zone. He yells that the kicker should back up five more yards. "I still need to finish strong, of course—don't want the offer rescinded."

"Would they do that?"

"They say they would. I think I would have to mess up pretty badly."

"Which you won't do. So enjoy relaxing outside while you can."

I nod. "Have you figured out next year yet?"

"Got a waitlist and an acceptance for now. Still waiting on everything to see for sure. If I don't like what I get, fuck it."

"What does that mean exactly?"

Byron shrugs. "If things don't work out with school, I'll probably just move to New York and start painting. Like, it's where I should be to do my best work."

"Wow."

"I need to follow in the footsteps of greatness, even if that greatness is long gone."

"That's inspiring."

"You ever heard of the Chelsea Hotel?"

"Sure."

"I need to pass through there, for starters. It's nonnegotiable."

"That shouldn't be too hard."

"But really *be* there. I need to live and breathe and exist inside those rooms. Arthur C. Clarke wrote *2001: A Space Odyssey* at that hotel. Allen Ginsberg stayed there. Dylan Thomas died there. Sid stabbed Nancy there. Jack Kerouac. Madonna. Valerie Solanas."

"Who's that?"

"She tried to kill Andy Warhol."

"Huh."

"Nico. Patti Smith. Dee Dee Ramone. Frank Bowling. Ching Ho Cheng. Robert Crumb. The list goes on and on and on. It's a ritual space like nothing else."

"Those are kind of big shoes to fill, don't you think?"

"Fuck it. Like, failure is not an option. But not trying? That's just unfathomable."

"You're saying your parents' house in Woodbury isn't doing it for you creatively?"

Byron snorts. "Put it this way. I'm terrified of dying, and the only way I can think to pump any meaning into myself is to create art in New York City."

"I can respect that, I think."

"And I'm being as pragmatic as I possibly can. Art is the pursuit of people with a certain amount of privilege. I get it. But this is also my life. This is my one goddamn shot. If not this, what the hell am I supposed to do? I'm not a mathematics freakazoid like you. I can't just show up and ace whatever I want without trying. This shit takes time."

"I work harder than you probably think, and it's not always fun."

"And you perform exceptionally."

"Plus, math and physics becomes extremely unpleasant if you're not careful."

"What do you mean?"

I shrug. "Physics studies movement of matter through space and time. You could end up doing something cool like working for NASA. You could also end up with a defence contractor designing missiles to kill people in the most cost-effective way possible. It would still be interesting work in an abstract sense, I guess."

"Probably not something you want to be doing."

"Agreed." I rub my chin. "It's also work that will be done one way or the other. If not me, then someone else. Food for thought."

"You don't want to be involved with that—killing people."

I nod and look toward the blond kicker. His form is elegant and seamless as his foot lifts back and whips forward, producing a powerful thwack and sending a football high into the air, flipping nose over tail through the uprights, landing just outside the Hula-Hoop, taking a sharp bounce off the end zone grass, and hitting Evan Friedman square in the face. Evan curses loudly.

"What I'm really interested in is forward-looking stuff. Like what civilization deep, deep into the future looks like."

Byron nods.

"For example, the luminosity of the sun is steadily increasing. That will increase radiation levels in our solar system, which will cause a decrease of carbon dioxide levels here on Earth. We're looking at the atmosphere being inhospitable to human life in six hundred million years."

"Is that true?"

"Uh-huh."

"I thought it was longer than that."

"Not according to the best information we have."

"Only six hundred million years?"

"It's a difficult thing to grasp, isn't it? That's an enormously long amount of time but also doesn't seem quite long enough. So, assuming we figure out a way to survive that, we're looking at the oceans evaporating in about a billion years. In four billion years all life down to the molecular level will be extinct. Between seven and eight billion years from now the Earth will be absorbed by the Sun. Our planet will cease to exist."

"Okay."

"And that's assuming we don't do something to ourselves first. Global warming. Nuclear war. Artificial intelligence run amuck."

"Right."

"So if we want to prolong humanity's existence, we need a hyperefficient way to travel enormous distances through space."

"And you want to keep humanity going?"

"That primal urge for self-preservation exists, doesn't it? These are mind-bendingly complex problems. The groundwork needs to be laid."

"So that's where you come in?"

"Might as well try! No one else in Woodbury is going to, that's for sure."

"I hate most of the people here," says Byron.

"I know you do."

"I like you, though. In a pleasant platonic way. You don't treat me like a goddamn freak, and I appreciate that."

"You stick to yourself and don't call me out for being a dweeb. I appreciate that."

Byron nods. I look back onto the football field and watch a custodian walking quickly toward the end zone. He gestures at Evan and shouts that he needs to put out the cigarette immediately. Evan nods and waves the custodian off, then points to the blond kicker and salutes him. I watch Evan pull the cigarette from his mouth and discreetly flick it into a garbage can. He walks around a corner wall and out of sight. The custodian stands with his hands on his hips and curses.

"Evan is a bit of a jerk, huh?"

"No doubt about that."

"He's so cocky, but he doesn't have much to offer other than baseball, if you ask me—just a really unpleasant guy."

"I've heard rumours about him. Apparently, he's treated some girls pretty badly. Gotten grabby and aggressive. Stuff like that."

"Not surprised." Byron nods. "Feels to me like all guys are ticking time bombs. They're going to behave poorly if you give them the opportunity."

"I hope not all guys."

"I think most guys."

I pause. "How is your painting going?"

Byron shakes his head. "This one is garbage, but I can just prime it over and start again. I'm in no rush. Creative energy is a weird, complicated thing. When I'm doing something, I want to channel everything I've got into it. That means everything. Insecurity, fear, jubilation, sexual energy, uncertainty. All of it. Then, the hope is it morphs into a product that an audience can understand and glean something from. With good art, you want to let it wash over you. It's an extraordinary experience when things connect just right. You know what I mean?"

"But this one isn't doing it for you?"

"Fuck it. This one is a bust."

I look back toward the school and see a thin trail of smoke rising from the garbage can. Soon, flames are visible. Principal Uppendahl exits the school and stands with her arms crossed. She holds a tense expression and watches the flames but makes no effort to extinguish them.

"I hate that woman."

"Ms. Uppendahl?"

"She's horrible," I say.

"She's extremely strict."

"She's a fascist. All she does is stifle and shut down. There's no care at all for us students. Nothing."

"I know." Byron shrugs. "I kind of respect her for it. Like, for being so good at what she does. She's authoritative, no doubt, but she's playing her role to perfection. Everyone needs an enemy. You've got yours."

***

The 2:00 p.m. sky was pale and clotted with dark clouds. Poncho-clad spectators occupied bleachers along the baseball diamond's first- and third-base lines. A life-sized fleece gladiator with zombie-coloured skin and a violet cape that billowed and snapped in the breeze paced along the bullpen. Murray slouched forward, leg guards strapped to his calves and hamstrings, his hands raised and fingers interlocked in the dugout's chain link fence. Sunflower seed shells littered the ground. His gums felt salted and punctured.

Middletown High School's starting pitcher stood a lanky six-foot-five. Murray watched the boy lift his hands above his head and bring his right arm whipping over his shoulder, then hop forward a step and release his pitch. All-district shortstop and noted coke enthusiast Evan Friedman held motionless at the plate. The ump called a strike.

Sunflower seeds leaked out the sides of Murray's mouth. "It's all timing with this guy."

"I still think that's a balk." Irwin Bullwright's voice was squeaky and hurried.

"Ump says the pitch is legal. Coach won't fight it. Especially if we pound 'em."

"Better get on with it then."

Bullwright held up a clipboard, his job as team scorekeeper a pity appointment after a pulled hamstring during tryouts ended his season.

"All he's got is an unorthodox windup. Figure out the timing and his stuff ain't so b—"

The ping of aluminum against cowhide echoed across the diamond. Evan Friedman took off running. The ball curled and dropped into the outfield for a stand-up double. Murray spat out a mash of seeds. His tone drawled. "See? Adapt to whatever gets thrown at you—just like Don always says."

"You talk to him much?"

"Sure do. He calls home after every game. Says the speed and strength in the NCAA is off the charts. It's a big adjustment, even for him. He's got two more years until he's draft-eligible again, so for now he's just putting in the work and making sure coaches see the potential he brings to the table." Murray hocked a loogie. "Trouble is, now that Don's out of the house, my dad has a whole lot more time to remind me what a disappointment I am. He says I might as well quit ball at this point—that there's no future in it."

"He said that?"

"Sure did, but I don't see it that way. I'm just a late bloomer, you know? Some guys bloom so late, they're out of the game before it's their time to peak. There's no way I'm letting that happen—no way."

A skull-rattling bang burst overhead. Murray jerked his neck skyward as a great crackling of pyrotechnic colour rained down over the diamond. A boy he recognized as a Monroe-Woodbury sophomore jeered and whooped in the parking lot. The umpire pointed in his direction. The boy took off running.

Murray let his hands drop from the chain link fence and slipped off his leg guards. He piled more sunflower seeds into his mouth and picked up a bat, squeezing its rubber handle and accentuating twisting movements of his wrists and forearms. Another metallic ping sliced the air. A junior named Nick Berenbaum scurried to first base. Evan Friedman advanced to third.

Murray moved into the on-deck circle and slipped a weight over the end of his bat. He timed his swing to the pitcher's throwing rhythm, willing himself to normalize the bizarre hitch and hop step. Balls were coming quickly—he estimated 80 mph. Monroe-Woodbury junior Phuc Tran got to a full count over eight pitches before a called strike sent him back to the dugout in a profanity-laced huff that earned him severe reprimand and a near-tossing from the umpire.

A sudden veil of darkness rolled north across the sky, causing a visible line to track over the field, and spectators to look up and mutter that rain must be imminent. Murray walked toward the batter's box and dug in his feet to the left of the plate. Fat water droplets began to fall. The sky was the colour of cold lead. Middletown's pitcher stared forward, his neck pimply and upper lip dotted with pubic-like smatterings of facial hair.

"I'm wearing a metal jock."

Murray looked behind him. The catcher grinned through his cage and dipped his chin. "All metal." He pointed from the sky to his crotch. "Lightning rod."

Murray grunted and tapped the plate with his bat. Middletown's pitcher brought his arm whipping over his shoulder, hopped forward, and released. The pitch exploded toward Murray's head. He ducked. The ball shot off the top of his bat and into the opposing dugout—a fluke foul ball and first strike. Murray's heart pumped furiously. He stared down the pitcher and kept expressionless. A bang sounded behind home plate. Murray's gut flipped. Spectators craned their necks toward the source of the disruption. The sophomore stood on the grass-covered hill behind home plate, hand extended up, holding a discharged firecracker as glowing magnesium rained down over the field. He pulled down his pants and mooned the field. The school mascot charged.

Murray dug his feet back into the batter's box. He kept his front elbow relaxed, weight favouring his back foot and both knees slightly bent. The pitch released, spinning furiously. Murray got a good look at the ball and swung late—a second strike. He heard whooping and hollering. The firecracker boy darted along the periphery of his vision toward the backside of the outfield fence, more canisters clutched in his hand and Monroe-Woodbury's gladiator mascot in close pursuit. Murray tapped the plate with his bat and resumed his stance. A pitch came in low and outside. The count was 2–1. The pitcher stared past Murray twitched. His throw tracked just outside. Murray swung. Reverberations coursed up his arm as the ball rocketed away from home plate in a high arc. Murray dropped his bat and ran toward first base. The ball dropped over the outfield fence and smacked the sophomore square in the head. His arms flailed, sending a lit firework shooting off into the mascot's face. Murray looked over his shoulder as he rounded second base. The gladiator wrapped the boy in a textbook prop tackle and dragged him toward the parking lot. Murray stepped onto home plate. He high-fived coach Sanderson and pushed through a sea of teammates hollering and back-slapping. Murray settled into his spot on the bench and turned to Irwin Bullwright. "Like I said. It's all about timing."

"You hung that guy out to dry."

"I studied the pitcher and got it right. Baseball is a cerebral game." Murray kicked his feet into the dirt and rested his hands on his stomach. "You ever feel like you're limited by your mind?"

"What do you mean?"

"Dunno. Maybe that you want to do something or say something, but you can't quite figure out how?"

"I guess I felt that way about calculus."

"Yeah," said Murray. "You ever felt that way about anything else? Confused like you're studying calculus, but something you know you should be good at?"

Irwin shook his head. "Nothing comes to mind. Is that the point?"

"Because since I got beaned by that ball that Don threw, fuck me, things have been a little off."

"Have you told your parents?"

"No."

"Have you seen a doctor?"

"At the time I did. Not since, really."

"You should."

"Yes. Maybe."

"Why not?"

"Don't want to cause alarm unless it's absolutely necessary. Right now, I'm just trying to figure it all out."

"How are you going to figure it out?"

"Not sure. Figuring that part out too."

There was a flash of lightning toward the west end of town. Moments later, thunder rolled in.

Chapter 9

June 2005

Byron sat on the Somerfields' living room couch and revelled in the feeling of a proper university acceptance letter between his own two hands. He especially liked the school's seal at the top of the page and being addressed as "Mr. Byron Somerfield," and the welcoming, upbeat, optimistic tone of the five short paragraphs explaining how the admissions department was confident he would thrive and was genuinely enthusiastic for him to join Boston College's class of 2009.

The school's fine arts program was a good one. Byron would spend four years receiving rigorous, thorough instruction that deconstructed and challenged what it meant to be a successful artist, then be reformed, built back up, and enter the world like a bat out of hell. Showings. Public sales. Commissions if necessary. This was the world Byron would inhabit, and there would be happiness no other way than that of a goddamn artistic being expressing himself for the public to experience.

There was a knock on the wall. Byron looked up to see his mother, Joy, standing on the threshold of the room holding a glass of wine. She smiled widely and sadly. James Somerfield was behind her, his frame squeezed into a t-shirt that clung to the little pooch of his belly.

"How are you doing?" said Joy.

"Fine."

"That's good."

Byron nodded silently.

"We just wanted to see how you were doing," said James.

"We?"

"Your parents."

"Oh." Byron paused. "Is something wrong?"

"What do you mean?"

"Well, it's rare that we'd be talking together. Unless it's bad news. I've noticed that. We only talk together if it's bad news."

"We just want to have a conversation," said Joy.

"About practical matters," said James. "A conversation between adults to tie up some loose ends, if that's alright with you."

"What sort of loose ends?"

"Is that your Boston College acceptance letter?"

Byron nodded. "The waitlist worked out in the end.

"Hmm."

"It's due by the end of next week. I'm excited."

"Does the letter mention anything about tuition fees?" said Joy.

"Not the letter explicitly—some other paperwork does."

"What does that paperwork say?"

"I don't remember exact numbers."

"We're looking at approximately $20,000," said James.

"Okay."

"That's per semester."

"Right."

"What do you think about that?" said Joy.

"Well, that's just what school costs, right?"

James shook his head. "If you pay it, it does."

"Someone has to pay it."

"If you choose to attend, someone has to pay it."

Byron stared. "What else am I going to do?"

"Your father and I have been saving for your education since you were born," said Joy. "There were some lean times with difficult decisions—times that contributions weren't made. But we want to help you out the best we can."

Byron nodded and remained silent.

"We've got $7,000 for you—a little over."

"Right."

"The rest of that, unfortunately, we don't have." Joy took a drink from her glass. "We can help you apply for bursaries if you'd like. I'd even be willing to co-sign on a loan."

Byron nodded. "So that $7,000…"

"A little over $7,000," said James.

"Is that...per semester?"

James shook his head. "That's all of it."

"I see."

"Your father was thinking there might have been an opportunity coming his way, in which case the amount we offered would have changed. Indeed, it still could change over the next four years."

"Those are all hypotheticals. Extreme hypotheticals," said James Somerfield. "Don't plan for any resources beyond the money we already have."

Byron nodded.

"We know you have big dreams," said Joy. "And you absolutely must follow them, to an extent." She smiled. "There are also, of course, practical matters to consider."

"I know you can appreciate practical matters," said James. "They make the world go round. Our bathroom, for example, is in dire need of renovation. Getting the landlord's support on that—another matter entirely."

"Okay."

"Do you understand what I'm saying?"

"Sometimes I don't like to consider practical matters."

"Who does? I'm saying you're looking at $150,000 in debt with no guarantee of career or financial success."

"Your father is an example of that—the elusive nature of success."

"An example of circumstance beyond one's control dictating success," said James. "There are education options that can set you up much better."

"Such as?"

"You got into a SUNY school, didn't you?"

"Plattsburgh and Buffalo."

"There you have it?"

"Gross," said Bryon.

Joy frowned. "Don't be a prick, dear."

"I'm just not interested in spending four years in Buffalo or Plattsburgh—I don't even really know where Plattsburgh is!"

"We want you to be aware of your options. A school like Boston College is a tough pill to swallow, financially speaking. If you really want to go, we can't stop you, bu—"

"I really want to go!"

"But we also can't support you in the way you deserve to be supported."

"Then fuck it. I'll go anyway and figure out the rest later."

"It's important to ask yourself what you're getting out of a place like that."

"Prestige. Superior Instruction. Superior facilities."

James Somerfield took a step forward. "That superior instruction is coming from failed artists using teaching as their only means of financial support—without people like you going into debt for tuition, they're out of a job. The problem with higher education is it's kind of a racket."

"Well, I need to put myself in a position to succeed." Byron's voice rose and cracked. "I'm going to die one day, so I might as well live now, and maybe I'll have a shot at making something that will be discovered, and be appreciated, and outlive me, and bring just a little bit of meaning to my existence."

"Relax. I want you to think about coming out of school with so much debt," said James. "The divide between you and your peers—the ones taking more practical paths—will be stark." He paused. "You also need to think critically about the quality of your output."

"I have faith in my abilities."

James crossed his arms over his belly. "There are mistakes I made early on—putting time and energy into futile pursuits—that I'd like you to learn from."

"My pursuits aren't futile."

"Think carefully. This is your life we're talking about!"

"Exactly! This is *my* life we're talking about." Byron rubbed his face and stared past his parents. "And it looks like I've hit a bit of a snag."

Chapter 10

October 2005

Since coming to MIT, I have been obsessive about wearing sandals while showering. Touching bare feet to the surface of a shared bathroom and risking skin-borne fungal infection is an unequivocal nonstarter. Sandals are necessary. They provide peace of mind.

The bathroom walls are a faint yellow and moist from the hot shower finished moments ago. I take a step onto the resin floor. My left foot sandal slides, and I yelp involuntarily, jamming my quadricep and nearly spread-eagling onto my backside. I move to a full standing position and wrap a towel around my chest and torso. Water beads on my skin. I clutch a bag of toiletries and ease open the door, running down the open hallway. My sandals make wet smacking noises against the bottoms of my feet. A feeling of vulnerability lingers over my bare shoulders and loose towel.

I reach my room at the precise moment my next-door neighbour, a scrawny mechanical engineering student named Jerry Fujimoto with whom I take Physics I and like to converse, steps into the hallway. He nods at me. "How are you?"

"Good." My exposed skin blushes.

"What are you doing tonight?"

"Studying, probably. Collision theory stuff."

"That's cool," said Jerry. "I'll be doing the same. Not collision theory, but other stuff."

I nod and enter my room, then close the door and dress in soft sweatpants and a t-shirt.

The Massachusetts Institute of Technology allocates undergraduate dormitory rooms by way of lottery, with weighted consideration given to need-based requests as necessary. Female-only accommodation tends to fill up quickly, as do so-called study floors, where stricter levels of noise and substance enforcement, not to mention the introverted personalities attracted to that sort of arrangement, provide an optimal environment with which to work through gargantuan mounds of assignments and class readings.

For most undergraduates, accommodation is a double room on a co-ed floor. The prospect of living alongside teenage males is an exciting, albeit foreign proposition. A roommate and the compromised control over my environment is unfathomable. This led to my fabrication of a chitinase allergy, whereby exposure to bananas caused wheezing, cramping, hives, swelling, diarrhea, and shortness of breath. Left unchecked, I was at risk of anaphylactic shock. MIT Housing acknowledged the condition without requirement of medical documentation and granted me sole occupation of a double room. I kept my mother ignorant of the arrangement. She would consider my deception morally questionable.

I open a spiral-bound notebook and pull Dourmashkin's *Classical Mechanics* from my bookshelf. My posture is congruent to the back of my chair as I flip to Chapter 15 and begin a passage on one-dimensional elastic collision between two objects. Explanatory figures are tightly packed in small font. I register a brief moment of appreciation, like I always do when mulling over the elegant completeness of a good formula. I am in my element.

My schedule for the fall semester is as follows: Physics I on Monday and Wednesday with a Friday morning seminar, Calculus I on Tuesday and Thursday with a Friday after-noon seminar, Mathematics for Computer Science on Wednesday evening, Computation Structures on Wednesday and Friday, and Media Studies—part of the humanities, arts, and sciences requirements all physics majors must complete—on Tuesday and Thursday. Monroe-Woodbury's guidance counsellor warned of the precipitous drop in grades many students experience between high school and first-year university. She was adamant I must not let this negatively affect my self-esteem, lest I throw off my confidence and spin out into a hole from which I might not escape. MIT, she said, was a world-class institution full of extraordinarily intelligent people. To expect a consistent standard of excellence from high school through a four-year university degree was simply not realistic. So far, I have bucked the trend. My performance across five classes and three months of school is a pristine 100%.

I hear shouting from the end of the hallway and look up toward my closed door. Most nights the dorm room is quiet, with weekends sometimes producing beer-fuelled spurts of rowdiness. My social life here consists of chatting with Jerry in either his room or mine and exchanging occasional emails with Byron Somerfield. My quiet existence is by design. I will need years of untarnished transcripts to make serious inroads in the physics community. Until then, my focus cannot be derailed.

My door rattles against the frame. There's a knock. Two boys from my floor, one a comparative media studies major and the other an anthropology major, stumble forward. The comparative media studies major holds a glazed-over expression. The anthropology major brims with substance-induced jolliness. Both speak with the over enunciation of serious inebriation. We converse for no more than thirty seconds before the comparative media studies major's face sours. His eyes widen, and he lurches forward, producing a hollow gagging noise as the evening's cafeteria dinner pours from his throat. Both boys flee. I squeal and run next door.

Jerry Fujimoto looks up as I barge into his room. "Hello?"

"Someone just puked in my room."

"Really?"

"Yes!"

"Who?"

"Some arts student."

"Who was it?"

"Not sure. A tall guy. Don't know his name."

"You should learn people's names, you know?"

"It's all over the carpet."

"Uh, is there someone you can call?"

"I don't know. Can you just help me deal with it?"

"Isn't there a facilities person or something?"

"Probably not at this time of night."

"I have work to do here."

"You think I don't?"

Jerry pushes back from his desk and groans. "You're lucky I like you."

"Tell me what we're going to do here."

Jerry shrugged. "Let's go find a bucket."

***

SUNY Buffalo's Goodyear Hall dormitory felt cramped even in the absence of visible light. Byron sat in bed with his back and head against the exterior-facing wall. He wore thin sweatpants and a white t-shirt. His roommate Doh-Keun slept. The space was no more than a hundred square feet.

Byron moved his hand lazily across the neck of an unamplified Stratocaster copy. He plucked strings with his fingers, producing noise that was feeble and limp. Little bits of oil paint crusted his cuticles. A telephone receiver, moist from human sweat, was pressed between his left ear and shoulder.

"What are you doing?" Byron's voice registered barely above a whisper.

"What do you mean?"

"I mean, I can hear you moving around, like you're not really listening."

"Uh-huh."

"You're the one who called me."

Byron heard slow intakes and exhales of breath. "You're coming around to being a SUNY student," said James Somerfield. "Your painting is going good, and you've started playing guitar."

"Just for fun. My academic focus is painting."

"It's a wonderful luxury, pursuing something for fun."

"I like being able to express myself. I'm looking at options to show in the spring. I've even started doing some research on commissions. Did you know the freakin' Mona Lisa was a commission?"

"I did."

"Because corporate commissions can be seriously lucrative."

"It's good work if you can get it."

"Right." Byron dragged his index finger along the guitar's low E string. "So, like, how's Woodbury?"

"Are you in touch with anyone from high school?"

"Like, one person."

"Is it a girl?"

"Yes, but not in that way."

"Well since you asked, things are difficult over here."

"W—"

"I've had a tough time recently finding my footing. I've been taking work where I can find it, and that's if I can find it at all."

"I'm sorry to hear that."

"I'm being candid with you because you're an adult now," said James.

"Right."

"These are adult matters."

Byron stayed silent. He sensed his father's voice hanging.

"I've been working on something that could change all that—really provide the stable foundation I need."

"Okay."

"There's this opportunity. It's in the food service industry."

"Okay..."

"Not really my preferred industry, but I'd get to be my own boss, and the return is practically guaranteed."

"This sounds like a get-rich-quick scheme."

"It's not a scheme, exactly."

"Then what is it?"

"Donuts."

"Huh?"

"Dunkin' Donuts."

"And?"

"Their franchisee buy-in program; $500,000 gets you everything you need."

"I don't understand."

"What's not to understand?"

"Since when do you know anything about donuts?"

"I know Dunkin' Donuts' revenue last year was $800 million."

"So what?"

"I'd like a piece of that if I could. Like it or not, you'll eventually need to make money. And if you fail? You humble yourself and keep going."

Byron's voice rose. "Who else have you told about this?"

"I'm only doing research for now. From what I understand, coffee is high-margin—just water and beans. If you get a decent volume going, you can make a fair living." Byron held his fingers still and let the guitar rest on his stomach. He liked the way its weight felt: an anticipation of production, like the ability to create important music was just waiting to be discovered.

"Are you listening?"

"Of course I am." Byron's tone was flat.

"I have a friend at head office. He says they're planning a franchisee hiring blitz late next month on account of a big expansion push. We could make a good run at this."

"We?"

"I mean me, us, whatever."

"What are you talking about?"

"Not going to college is one of the biggest regrets of my life."

"Never too late."

"You have access to so many connections right now."

"I guess so?"

"I bet a few of your classmates come from considerable means."

"I d—"

"Even if UB is just a SUNY school."

"Uh, maybe."

"And the rich are always looking for ways to get richer."

"Like, isn't everyone?"

"So this is a place for them to park money. I would manage the day-to-day."

"Okay."

"I worry that you don't appreciate the significance of this."

"Why n—"

"You've never had a real job, for starters."

"I w—"

"I understand you've committed time to stuff that interests you. I'm talking about working for a revenue-generating organization—one where you're paid in exchange for your skills."

"W—"

"I'm not blaming you. Your mother and I provided this flexibility, at a considerable cost to ourselves."

"Why are you telling me this?"

"To get your foot in the door."

"The Dunkin' Donuts door?"

"You could find me investors."

"W—"

"You can't make money without a little something to get started. You know that."

Byron moved the phone to his right ear. "You don't have any money?"

"It's tied up."

"What about Mom?"

"I'd prefer to keep start-up costs outside the family."

"Don't you have, like, a network of people you can draw on?"

"That network runs hot and cold, Byron."

"So right no—"

"Cold. Extremely cold. And timing is everything."

"I think I need to focus on my work—school and all that."

"Look, I'm talking about a simple conversation to get the ball rolling."

Byron exhaled and rubbed his forehead. His calves ached from an afternoon standing in the undergraduate studio. The day had been productive. Tomorrow would be spent catching up with a week's worth of assigned reading on early Impressionist art and their relationship to the work of Vincent van Gogh.

"There could be access to a lot of money walking around your campus. Consider it."

Byron rubbed his chin. "I've been thinking about perfection in art." He spoke slowly. "Like, do you think anyone has ever written a perfect album?"

"I don't know, Byron."

"And if not, do you think anyone ever will?"

"I don't have the time for this right now."

"Just consider it."

"Fine." Byron's father's tone was short. "What about Bob Dylan?"

"Sure. Bob Dylan is a once-in-a-generation poet."

"But?"

"He's also a subpar vocalist. His recordings are iconic, but they're not perfect."

"What about Pink Floyd?"

"Extraordinary instrumentalists. They've got some real cornball lyrics, though, don't you think?"

"The Beatles?"

"Too simplistic to be truly great."

"You're telling me the Beatles are too simplistic?"

"Think about it."

"You're wrong. Consider it in the context of their era."

"Joni Mitchell?"

"The same."

"Then you've never *really* heard her voice."

"Pass."

"What about Charlie Parker?"

"Too sloppy."

"Led Zeppelin?"

"Plagiarists."

"Uh, Depeche Mode?"

"Next."

"Whitney Houston?"

"Too produced."

"Miles Davis?"

"Too mellow."

"Have you actually listened to Miles Davis?"

"Sure."

"U2?"

"Too many pedals."

"Jimi Hendrix?"

"Too drug-fuelled."

"The Doors?"

"The most overrated band in the history of music."

"What are you trying to tell me?"

"I'm saying art is a relentless pursuit of unachievable perfection. Even the best in the world haven't gotten it right."

"I understand. No—"

"How is Mom doing?"

"Your mother is good."

"And her work?"

"She's fed up, but she's a resilient woman."

There was rustling through the phone line. "Now, can we just focus for a second—back to what we were talking about earlier."

"If you want."

"Cut the smug bullshit, would you? I'm trying to do the right thing here. All I ask is you put the idea forward to people who might be interested. Can you do that for me? What's so hard about that?"

Doh-Keun stirred across the room. Byron squeezed the phone harder into his right ear and lifted the guitar off his body. "I have to get to bed."

"I'm just saying think about it."

***

Murray's body felt heavy and languid. He had left Polymer Imports' warehouse at exactly 5:05 p.m. The bike ride home took forty minutes. Now, he swayed on the spot and feared he would fall asleep while standing. He knew a nap before dinner would throw his sleep schedule into disarray. Murray shuffled toward his bedroom. He did not care.

The feeling of lying in bed fully clothed was unusual. Murray's consciousness faded into pleasant nothingness. He awoke an hour later to a blaring alarm clock and shifted, causing his jeans to rise past his belly button. He sat up and tasted stale saliva. He longed to return to sleep.

Murray moved sloppily down the hallway as the sounds of Bob Costas's Yankees pregame floated in from the living room. He spotted his father against the warm flicker of the television, collar unbuttoned and face buried in his phone, reading emails. Murray walked into the kitchen and opened the refrigerator. Condiment containers jangled from the door.

"What can I get you, my dear?"

Murray turned. His mother, April, materialized from the hallway. She wore tights and a sleeveless shirt, her figure toned from thrice-weekly yoga classes. She reached into the refrigerator and removed a plate of casserole. Murray sat down at the kitchen table. He held his spoon like a shovel and ate quickly. His mother folded her hands. "How's work?"

Murray swallowed. "Boring."

"What do they have you doing?"

"Usual warehouse stuff."

"What's usual warehouse stuff?"

"Picking, organizing. Things like that."

"Do you see yourself working there long-term?"

"Not a chance."

April's tone sharpened. "Your father thinks warehouse work is good for young people."

"How so?"

"He believes it's motivating."

"Dad might be onto something. I'm quitting in December."

April raised her chin. "Really?"

"I enrolled in Rockland College for winter semester."

"You did?"

"Uh-huh."

"They accepted you?"

"Of course they did."

"When did you find out?"

"Today at work."

"Well, this is extraordinary!"

"It's not bad. Got accepted for Business. Comes with the option to transfer to a four-year school."

"That's wonderful news."

"Plus, the baseball team is pretty good. I talked to the coach yesterday."

"That's nice."

Murray pushed a cheese-crusted noodle toward the end of his plate. "Don't say anything to Dad. I want to tell him myself."

April Buchanan made a lip-zipping motion with her hand. Murray stood up from the table and scrubbed his plate into the sink. He moved out of the kitchen and descended the basement stairs. It was here, the summer Don Jr. turned thirteen, that their father commissioned the creation of a serious workout space. Carpet was replaced with rubberized matting. A bench facilitated shoulder press, bench press, and seated bicep curls. A squat rack faced a floor-to-ceiling mirror. Interchangeable plates ranged from five to forty-five pounds.

Murray put on mesh shorts and running shoes. He climbed onto the stationary bike, pedalling slowly and methodically to the whir of the spinning flywheel. His hamstrings and calves felt warm. He watched his reflection in the mirror and puffed out his chest, his mind a dense cloud. He thought of Don Jr. in the NCAA.

Murray dismounted. He approached the squat rack, micro-adjusting his stance into a comfortable position and lowering his quadriceps until perpendicular to his calves. He rose, keeping his back straight and body weight in the middle of his feet. Murray repeated the motion. He tightened the inside of his mouth and exhaled, then stepped forward and raised his body until his shoulders lifted the empty bar from its cradle. He took two steps backward and lowered himself, his legs noticing but not straining under the new weight. He reracked and loaded up plates on either end of the bar, then took the weight on his shoulders and waddled backward. Murray exhaled loudly. He lowered his legs. His hamstrings and quadriceps strained. He grunted and returned to a standing position.

It was nearing 10:00 p.m. when Murray ascended from the basement. His legs and core burned. Endorphins pumped. The living room television was quiet. His father would be asleep already, an early bedtime critical to his unflappable 4:45 a.m. wake-up. Murray moved into the main-floor bathroom. He stripped. His body was tight and chiselled. He turned forty-five degrees left. His quads and hamstrings popped—a foundation of power crucial for elite catchers. Murray showered. He felt warm as he lay down in bed. Sleep took an hour to arrive.

Murray awoke to his alarm. His head felt heavy and pained, as if hungover from a night of hard partying. He rose partially and pressed the snooze button, then lay down and closed his eyes. His alarm sounded a second time. Murray sat up. He showered quickly and dressed indifferently. The kitchen was dark as he ate breakfast. Murray placed his empty bowl in the sink next to his father's. He exited the house. Dawn had not broken, and the air was cold. Woodbury felt peaceful and still.

Route 32 was void of traffic. Murray hugged the white line and pedalled his twelve-speed. He liked the way he could zip along the road at great speeds and hop onto the sidewalk on a whim. He arrived at Polymer Imports with bits of moisture dotting his back and underarms. He broke a sweat even on the coldest mornings.

Murray chained his bike to a lamppost and moved along the brick walkway toward the warehouse's receiving entrance. He nodded to a middle-aged woman puffing on a cigarette and pressed his key card against a black sensor. A green light flashed. He pulled open the door. The hallway walls were bare and painted in light pastel colours. Murray tapped his key card again and passed through a second set of doors. Rows of shelves ran lengthwise through the warehouse space. Enormous cardboard packing boxes were stacked from floor to ceiling. The air smelled musty and industrial.

Polymer Imports' logistics manager was a slight woman in her forties named Brenda Trinh. She smiled at Murray—her one-time professional association with his father was the driving force behind Murray's present employment—then went back to speaking with a bearded man named Brian on the matter of a lost shipment bound for San Diego.

Murray changed into work boots and retrieved a grey flatbed cart. He wheeled it to the printer bay and collected a stack of paper purchase orders from the output tray. Brian approached Murray and nodded. "More of this shit, huh?"

"That's right."

Brian took a long pull of coffee. He said he'd been at Polymer Imports every day for almost five years, and if it wasn't for his two little girls, he'd have quit a long time ago and probably be done with everything by now. Murray grunted in acknowledgement and ran his finger down the first order. Each printed line indicated a product category, model number, and pick quantity, all locatable within the rows and shelves inside the warehouse's ten thousand square feet.

"It's bullshit, of course."

Murray looked up. "What's that?"

"I said it's all a crock of shit. Everything this company sells is garbage." Brian pointed around the warehouse. "Imitation Tupperware, plastic spoons, dog toys, hairbrushes. Give me a fucking break."

Murray nodded. "I feel like we've had this conversation before."

"We buy the stuff from China, ship it to Los Angeles, truck it to New York, then sell it to stores across the damn continent. That much hassle for a paper plate or a piece-of-shit lightbulb? Seems like bullshit, don't you think?"

Murray shrugged. "I'm out of here in a month—not going to let it bother me."

"Really?"

"Going to school."

"Fuck it. That's a racket too. Why not just keep earning money?"

Murray shrugged again. "Maybe."

Brian shook his head and rolled his cart away. Murray looked back to his stack of purchase orders. The next ninety minutes were spent in a bored state of low-level concentration moving through rows of inventory stocked three shelves high. Fast-moving items were kept at arm's height. Obscure buys sat on lower shelves, requiring awkward bending and reaching. Murray took his route methodically, salvaging pleasure from arranging packing boxes in neat stacks on his cart, then sliding them onto the checkout table in a clean motion for a fleet of women to scan and package before they were loaded into eighteen-wheelers driven almost exclusively by—near as Murray could tell—middle-aged Polish men.

Murray's mind ticked slowly. He parked his cart and walked into the break room. Outside light shone through the north-facing windows. He looked out over the lawn at smokers gathered by the receiving entrance, bodies tensed against the cold October wind. Murray approached a stainless-steel urn and poured coffee into a paper cup. He sipped slowly. The coffee was lukewarm. Murray puckered his lips. He just needed to make it until the start of winter semester. After that, everything would happen.

Chapter 11

December 2005

Byron swung the steering wheel left and pulled his mother's Mercury Sable off Estrada Road. Lesley Chang's driveway was long and recently paved, her house symmetrical and two stories high. Byron coasted the car to a stop as Lesley stepped onto the porch wearing a puffy blue parka. She entered the front passenger-side door.

"I like your place," said Bryon.

Lesley shrugged. "Thanks."

"It's tidy."

"My mom hires someone to do the lawn."

"My parents would never do that."

"My mom says it wouldn't get done otherwise." Lesley paused. "I think my dad pays her a lot of child support."

Byron twisted his head over his shoulder and reversed out the driveway. "If my parents divorced, it would definitely be my dad getting support."

"Seems like your dad's lived an interesting life."

"Are you being condescending?"

"I hope not."

Byron shifted the car into drive and accelerated west toward Route 32. "Because I am."

"From what you say, he marches to the beat of his own drum, which I like."

"I guess."

"And scientifically speaking, we're all just molecules."

"Well, that bunch of molecules is losing it. He keeps talking about investing in a Dunkin' Donuts franchise."

Lesley snorted. "Really?"

"He called me about it a few months ago. I was hoping he'd forget, but it was the first thing he mentioned when I came back from Buffalo. Are you kidding me? Dunkin' Donuts?!"

"Do you think we're all doomed to become our parents?"

"Your mom seems cool."

"She is cool, but I still have my life to live."

"I'll never let myself be like my dad. Never, ever, ever. I won't let it happen."

"Are they at least happy to have you home for a bit?"

"Uh, I think so. They're empty-nesters now—first time."

"My mom is too," said Lesley. "Hopefully she stays an empty-nester."

Byron reached above his head and pulled out a CD wedged between the Sable's sun visor and cloth roof. "Check this out." He slid the CD into the dashboard player and pressed play. "Brian Eno."

"Huh?"

"Dig it."

"That's the weird atmospheric space guy, right?"

"Among other things. You have to let it wash over you. The stuff he does—it's amazing."

"Got it."

"And even if it's not amazing, it's abstract and he's got a reputation as a genius, so that's half the battle."

"You should beware the complacent genius."

"He's worked with everyone. Bowie, Genesis, Nico...Coldplay. Microsoft paid him $35,000 to compose that sound Windows 95 made when it booted up."

"I think I remember that."

"Everyone does, whether they know it or not."

"Brian Eno did that?"

"Sure did."

"Huh."

"Exactly." Byron nodded out the passenger window. The top edge of Monroe-Woodbury High School slid in and out of view as they drove. "Eh?" He looked to Lesley. "You miss that place?"

"Nah."

"Come on."

"Not most of it. Maybe a little here and there."

"I don't miss it a whole lot."

"I miss Marcotte. He was cool—beyond cool. He's all that I miss."

"You loved that guy."

"All I know is he was the only teacher who seemed genuinely interested in me and my success. That's saying something!"

"Maybe I'll miss it at some point," said Byron. "We're going to hit twenty. Then we're going to hit twenty-five. If I'm looking at thirty not having accomplished what I want to accomplish, that's going to be a problem. Maybe then I'll start to miss Woodbury." He turned west onto Route 6. "Until then, I continue forward. No looking back and no bullshit nostalgia."

"I'm going to be in a much different place at thirty than I am now. At least I better," said Lesley. "First semester at MIT has been no sweat. I've been reading ahead and poking around upper-year coursework—it should pick up. Plus, I might already have a job arranged for next summer."

"Really?"

"In a lab."

"Doing what?"

"Astrophysics stuff for an extremely smart woman. It would mostly be grunt work. Sounds more impressive than it is at this point."

"It sounds extremely impressive."

"It's entry-level, but it's still a big deal."

"That's great for you!"

"It is," said Lesley. "Do you like Buffalo?"

"Oh, it's not so bad. Maybe even an underrated city."

"I used to visit my dad up there sometimes."

"I get lots of time to do what I do—art and all that. I manage."

"But it's not Manhattan."

"Buffalo shares a border with fucking Canada, so it's definitely not Manhattan. I'm making the best of it." Byron steered south off the highway and looped into Kiryas Joel. He grinned. "What do you think of this place?"

"Not sure. Don't come here much ever, really."

"Did you know I'm a quarter Jewish? On my mom's side, which counts extra, apparently."

"Huh."

"And I like coming through here sometimes."

"It's unusual."

"There's nothing quite like it."

"My mom says there's all sorts of shady manoeuvring between the Hasidim and the school district."

"I like it for all its uniqueness." Byron pulled into a plaza made up of two-story beige buildings with matching maroon signage. "Weird place to be over Christmas though."

Lesley chuckled.

"But I still like it."

"When are you going back to school?"

"A few days after New Year's, probably."

"Me too." Lesley pointed to a woman on the sidewalk pushing a stroller and holding the hand of a toddler. "She looks like she's our age."

"She could be."

"What do you think about that?"

"Kids are not my first choice right now."

"It would be terrible."

"Think so?"

"Kids? Now? Definitely."

"So motherhood isn't for you?"

"Probably not ever, and definitely not now."

"Are you seeing anyone in Boston?"

"Romantically?"

"That's right."

"No." Lesley grinned. "But there's a prospect."

Byron tilted his head. "A 'him'?"

"Yes, a 'him.'"

"What do you like about 'him'?"

"Not sure."

"Anything?"

"That I can like him without even trying. Maybe that's something?"

"Sure is. Does he have a name?"

"He does."

"And that is?"

"Jerry. He's interesting. Smart as a whip. I like being in his presence, and he likes being in my presence—at least I think he does."

"What's he studying?"

"Mechanical Engineering."

"And he likes it?"

"He's a fanatic."

"So he's got a lucrative career ahead of him."

"He certainly seems to think so." Lesley rolled her eyes. "Stop feeling sorry for yourself."

"I'm not."

"Are you seeing anyone?"

"What do you think?"

"Uh, you tell me."

Byron fiddled with his seatbelt. "If you had to guess, what would you say?"

"I'd say 'yes'?"

"And then what if I told you something else?"

"What?"

Byron paused before he spoke. His voice rose. "That my preferences are...not heterosexual?"

"You mean you're...gay?"

"That's correct."

"Are you sure?"

"Sure am."

"Positive?"

"Yes."

Lesley paused. "I'd say that fits."

"Full gay."

"I think I basically knew that."

"You did?"

"Uh-huh."

"How the hell could you tell?"

"It all just fits."

"I don't know what to make of that."

"So? Are you seeing anyone?"

"Not specifically."

"Anyone you have your eye on?"

"I guess I'm looking for someone special, but there's no hurry. I want to worry about school and my work. That shit is time-consuming."

"Have you told your parents?"

"No way! They're on an information drip—need-to-know basis only."

"How come?"

"My mom, I think, would be cool. My dad would be a shithead. He'd make a damn scene, but he's kind of a loser, so it would be this weird, limp, sad scene."

"That's too bad."

Byron parted his hands. "Whatever. This is my life. I'm committed to living it."

CHAPTER 12

MARCH 2006

Room 1217 in Academic I, on the northwest end of Rockland Community College, was at full capacity. The student body numbered thirty and was a hodge-podge of middle-agers, ESL, and burn-out GEDs. Murray occupied the end aisle seat in the room's second-to-last row. Haze lingered in his eyes.

Professor Alan Flannigan entered from the classroom's front side door at five minutes past 9:00 a.m. He wore a green button-down shirt and cheap Walmart slacks. His hairline formed a glossy dome over his scalp. He took shallow breaths and muttered apologies for being late.

Murray slouched forward, elbows on the ledge in front of him and gaze on the floor. He liked the way his calves protruded from below his khaki shorts. He looked to his right—his bicep popped. He would join the Rockland Hawks' lineup as a spring walk-on. Not to would be unacceptable.

Professor Flannigan stood beside his desk. His physique was doughy and posture slouched. He ran his tongue across his lips and began to lecture on the topic of marketing excellence in the beverage industry. The class took sleepy notes.

Murray looked down at his notebook. He had previously secured a meeting with Rockland's head coach, John Greeley, during which he was regaled with stories of playing Class A ball against Roberto Alomar and once being cut during Milwaukee Brewers' spring training. For some, Junior College baseball—as explained by Coach Greeley—was preferable to Division I for its less competitive positional battles and draft eligibility after both freshman and sophomore years. An exceptional player would have every opportunity to shine.

"The Coca-Cola Company does $20 billion in sales a year. They spend 15% of that—$3 billion—on marketing." Professor Flannigan rested his hands on the pooch of his belly. "Starting in the late 1970s, we saw the Cola Wars. Coke and Pepsi invested enormous sums of money to out-market one another in the name of growing top-line sales. Investors demanded it. Consumers took notice. Lowly marketing professors collected limitless lecture fodder." He paused expectantly. The class held silent. Some looked up in confusion.

Murray flexed his calves. The last three months had been an extensive training regimen designed to crack a postsecondary baseball roster. According to Coach Greeley, this year's starting catcher position was wide open for anyone with the talent to take it. Serious playing time as a freshman would be an enormous boost to Murray's career. Even if the MLB didn't take notice, two standout JUCO seasons could earn him a Division I offer for his remaining years of eligibility. There, the stage would be bigger and the opportunities for exposure significantly improved.

Professor Flannigan sneezed three times in quick succession. He removed a handkerchief from his pocket and hastily wiped his nose. "Coca-Cola is extremely good at projecting global consistency across its branding. Coke position itself not as a product to be consumed, but as a lifestyle to be embraced. 'Coke is Happiness'; 'Refreshing New Feeling'; 'Keeping it Real.'" Professor Flannigan paused. "Their brand recognition is the envy of just about every organization on Earth." He began to pace the room. "There are, of course, enormous failures. A classic example that comes to mind is New Coke."

He paused and smiled smugly. "Anyone?" He rubbed his hands together. "Declining market share led the Coca-Cola company to tweak the formula of its flagship beverage. Prelaunch market research determined the drink, called New Coke, beat out both Pepsi and traditional Coke in blind taste tests. The product launched, and sales were abysmal. New Coke was pulled from shelves three months later. The gaffe cost the company millions." Professor Flannigan stopped pacing. "What the company failed to account for is the symbolic significance of Coke to its core drinkers. Marketing has the power to fundamentally ingrain itself in our lives. As future business professionals, you'll be living this day in and day out."

Murray looked down at his vein-riddled forearms. Success as a Rockland Hawk would require significant improvement from his time at Monroe-Woodbury. He had packed fifteen pounds onto his frame since the fall and needed more. Increased muscle mass meant greater hitting strength and faster pickoff throws from behind the plate. A round of HGH during the off-season could provide an additional boost to his mass and power. He was fuzzy on both a reliable source and the required financial investment but suspected the enormous man of indeterminate age known to haunt Rockland's athletic centre weight room could point him in the right direction. The upside was high. Risk, especially in the NCJAA, was minimal.

Alan Flannigan coughed. He returned his hands to his belly and smiled blandly. "Before I forget, a reminder to everyone that your case study assignments are due. You can hand them in at the end of class."

Murray stiffened. His gaze swivelled from side to side as his classmates nodded. Some pulled thin stacks of stapled papers from their bags. Murray turned to a dumpy, middle-aged woman with a loose ponytail. "You did this?"

"I'm sorry?"

"I mean, you knew about the assignment?"

"Of course I did."

Murray nodded slowly. "Right."

"Did you forget?"

Murray groaned and squeezed his eyes shut. "I think I did."

"You mean entirely?"

"Uh-huh."

"Oh....how?"

"I guess it slipped my mind."

"Oh....are you okay?"

"I don't know." Murray raised his hand. "Professor?"

Alan Flannigan's expression registered shock. "Why, yes?"

"How much is the assignment worth?"

"For those who read the syllabus, they'll know this assignment is worth 20% of the final grade. If it's not handed in today, it's late, which means a big fat goose egg."

"Right."

"Anything else?"

Murray shook his head. He drummed his fingers on his desk and rubbed his face. His vision narrowed. He watched Alan Flannigan's lips curl. Murray weighed his options. Flannigan's chin wobbled from side to side. Murray decided right then to drop the class. He looked around the room again. A man with a drooping eyelid and fifty pounds of extraneous girth ate a sandwich from a clear plastic bag. Near the back of the class, a thin-nosed man with uneven red hair picked at a pimple the size of a pea. A woman lifted her leg to pass gas and acted as if she had not done so. The room caved in. Murray did not know what would come next.

CHAPTER 13

JUNE 2006

Now, BARELY OUT OF May, Woodbury was already immersed in full summertime heat. Byron sat slightly reclined in a folding chaise lounge and strummed loosely on his Stratocaster. His arms sizzled under the unshaded sun.

In the neighbouring yard, Mrs. Wasser, on indefinite leave from her job as a corporate accountant, lobbed a Wiffle ball to her four-year-old daughter, Sarah, who swung a plastic bat and missed badly. Mrs. Wasser cooed. Sarah giggled.

The Somerfields' backyard screen door clicked and slid open. "Can you help me here, Byron?"

"Huh?" Byron lifted his chin and rolled his eyes toward his forehead. His father stood in the doorway in jeans and an old t-shirt.

"It's a beautiful day, don't you think?"

Byron readjusted his back. "It's fine—a little hot."

"Good grilling weather. Can you help me with the BBQ?"

"What?"

"The BBQ."

"You mean the old one in the back of the garage?"

"Uh-huh."

"That thing works?"

"Went and got a new propane tank yesterday."

"Have you tested it out?"

James rubbed his hands together. "Not yet. I need your help."

Byron rocked into a sitting position. He placed the Stratocaster widthwise across the chaise lounge and stepped to his feet. Sweat tickled his lower back. He stretched his arms above his head and followed his father into the garage. An old two-burner BBQ was slotted into a space between the outside-facing concrete wall and Joy Somerfield's red Buick.

Byron's father shimmied around a tool bench and a pile of extension cords. He cracked his knuckles. "Come over here and take a side, could you?"

"Okay."

"And make sure you have a good hold on the body. Don't trust the handles."

Byron grasped the grill at its steel legs. "Got it."

"Now lift."

"When was the last time we used this thing?"

"Lift it, would you?"

Byron tightened his grip and took the weight onto his hands and forearms. The grill rose unsteadily. He stepped backward and felt resistance.

"We're going out of the garage and onto the lawn. Got it?"

Byron nodded.

James pushed the grill forward. Byron, his back to the garage's rear exit, manoeuvred blindly through the stored clutter. Weight pulled. The BBQ tipped toward Joy's Buick. James's face flashed panic, and he heaved. Together, father and son steered the BBQ away from the car and onto the threshold between garage and backyard. Byron stepped down the foot-high incline. Shrill screeching sounded. Sparks flickered and shot up from the grill carriage's metal underside. "Shit, Byron. Watch it."

"I have it."

"Could you lift it?"

"I have it."

James Somerfield grunted and brought his side over the threshold. "Put it down over there."

Byron guided the grill toward a spot in the grass off the back deck. His wrists and forearms ached. He released the weight. The grill settled. James disappeared around the side of the house and returned with a fresh propane tank that glimmered against the midday sun. Byron watched his father attach the supply hose to the tank valve then scurry into the house and emerge with a book of matches and hamburger patties wrapped in butcher paper. James turned the propane gauge and threw a lit match. A great whooshing sounded. Flames danced along the grill's burners. James Somerfield closed the lid. "We can get some meat going once this heats up."

Byron nodded and rubbed at a spot on his elbow. Laughter carried from the neighbour's backyard. He watched Sarah Wasser contact the Wiffle ball and send it forward into a shallow arc. Mrs. Wasser cheered. She retrieved the ball and squared herself to Sarah, then lobbed another throw. Sarah swung and missed. Mrs. Wasser jogged forward and bent down. Sarah let out a shrill yell, whipping the plastic bat against her mother's head with a hollow thud. Mrs. Wasser cried out and scolded Sarah. She lifted her daughter onto her hip and pulled the bat from her hand.

James Somerfield cleared his throat. Byron looked at his father. "Yes?"

"Did you make any progress with what we talked about?"

"Kind of. I've started putting together some ambient recordings—not sure what it is yet, exactly, but you never know. I'm still learning."

"No. The other thing."

"What?"

"Dunkin' Donuts."

"Oh." Byron titled his head. "You're still doing that?"

"I'd like to."

"That was months ago."

"I still think it's a great opportunity."

Byron rubbed the back of his neck. "No one comes to mind."

"I'm disappointed to hear that."

"And, like, Dunkin' Donuts is lame. Ugly uniforms. Shitty coffee. What's good about it?"

"It could be a serious money-maker. Start-up costs are all you need." James enunciated each word carefully. "Figure out which families at SUNY Buffalo have money and then make an introduction."

"Yeah, maybe. The moment should be just right. Sometimes you only get one chance with these things."

"These things?" James's voice rose. "Like you're some kind of expert?"

"Are you?"

"I'm out here trying to make a living any way I can. What are you doing this summer, other than taking up space?"

"Not sure. I'm enjoying time. You know, recharging and finding inspiration."

"Mmmm." James opened the BBQ lid. He ran a brush along the metal grill and placed sirloin patties in two rows. "You know, back in high school I took a door-to-door job selling lawn fertilizer so I could buy comics?"

"You've never mentioned it."

"Earnings were dictated by the effort you put in. So I took out a map and strategically targeted the richest pockets of my territory. The first sunny weekend of spring, I pounded the pavement. Guess what? I made a killing. The boss said I did a month's worth of business in a single weekend. Can you imagine that? A single damn weekend."

"That's impressive."

"It was the desire to succeed that did it."

"Yeah." Byron paused. "I'm motivated in the same way—sort of. I want to make my living from art and nothing else."

"Take it from me: life has a way of changing even the best-laid plans."

"I don't want it to. I just need to stay focused and not give in when things get tough."

"It happens to most people sooner or later."

"Well, hell, then I'll burn money if I make it any other way."

James waved a hand dismissively.

"I'm serious."

"Guess what I did with my fertilizer earnings?"

"What?"

"Bought a lawn mower and cut lawns. Think about it. I had a built-in customer base ready to go. That fall, I bought a rake. My energy was infectious. Customers couldn't say no. What do you think I did when winter came around? Found a deal on a snowblower."

"That's a lot of comic books."

"You're damn right it is."

"So what happened?"

"I spent the winter clearing driveways and made a bundle."

"Then what?"

"I learned the importance of being humble."

"How?"

James Somerfield shrugged. "I bragged a lot. Someone at school figured out there was money to be made and undercut me. I lost 90% of my clients that spring—didn't make sense to continue. The kid got a reputation for being a weasel, but he didn't care. Money is money."

"Mmm." Byron looked down at his feet. "What was the point of that story?"

"Hustle and hard work can pay the bills."

"I want giving a crap about what I'm doing to be more important than paying the bills."

"No offence, but that's because you're living in a fantasy world."

Byron removed a $20 bill from his pocket. He folded it lengthwise and held it over the BBQ. Heat toasted his fingers. He lowered his hand until the ends of the bill sizzled and curled.

"What the heck do you think you're doing?"

"There's always more money to make. What's $20?"

Byron watched the bill burn down toward his fingers then dropped the charred remains into the grass.

James flipped a burger and shook his head.

"What?"

"How about you go inside?"

"Why?"

"Just do it."

"Aren't we eating out here?"

"Just do it."

"Whatever you want." Byron lifted his guitar by its neck and walked into the house. His mother sat at the kitchen table reading a James Patterson paperback. She smiled. "When's lunch, dear?"

"Dad got pissed at me."

"What happened?"

"We were out there grilling, th—"

"Since when do we have a BBQ?"

"He was going on about this old job he had, and I said I wasn't interested in any of it. He seemed to think, like, my values are out of whack or something."

Joy nodded.

"I burned a $20 bill to prove a point."

"Oh." Her eyebrows rose. "What point was that exactly?"

"Fuck it."

"You know that money is tight around here?"

"Yes."

"You do?"

"I mean, isn't money always tight?"

"It often is."

"I've been noticing something," said Byron.

"What's that?"

"Dad's, like, kind of a loser."

"Your father's been moping around a lot lately. More so than usual. He's a bit of a mope in general, mind you." Joy cleared her throat and traced her thumb over the kitchen table. "What would you say if I said we were considering separating?"

"Uuhh, I'd say I don't like that."

"It's something we've been thinking about for a while now."

"It is?"

"I have, anyway. Your father can speak for himself."

Byron exhaled slowly.

"You'd prefer we stay together?"

"Of course I want you to stay together."

"Why is that?"

"Because I don't want to have divorced parents."

"You're an adult now."

"You're still my parents."

"Sometimes these things are inevitable."

"Hey!" Byron's father waved through the screen door. "Lunch is ready."

"Thank you, dear." Joy locked eyes with her son. "Everything's going to be just fine." She stepped into the backyard. Byron followed. The family sat down to a lunch of grilled hamburgers and Safeway potato salad. Sweat beaded across Byron's hairline and tricked down the side of his face. His parents were wordless.

A car door closed in the driveway next door. Mr. Wasser walked up the driveway and into his backyard, his tailored slacks and pressed shirt—even on a Saturday—confirming his recent ascent to partner at a law firm in Danby. He embraced his wife and daughter then looked toward the Somerfields and raised a hand in greeting. Byron watched his father's eyes widen. Clutched between thumb and index finger was a Dunkin' Donuts coffee cup. James waved back at Mr. Wasser and turned to his son. "You see that?!"

"What?"

"Donuts and coffee can make you rich, assuming you've got a guy like me willing to do the leg work."

"Okay."

"Take the opportunities wherever you can." He paused and grinned. "This might be the start of something really big."

***

"Hey, Don."

"Hi, Mur."

"What's going on?"

"Just relaxing, Mur."

"Are you with a girl?"

"You mean right now?"

"Yeah."

"No," said Don. "Not right now."

"But you've met some girls at Vanderbilt?"

Don chuckled through the phone. "Of course."

"Why is that funny?"

"Because I'm a DI athlete with moderate pro potential. There have been some girls."

"Do you have a girlfriend?"

"No," said Don. "Not right now."

"Why not?"

"Not interested."

"Because," said Murray. "If I was in your position I'd be interested."

"I'm draft-eligible again this year and projecting to be a decent pick. Need to put my best foot forward."

"Right."

"Competing with seniors and high school hotshots for the pro's attention. Baseball needs to be my priority."

"How's that going?"

"Focusing on bulking up, but in a disciplined way. Like I always told you."

"Lifting smart is better than lifting heavy. That's what you told me."

"Exactly. I keep improving my power and stay focused on injury prevention. Protect the shoulders, protect the elbows, protect the wrists, protect the knees. All of it."

"That's really exciting."

"I feel like I'm close, Mur. Real close to achieving my dreams. Closer than I've ever been."

"And you will."

"I might, but there's still work to be done."

"And you will take care of that work."

"Enough about that," said Don. "I want to hear about you."

"Don't worry about me."

"I want to hear about what you have going on."

"I'm okay," said Murray.

"But not great?"

"I'm more than okay. I'm good."

"Uh-huh," said Don. "Ball is good?"

"The season was fun. The talent was better than I expected. Lots of good players. Seems like a few guys could move up to DI."

"I'm happy to hear that."

"So things are good, but they're also kind of fucked up."

"Why's that?"

"I'm fine, by the way."

"Uh-huh..."

"But, like, I dropped out of Rockland and haven't told Mom and Dad yet."

"Right..."

"They won't even notice when I'm not playing next year."

"You just dropped your classes?"

"Uh-huh?"

"Why?"

"I dropped one. Then I dropped the rest."

"Come on."

"Couldn't stay focused and just stopped caring."

"What the fuck are you talking about, Mur? You're a smart guy. You shouldn't even be in a place like that to begin with."

"If I'm so smart, why are you the one in college?"

"We have tutors and coaches to make sure we're taking care of classes. We jump through the hoops and everyone is happy. You're a goddamn rocket scientist compared to me, and you probably really *could* be a rocket scientist if you wanted to."

"Like, I've been struggling, Don."

"No kidding."

"I mean really." Murray pushed his face into the phone. "That baseball thing. When you beaned me in the head, and I had to go to the hospital." He spoke slowly. "I don't think I've ever been the same after that."

"Okay…"

"And I'm not sure I ever will be."

"What do you mean?"

"I'm saying it fucked me up."

"Like how?"

"Like, my cognitive abilities."

"Are you being serious?"

"I think so. I mean, we know getting hit in the head with a fastball isn't good."

"Right."

"And when my head hit the ground, it definitely smacked against a rock. Like, the ground was hard, but the rock was harder."

Don Jr. groaned.

"So that's a fastball to the temple, and then my head smacking the hard ground right into a rock. I'm not quite sure what the way forward is."

"I didn't know it was that bad."

"It wasn't your fault."

"Well, it wasn't my intention, but it kind of was my fault."

"It was no one's fault."

"I was the one who threw the pitch. I was the one who got distracted by Lillian Monk right at the end of my windup and let the ball get away from me. That was me."

"Maybe, but I was still there with a bucket on my head and a shirt wrapped around my face so I wouldn't flinch." Murray rubbed his head. "In retrospect, I wish I had flinched."

"What are you saying?"

"I'm saying I've dropped out of community college and baseball might be over. I'm also saying that I'm feeling pretty useless."

"It sounds like you're feeling dissatisfied."

"I'm saying I feel real useless. Concentration is hard. Like, the things I used to be able to focus on—to be good at and excel at—that's gone now."

"Did you talk to a doctor?"

"Of course I did, at the time."

"But you should again. Now. You need to get into treatment."

"Treatment of what? For what? It was three years ago."

"For your head. Something is better than nothing."

"Maybe. But I need a job first."

"A job will come with time."

"Well, it better come soon!" Murray looked at his bedroom ceiling through the dark. "I'm open to whatever is available. I'll be a corporate drone. I'll flip houses. I'll sell insurance."

"I think I know what you mean."

"Imagine being able to renovate a house. What a serious, practical skill!"

"Are you interested in renovating houses?"

"Why not? I'm ready for a second act."

"Fuck, Mur. I feel awful."

"You can't feel awful."

"Sure I can. I do!"

"Well, you can't let it derail you. Just keep on doing what you're doing. I want to see you play in the majors."

"Yeah." Don breathed out through his nose. "The opportunity is there. A contract, a signing bonus, all that. There are people who will make it and people who won't. Most won't. I might. Maybe."

"You will, and it will be amazing."

"Are you living with Mom and Dad right now?"

"I am."

"How's that going?"

"Mom is supportive as usual. Dad is an overbearing bully, also as usual. All bets are off if I tell them I dropped out."

"Mom mentioned to me she was thinking about going back to work."

"As a lawyer?"

"That's right. Mom's a smart lady. You just might not know it because she plays second fiddle to Dad. She said once you're out of the house, she wants to start practising again. Her licensing is up to date and everything."

"She never said anything to me."

Don laughed. "No pressure."

"Right."

"You spend time getting yourself together and don't worry about anything else. We both know you're capable of greatness. And greatness is subjective, and that's entirely the point. It's all about personal greatness, given your circumstances, however fucked up they might be. So go do it!"

***

The summer dorm room in Random Hall is a temporary arrangement made necessary by my recently won research assistant position in Nergis Mavalvala's astrophysics lab. Professor Mavalvala is a scientific God. She is everything I aspire to be.

The room's walls are white and uninspired. I have not bothered with personal touches other than the stack of textbooks on the corner of my desk and a small collection of closet-hung clothes. My present wardrobe is three pairs of pants, two collared shirts, two t-shirts, and a single blouse. This far exceeds my lab's unwritten dress code standards, especially within a dweeb-heavy space like Professor Mavalvala's.

I sit on the edge of my bed and browse a copy of *Computational Science and Engineering* by Gilbert Strang. There is a constant pressure on my forehead—a sure by-product of the previous night's house party that lasted well past midnight. As a rule, I find drinking a gargantuan waste of time and successfully abstained from alcohol for the entirety of my freshman year. I have loosened my stance since spring term ended, especially when socializing with older labmates.

My mother took the news of my summertime employment unexpectedly hard. She made worried throat noises as I explained my admittance into the lab, the complex research being done, and the subsidized dorm room where I would be staying. It was less than a week after semester finished that she announced her intention to visit campus. She is due to arrive imminently.

I feel a slight—though noticeable—nausea when moving my head up, down, or side to side. I spent an hour last night drinking and chatting with the cute friend of a lab research assistant. He left to get pizza around 1:30 a.m. and did not invite me along, though in retrospect he also did not explicitly forbid me from joining. I walked back to the dormitory alone, feeling buzzed and bland.

There is movement down the hallway. I hear a knock, then the turning of a knob, and the squeaking of hinges. The door swings open. My mother stands before me. Her boyfriend Daryl is to her right. They smile in a way that makes the room feel immediately claustrophobic. My personal space evaporates.

"Hello, dear!" My mother's face beams. "How are you?"

I rise from my bed, and we embrace in a long hug.

"The parking here is god-awful."

"Most people just walk."

"We drove around for fifteen minutes before Daryl found a spot." My mother pushes me out to arm's length. "Your room's a little bare, don't you think?"

"It doesn't matter. I'm just here for the summer."

"It's important to take pride in your living space! Would you like us to take you shopping?"

I exhale and feel my jaw tighten. "For what?"

My mother points to the bed. "New sheets, for starters. We could get you a nightstand or a bookshelf."

"I don't need any of it. I'm just fine here."

"Are you sure?"

"Everything is fine."

"Whatever you say." My mother waves her hand indifferently. "What would you like to do?"

I poke at the mole on my forehead. Jerry Fujimoto is home in Milwaukee for the summer. Byron is still in Woodbury. I stare longingly at *Computational Science and Engineering* and shrug. "How about a walk?"

"Show us the campus! That sounds like a lovely idea." My mother looks at Daryl. "What do you think?"

Daryl smiles. "Lovely."

"Right then. Follow me." I slip on shoes and move past my mother and Daryl out into the hallway. We descend two flights of stairs and exit onto Massachusetts Avenue, then walk south toward the Charles, and turn east on Vassar Street. My mother gasps in delight at the Stata Center's disorderly architectural lines and cartoonish perspectives. Daryl says that the campus is electric, and isn't it wonderful to see a university properly investing in the advancement of scientific study. He asks what sort of work Professor Mavalvala's lab does, and I stumble through a layman's explanation on the ins and outs of quantum measurement as it relates to the study of radiation pressure and gravitational waves. Daryl is thrilled.

We walk to Memorial Drive. The Charles River stretches out before us. A women's eight holds still on the water. My mother asks if I'd consider joining crew and says that any team worth a damn would be lucky to have me as a coxswain on account of my small stature and unshakeable focus. I shrug and say I don't have time to bother with that. My mom slows her pace. "You're not working too hard, are you?"

"It's MIT. You have to work hard."

"Not harder than everyone else, I hope?"

"How could you even quantify that? I'm working as hard as I need to work to get things done."

"Uh-huh. Have you ever considered getting involved in student government?"

"What? No, of course not."

"It's a unique opportunity to shape how your school functions. Grad school admission boards will love it."

"I don't have time."

"How about a boyfriend?"

"No, Mom." My voice's pitch rises involuntarily, and I think of Jerry again.

"How about dates? Anyone? And if so, who initiated the request?"

"None of that, that you need to know about."

My mother smirks. "The person you meet swaying through a wine haze could be the one to completely change your life."

I explain that my focus is studying and steer my mother and Daryl north up Fowler Street. We move past tennis courts with professorial-looking players showing off halting and uncoordinated swings, then through Roberts Field, where Daryl gets excited and asks about the football team, to which I cannot offer an iota of reliable information. I point out the physics department off Albany Avenue, the nuclear reactor lab, and the coffee shop where Professor Mavalvala buys us lattes sometimes. Random Hall comes back into view. I kick at the ground and make a farting noise with my mouth. "Is there anything else you wanted to see?"

My mother rolls her eyes. "Are you trying to get rid of us?"

"I—"

"We shouldn't stay too long. Right, Daryl?"

Daryl smiles evenly. "Whatever you'd like."

"We're on our way to New Brunswick," says my mother.

"You're going to Canada?"

"Last I checked."

"Why?"

"Daryl's Canadian, didn't you know?"

Daryl nods. "Born and raised in Moncton. Went to university in Toronto then got hired by a New York firm after graduation. I've been here ever since."

I nod and say that's interesting. We settle into silence. My mother suggests lunch, and we walk north on Massachusetts Avenue, ending up at an expensive Mediterranean place I would never otherwise patronize. The interior is quiet, aside from the constant low-level babbling of a floor-to-ceiling glass-walled waterfall. A hostess dressed in tight black leads us to a table near the front of the restaurant. Daryl quickly excuses himself to use the bathroom.

I sit. My mother smiles across from me. We are brought bread and olive oil by a well-dressed server with a gaunt build. My mother asks his favourite appetizer, to which he replies Tirokafteri with vegetables and flatbread. She requests enough be brought out for the three of us. My mother watches the man turn and disappear into the kitchen. Her gaze settles onto me. She does not speak.

I look down at the menu, and my eyes bulge. "Expensive."

"It's no trouble, dear."

"I mean really expensive."

My mother scans the specials. "My commitment is to you. You know that, don't you?"

I focus on the menu and nod.

"I've been given a promotion at work. Starting next month, I'm the new chief of nursing for Orange Regional." My mother tears a piece of bread in two. "The old chief resigned over a big sex scandal: subordinates, contractors, more than a few inanimate objects, apparently." She smiles thinly. "He was a skilled medical professional, but he was also a monster."

"Oh."

"Watch out for the monsters. You'll meet plenty of them, if you haven't already."

I nod. "Sure."

My mother lifts her hand and places the bread in her mouth. She chews slowly. "The money is good, of course. I'll be extremely busy."

"I'm happy for you."

"But there is, and always will be, a home for you in Woodbury. You know that, don't you?"

"Sure."

"No matter what's going on."

"I know."

"With anything."

"Right."

"I mean with anything."

"Are you and Daryl getting married?"

My mother lets out a high-pitched laugh. "Goodness no."

"Why not?"

"The decision to have a man in my life again was not made lightly."

"Because he seems nice enough."

"He's a little bland, don't you think? Like cardboard, sometimes."

"I hadn't noticed."

"Did you know he's three years older than me? He's turning fifty next year."

"Is that a problem?"

"Maybe." My mother shakes her head. Her eyes narrow. "He's smart, but he doesn't always show it, necessarily. His friends are degenerates. He turns into a moron whenever he's around them."

"But that's just a male defensive mechanism for handling insecurity. You told me that when Dad left, remember?"

"He doesn't vote."

"A lot of people don't vote."

"And when he does, it's Libertarian." My mother rolls her eyes. "Give me a goddamn break. Choose a side, please."

"Why are you telling me all this?"

"You're my daughter, Lesley. I'm telling you about my life. Suffice to say, I wouldn't get too attached to him."

I nod and go silent. My gaze drifts as Daryl emerges from the bathroom. He approaches the table and puts his hand on my mother's shoulder. "What are you ladies talking about?"

My mother looks up at him and smiles. "Just girl stuff, dear."

Chapter 14

February 2007

THE STUDIO SPACE INSIDE the Center for the Arts, toward the east end of SUNY Buffalo's campus, was Byron's creative mecca. Nights were particularly fruitful. After-hours building access required a key from the College of Art be signed out for a period not to exceed twenty-four hours—a minor inconvenience Byron remedied by having a hardware store cut a copy from the department's original. He enjoyed the ritual of the dark walk through campus, usually quiet when streets were abandoned and nearby bars were barely breathing, but occasionally chock full of students drunk and headed out or back, or wherever it was they were coming or going. Overnights were the magic time.

Byron stood, back hunched, in front of a 36" x 36" cloth canvas, primed the previous day with two coats of gesso. The studio was open-concept and cluttered. Easels were arranged haphazardly, and years of paint and assorted material stuck to the floor. A JVC camcorder was rigged up in the corner—the process of creation provided critical context to the understanding and appreciation of his work.

Byron eyed a landscape photograph taken near Olcott and began to sketch an outline: horizon, land, water, sky, clouds, rock, foliage. He worked from the centre out and paused at regular intervals. Pencil lines were light, the movements of his hands were subtle.

The time neared midnight. During overnight sessions, Byron and class wunderkind Phil Paxton usually had the studio to themselves. Phil's enormous abstract canvases had caused a minor stir up and down the local art scene. He was sometimes spotted sleeping in discrete spots around the studio and at least once emerging from the bathroom in a robe and brushing his teeth.

Byron held up the landscape photograph. He relaxed his eyes then lowered his hand, allowing the canvas and photo to occupy his field of view simultaneously. Phil approached from a corner. He took a long drag on a cigarette and pointed a finger. "South shore of Lake Ontario?"

"That's right," said Byron.

Phil crossed his thick arms over his chest. His hair was past his shoulders. "That was rude of me. Your work is your work. Fuck what I have to say about it."

"I can't believe you don't get busted for smoking in here."

"What's the worst that could happen?"

"Dunno. You get banned?"

"Not going to happen."

"Whatever you say." Byron shrugged. "How is your stuff going?"

Phil took another pull on his cigarette. "I'll know when I'm done."

"You doing another big one?"

"Fuck yes. Biggest one yet. Painting over an old billboard."

"How'd you get it inside?"

"Sawed it up." Phil pointed a knuckle behind him. "Working on the first square right now."

"Wow."

Phil shoved his cigarette into an empty coffee mug. "Don't let me keep you."

"Right."

"Good luck with your thing."

Byron nodded. He squeezed dollops of oil paint onto a palette, dipping his brush into vibrant yellow and cutting it with titanium white. He swirled his hand clockwise then touched brush to canvas—a faint yellow streak clung to its surface. Byron worked his way through the canvas, starting with the sky's blues, yellows, and purples, then bringing in the deep browns and blacks of the horizon, and then the dense greens of the foreground.

It was past 3:00 a.m. when Byron pried his gaze from his work. He arched his upper back and stretched. "How are you doing, Phil?"

"Huh?" Phil's voice was muffled.

"How are you doing?"

"Not really sure."

"You make progress tonight?"

"Don't know. I tend not to think about the outcome. Not one bit. I create, and I don't care if I succeed or fail."

"Is that, like, really true?"

Phil approached Byron and grinned. "Sure is."

"You're telling me you don't care one bit if a massive canvas you're spending days on is any good?"

"That's right."

"Not even a bit?"

"Don't care about any of it. If you're asking me, I'm saying nothing matters. If I want to do a painting, I do. Otherwise, I say fuck it."

"Then why are you bothering?"

Phil shrugged. "Being a painter seems like a good way to shirk responsibility. Also, if things break in your favour, the women and the drugs are great. Mostly it's the women and the drugs."

"I guess that's one way to look at it." Byron felt a tingling in his nose. He shut his eyes and took in a deep breath—his face kicked forward, and he sneezed aggressively. His elbow jutted out and knocked the canvas, tipping it off the easel and smacking it into the corner of an apple box before it settled face-down on the floor. "Fuck."

"Oh, shit."

Byron picked up the canvas and held it at arm's length. His freshly laid foreground was smudged. A small tear was visible in the canvas's bottom right corner. "I've been working five hours on this."

"Tough break."

"I'll say."

"That one didn't go your way."

Byron returned the canvas to the easel. "Fuck, that's frustrating."

"Really shitty."

Byron lowered his head to one side. "You know what?"

"What's that?"

"I'm not going to let it bother me."

"Good for you."

"I'm just not. This was a moment of authenticity—an honest-to-goodness human experience. What happened just now is real and makes the painting interesting. The sneeze. The canvas falling and ripping. That becomes part of the experience of the art. I'm not a robot. I'm an imperfect sentient being."

"Love that," said Phil.

"You think so?"

"I mean, sure. Whatever. I don't care either way." Phil opened a plastic baggie and pulled out a shrivelled psilocybin mushroom. He grinned at Byron and popped it into his mouth. "They taste so bad." He chewed and made an awful face then swallowed. "You want one?"

"No, thanks," said Byron. "Need to finish this."

"Could make finishing it a whole later easier—or harder. Tough to say."

"I have to focus."

"Whatever you want. I'll see you when I'm out of whatever it is I get myself into." Phil disappeared into the back of the studio. Byron continued to stare at his landscape. The work was coming together nicely, though its definitive quality was difficult to judge. He ran a hand through his hair. Byron would let the painting sit. Time would be the truest test of his work.

***

I sit in Barker Library. The oculus at the room's apex is dark with penetrating night. My back is stiff from poor posture, and my eyes sting with dryness. It's past 4:00 a.m., though I tend not to fixate on time when locked into serious studying runs. A Glenn Gould recording of "The Goldberg Variations" plays through my over-ear Sennheisers. I am one of four bodies present.

On the desk in front of me is *Planetary Sciences* by de Pater, Imke, and Lissauer. Its pages are pristine, as if the book's previous owner took great pains at preservation or completely shunned studying the material. I scan paragraphs. Interior densities. Gigapascals. Hydrostatic equilibriums. My brain buzzes.

A draft crosses my face. I look up and see Jerry Fujimoto enter the library. He makes eye contact and smiles, then settles into the desk across from mine. Jerry wears sweatpants and a white t-shirt. His posture is erect, and his eyeballs move methodically, scanning textbook pages from one side to the other with mechanized precision. I watch his mouth open and hear muffled noise. He stares expectantly at me. I lift the headphone off my left ear and speak quietly. "What's that?"

"I said, 'What are you working on?'"

I shrug. "Physics stuff."

"What sort of 'physics stuff'?"

"Extrasolar planet theory—deep space."

"How's that going?"

"Fine."

Jerry nods and returns to his book. His lips are open and twitch slightly as he reads. I watch his gaze scan the page, then pull up and float toward me. We don't make eye contact. He does not know that I know that he looked in my direction. "What are you working on?"

"It's pretty complicated." Jerry exhales and rests a bony forearm on his head. "Lots of cutting-edge concepts."

"We're second-year undergrad."

"How much do you know about mechanical engineering?"

"Some. You're working on hydraulics, right?"

"Energy storage."

"You looked focused."

"We're talking technology to phase out the combustion engine—think of the ramifications."

"Is that true?"

"Of course it's true." Jerry jabs a finger into his notebook. "This is serious business." He pauses. "You have an assignment due?"

I shake my head. "Just studying—exams coming up."

Jerry nods and drifts back to his textbook. I slip my left headphone back over my ear and rejoin Glenn Gould. The complexity of the sounds is enchanting. I look up sometime later. Jerry is leaning forward rocking his body to and fro—behaviour I have previously observed in him during great bouts of prolonged concentration. The waist of his hooded sweatshirt rides up and exposes a flabby lower back. Jerry leans farther forward, revealing a red strip of Hanes-brand male underwear and an olive-coloured butt crack. I feel heat and pinch my fleshy midriff. I have gained noticeable girth around my stomach and thighs since starting at MIT.

Jerry catches my eye. I look back to my book. He points to his ears and mimes that I should lift my headphones again. I oblige.

"I'm going to be a great engineer, you know."

"Okay..."

"I really am."

"You said you aced your first semester, right?"

"I sure did."

"Really?"

"Absolutely."

"Then you're on your way."

Jerry raps his fingers on the desk in front of him and sucks in a breath. "My mom studied engineering."

"So it runs in the family."

"Her family was dirt-poor. She went to a shitty technical college—the polar opposite of a place like this."

"What did she do when she graduated?"

"Worked IT for a bank in Milwaukee. After a few years, she got squeezed out. The job market sucked, and she had to take a gig at the mall selling TVs."

"That's sad."

"Uh-huh. But she's a natural introvert and had a hard time making her sales numbers. Eventually she got fired and started working at an HVAC warehouse. My older brother says that's when her drug dependency really started."

"Oh."

"Uh-huh."

"How is she now?"

Jerry shrugs. "She got really into coke—most days before work and everything." He smirks. "Turns out being jacked up on the job is exactly what her career needed. There's something liberating about not caring whether you succeed or fail, you know?"

"I guess."

"The more coke she railed, the more she didn't give a shit about telling people what she really thought. Her performance got noticed, and she was promoted, first to a warehouse supervisor, then manager, then operations director. Now she's a global VP."

"Is that really true?"

"I swear to you it is. Mom's success was tough on my dad. She'd come home high and berate him—hit him over the head with shoes and stuff. He was too principled to hit her back and too much of a pushover to stand up to her emotionally. Finally, it got so bad that she agreed to go to rehab. She went right back to being an introvert, and her performance tanked. Now she's back on the powder again and making more money than ever."

"Oh," I say. "I'm not sure if that's a happy story or a sad story."

"It's an interesting story."

"Are your parents still together?"

"Somehow. Their marriage is a mystery to me, but it works for them." Jerry exhales. "What about your parents?"

"Divorced years ago."

"Sorry to hear that."

"These things happen." I smile. "There was no clue that anything was wrong. I had to piece everything together after the fact."

"What did you find?"

"Reckless spending and a little infidelity."

"I'm sorry."

"My mom's happier now than she ever was married. I'm fine as long as she's fine."

"Then that's good."

"Uh-huh."

Jerry pauses. "When do you think you'll have some free time?"

"I don't know. Why?"

"I was thinking that maybe we could go somewhere together. Like to eat. Or study. Or a walk by the river. I don't care, really."

"You don't care?"

"I mean, I'm indifferent to the activity. But I am interested in you being there—wherever 'there' is."

I feel my body go warm.

"What do you think?"

"I think we could do that."

"Great." Jerry smiles a wonderful toothy smile. "I look forward to it."

"Me too."

Jerry continues to smile as he drifts back to his studying. I return to *Planetary Sciences* and feel the creep of serious exhaustion. Tomorrow's schedule is jammed from noon onward, with Introduction to Aerospace Engineering and Design, Principles of Automatic Control, Electricity and Magnetism, dinner, a Society of Physics Students meeting, Introduction to Propulsion Systems, and studying. I have not slept. My mind is finely tuned. I will ace this semester, and the year, and graduate summa cum laude. My parents will be speechless. I squint toward the domed ceiling. Faint orange is visible through the oculus. "Oh, God. Dawn."

CHAPTER 15

JULY 2007

BEING CONSCIOUS OF ONE'S mortality defines what it means to be a goddamn human being. The certainty of life ending—and the enormous amount of private energy spent trying to rationalize that certainty—is challenging to discuss in any sort of serious way. For a shared inevitability, self-awareness of human fragility is heart-wrenchingly lonely. Death may come by way of terminal illness, bringing with it a timeline for remaining months or years of good health and affording late-stage opportunities to experience the world with a great, aching urgency. Death might also be marred in a murky prognosis, forcing the sufferer into a horrid coexistence with illness for an indeterminate length of time. Here, the sufferer has hope—the possibility that whatever is wrong will be made right. The sufferer fights. The sufferer may win, or they may lose.

Then there are unexpected deaths. Accidents. Violence. Undiagnosed acute medical conditions. These deaths leave messy loose ends and lingering questions that will never be satisfactorily resolved. Sudden deaths are uniquely challenging to overcome. This was how Don Jr. and April Buchanan died.

It was shortly after sunup when Murray received the news. Information had been relayed mechanically and without tangible emotion. As his father explained it, Murray's mother and brother—the now late April Buchanan née Stephenson and Donald Buchanan Jr., home for the summer after his junior year at Vanderbilt—were involved in a car accident. There were no survivors. The elder Don's face, usually hyper-engaged and several steps ahead of the present, was dull and empty. His skin was the colour of porridge.

Murray sat up in bed and filtered the information through a confused morning fog. His mind was a mess of sheets and warm drool. His brother and mother were—apparently—gone. Forever. Dead. Incomprehensible. He would need to attend a funeral and be spoken to by friends and relatives. People would lavish him with sympathetic attention.

He would probably be made to see a therapist. Everything was horrible, and it was all falling apart.

Traffic was light as Murray and his father travelled down Highway 87 in the family's Lincoln Continental. They turned east just short of the state line, passing through Nyacks West, Central, and South, then crossing the Hudson River by way of the Tappan Zee Bridge. The water was dark brown and heaved rhythmically under the great mass of steel and concrete. Gusts of wind hit the car, straining its body against its chassis and causing Murray's father to curse under his breath. They moved north through Tarrytown and Sleepy Hollow, winding along old tree-lined roads and onto the Phelps Memorial grounds.

The hospital floor was linoleum, patterned in two different tones of beige and intersected with thin blue highlights. Walls were cotton-white and held, at regular frequency, water fountains, fire extinguishers, and closed doors to rooms of indeterminate usage. The ceiling was lined with white 2' by 4' panels and tube lights giving off a yellow-hued glow. A round-faced orderly ushered Murray and his father to a smaller room that was similarly cotton-walled and beige-floored, inside which sat a slender bearded man who stood up and introduced himself as the coroner, then handed Don Sr. a printed sheet of paper saying it contained identifying photos of April and Don Jr. It would be helpful, the coroner said, if he could provide confirmation as to the persons in the photos.

Don Sr. nodded and turned the page over. His face was unchanged. "That's them."

"Both your wife and son?"

"Yes."

The coroner nodded. "We try to give family members the option to see deceased loved ones, if they so choose."

Don Sr. shook his head.

"Are you sure?"

"I don't believe there's any need."

Murray's breathing increased. "What ab—"

"I've never been one for hospitals."

The coroner nodded and ran his hand through his beard. The orderly led Don Sr. and Murray back down the hallway. He presented Don Sr. with a thick plastic bag filled with personal effects collected from the scene of the accident. There was no reasonable use for any of it now. The orderly pushed a pen and single sheet of typed paper forward. Murray watched his father look over the page then let out a cough and scrawl a faint, sad signature.

The Buchanan house stood monolithic and still, its appearance unchanged since the radically life-altering events of the last twelve hours. Murray followed his father up the stone walk and through the front door. He moved stiffly down the hallway and perched on the end of the mattress.

In time, there was a knock on the door. Murray heard his father conversing in low tones with a female voice. Murray crept along the hallway's tile floor and listened as details of the accident were discussed with a grim-faced woman in standard-issue New York State Police grey. From what he could glean, Don Jr. and April were travelling northbound on Route 9 around 8:00 p.m. when the car veered from the road, flipped, hit a tree, and landed roof-down in a ditch. The scene had been gruesome. His mother, tended to as a matter of formality, was dead at the scene. Don had remained lucid through early parts of the ordeal and engaged in coherent conversation with first responders before losing consciousness.

Murray took shallow breaths in through his nose and steadied his body. Don Jr.'s last days oozed of ongoing excitement and promise for future greatness. His first three seasons at Vanderbilt saw steady improvement in playing time and on-field performance. Their father speculated to anyone who would listen that his son would be chosen in the first ten rounds of that summer's draft but would return to school for a final year to further raise his draft stock, at which point he was likely to be one of the top sixty players selected, bringing with it a lucrative signing bonus, enormous development resources, and a path to the Major Leagues. Now all that was gone. Murray shuddered. He felt aching and unresolvable pain.

Conversation had trailed off. The grim-faced officer exited the house, and Murray stood still, his heels hovering off the floor. He heard the police cruiser's engine engage and the noise of rubber, first against compacted driveway gravel then onto paved asphalt. His father shuffled down the hallway. Murray retreated to his bedroom. The staircase groaned reliably as Don Sr. ascended. Murray heard footsteps pause at the threshold of Don Jr.'s bedroom. There was silence for a remarkably long period of time, and then the terrible sound of a grown man sobbing.

Chapter 16

JANUARY 2008

Jerry's mattress is a twin, so we lie overlapping with limbs intertwined. We are naked and partially covered by beige cotton sheets, our clothes discarded on his dormitory floor. The whole thing lasted about twenty minutes. We watched pornography together on my laptop beforehand—something I am indifferent to but Jerry says heightens his experience. The feeling of a warm body pressing against my own, grunting and thrusting, was exhilarating.

Jerry's left side is visible from his shoulder past his pectoral to his waist. He rests his head on a pillow propped up at forty-five degrees, his stomach rising and falling with slow breaths. His eyes are pensive.

"I think I'm hungry," I say.

"You think?"

"I mean, I know I am." I smile. "It's kind of an odd time of the day to do what we just did, don't you think? I need some breakfast."

Jerry yawned. "I'm skipping my first class."

"You do that a lot."

"Whatever. I'm ahead on the material. It's just a lecture today—no quiz and no participation marks."

"If it was me I'd still go."

"Because you crave validation from your professors."

"I guess."

"It's fine. I talked to some of the other guys in the class. We've got it locked up."

"I don't talk to anyone here, really, other than you."

Jerry shrugs. "It's not hard."

"I just can't get interesting conversations going. That's not a judgment call. I don't think I'm better than people. I'm saying how it is." I count on my fingers. "In my life there's been you, this guy Byron from high school, my mom, and one old teacher. Everyone else is just kind of a bore. And you know what? I'm not disappointed about it."

"What happened to the guy from high school?"

"We still keep in touch. He's gay, so you have nothing to worry about."

"Really?"

"He came out to me back in first year. I had my suspicions."

"Well, I'm glad I made the cut."

"That's because you're smart and I care about what you have to say. I'm interested in who I'm interested in."

"I'm interested in getting out of here."

I snicker. "Like, out of this room or out of Boston?"

Jerry sits up. "I want Silicon Valley bad. Apple. Facebook. Oracle. Microsoft. PayPal. Yahoo. Intel. Cisco. Adobe. I want all of it."

"Okay."

"I do!"

"Why is that, do you think?"

"Because it's cool as shit."

"Yahoo hasn't been cool in like five years."

"I mean in principle. You go to a place like Silicon Valley—anything can happen."

"I can appreciate that."

"Especially if you're smart, you're motivated, and you know how to work a room. I've considered leaving here early. I know I have the baseline skills to succeed. I just need to improve my body of work." Jerry pauses. "I could probably build up my skills faster working out west. But having a degree might also be helpful."

"There are plenty of ridiculously smart people here doing ridiculously cool things. Graduating from MIT is the right move."

"I know."

I rest my hand on Jerry's chest. "I think I want more school."

"That doesn't surprise me."

"A lot of PhD programs let you apply right out of undergrad."

"But will they accept you?"

"I hope so."

"If you're sharp as a tack they will, which you are."

"Stanford is on my shortlist."

"Th—"

"Not to say that I'm trying to go out west because you're trying to go out west." I pause. "It's also not specifically not related to you wanting to go out west."

"I get it."

"Going across the country is a big deal. A Master's and then a PhD—that's years of my life. It's a huge commitment! It feels like my point of no return."

"What do your parents think?"

I shrug. "My dad will be proud but emotionally distant."

"Okay."

"I think it will hurt my mom. She wants me to stay on the east coast, but I don't know if that's realistic. She won't say it, but she'd be happy for me to move back home. That's not going to happen. It's never, ever going to happen."

Jerry chuckles. "Why not?"

"I love my mom dearly."

"And?"

"I need to allow myself to be my own person, emotionally. Can't do that living at home."

"When did your parents split up?"

"A while ago."

"Like when?"

"I was fifteen."

"So you were old enough to get it?"

"I guess."

"And what happened?"

"Why do you want to know?"

"We're a couple, aren't we? This is what couples talk about."

"It is?"

Jerry shrugs and closes his eyes. "I just like hearing about you."

"Well," I say. "My dad was extremely career-focused. Being a surgeon is a big deal. He wanted to do everything he could to excel."

"So he left?"

"He moved to Buffalo to take a promotion."

"Promotion to what?"

"Head of Otolaryngology at Buffalo General."

"So tha—"

"Ear, Nose, and Throat."

"And your mom didn't go with him?"

"No."

"That didn't seem weird?"

I shrug. "My parents are a little bit weird."

"Everybody says that."

"I don't know what to tell you. They drifted apart. To me they felt like two people living in the same house who happened to be raising a child together."

"And your dad slept around?"

I slap Jerry's chest. "What the fuck is wrong with you?"

"I'm curious."

I curl my lips inward slightly and exhale. "Yes, but it's complicated."

"What do you mean?"

"I think there was some uncertainty about timing. When exactly did my parents split up? When did my dad get offered the job in Buffalo? When did he start dating again? I'm not clear on what the precipitating event was." I pause. "What I do know is my mom caught my dad with a prostitute." I take a breath. "She turned on the home computer one day and found a raunchy email saved to the clipboard. There was also a web browser open to a Best Western in Rochester—sloppy moves on my dad's part."

"Unless he wanted to get caught."

"Maybe. It's possible." I shrug. "My mom drove to the hotel and got my dad's room information from the concierge. She knocked on the door and there was no answer, so she sat down on a chair and waited in the hallway. Meanwhile, my dad was inside the room freaking out. He tried to escape out the second-floor window but slipped and fell into a dumpster. He broke his wrists—both of them. It set his surgery career back six months."

"Is that story true?"

"According to my mom it is."

"Have you talked to your dad about it?"

I shake my head. "Not a chance."

"Why not?"

"It's not something we'd ever discuss."

"So what do you talk about?"

"Dunno. His work. My work."

"What does he say about your work?"

"He says he's proud of me."

"That's nice."

I nod and say nothing.

"What did your mom think about your dad leaving?"

"She probably wasn't thrilled."

"No doubt."

"My mom is an extraordinary woman. She's accomplished much and will continue to accomplish much." I pause and smile. "She's also known to have boundary issues."

"What do you mean?"

"I'm her daughter, but sometimes I'm also her confidant. She burdened me with lots of messy stuff when their marriage fell apart. Jealousy, legal arrangements—shit like that."

"Sounds bad."

"Who am I to judge?"

"Her daughter!"

"From my parents' marriage I take away that relationships are difficult—all relationships. A relationship for a lifetime? A marriage? How do you do that? Especially without compromising."

Jerry continues to keep his eyes closed. "I think you have to compromise. There's no other way."

"Kind of depressing."

I can hear Jerry's nose whistle as he takes in slow breaths. "Going home for me is out of the goddamn question. There's plenty I want to do with my life and plenty I want to experience. The state of fucking Wisconsin has nothing to do with any of that. Never going back."

I nod slowly and run my finger in a circle over Jerry's skin. "Do you think you'll be sad when your parents die?"

"Why would you say that?"

"Will you?"

Jerry tilts his head toward the ceiling. "Uh, I don't know."

"Are you serious?"

"I mean, of course I will. I just don't think about it."

"Because you hear stories about people never properly reconciling—or just sort of drifting apart. That would be sad, wouldn't it? To have that happen? To be with a parent as their life was ending, both aware that time was limited and not really knowing what to say."

"I think people are in a coma a lot of the time."

"What do you mean?"

"Just practically speaking. I think when the end is close, the person passing away is already unconscious. And if they're not unconscious, they're probably on serious meds. That's the way it was when my grandfather passed. It was sad, of course. But he didn't know where he was. His reality was disconnected from my reality."

"Right."

"What made you bring that up?"

"I just don't want to be regretting choices I've made with the few people I'm interested in having a relationship with."

Jerry exhales. "That makes sense."

The mattress squeaks as I step onto the floor. I pull on leggings and a t-shirt and then lean toward Jerry and place my lips on his forehead. "I'm hungry, and I have class."

"Enjoy."

"Don't sleep all day. You have work to do."

Jerry nods and smiles. "Go to class."

***

It was the smell that had hit Murray hardest when he reentered Polymer Imports' head office after more than two years away—a mustiness mixed with heavy cleaning solution that kicked up a slew of unpleasant memories. A quick meeting with human resources arranged by Brenda Trinh at his father's behest was all it took for employment to rematerialize. This was a nepotistic backslide that reeked of failure and wasted promise.

Murray walked the familiar hallway toward the building's rear as dread percolated. The arrangement would not be so bad, he thought, if the work was at all stimulating or engaging, or the packing team hired an attractive woman, or if his present employment was a stepping stone to something more lucrative or fulfilling. He tapped his key card and entered the warehouse floor. He was at risk of becoming a lifer.

Murray worked off his utility cart in a resigned and mechanical way. The company had reimbursed him for new steel-toe boots, and he could already feel a blister forming on the inside edge of his big toe. He rolled his cart along the rows of shelving and locked eyes with a stocky, bearded man. "How are you, Brian?"

"Surviving. What the hell are you doing back here?"

Murray shrugged. "Working."

"You still playing ball?"

"Not competitively at the moment."

"What happened?"

"Just figuring out what comes next."

"Did you fuck up?"

"Not really."

"Was it drugs?"

Murray shook his head slowly. "Nothing like that. I just need to make a plan for what to do now." He held up a stack of printed orders. "Is it just me, or has it gotten busier around here?"

"Sure has." Brian exhaled. "We just wrapped up another acquisition."

"I think my dad mentioned something about that."

"The integration was a fucking nightmare. A whole new set of inventory to deal with and no headcount increase. It's bullshit if you ask me."

"That sucks."

"Sure does, but a job is a job."

"Pretty shitty job, if you ask me."

"Just wait until you've got no other choice."

"What do you mean?"

"Until you've got a family and all that shit."

"That's not me, thankfully."

Brian lowered his voice. "Well then, enjoy it here while you can. We're all at risk of being automated out of existence, and anyone with half a brain knows it." He made electronic beeping noises and moved mechanically toward a row of shelving, picked an order, and dropped it into a box. "Think some egghead can't figure out how to make a computer do that?"

"Point taken."

"That's why you need an exit plan."

Murray nodded.

"I'm working on some big things."

Murray remained silent.

"You need to think about work that computers can't replicate. For all the hype about technology, business is still built on relationships. There's always going to be jobs for people who know how to connect and know how to sell."

"I guess you're right."

"Think about it!"

"So...you're going to be a salesman?"

"It's a no-brainer."

"Selling what?"

"Whatever I can get my hands on. The fundamentals are all the same. I'll be out of here in a year, I promise you that." Brian smiled smugly. "I suggest you do the same."

Murray heard his name across the warehouse. He looked up and saw Brenda Trinh moving toward him, her face sympathetic. "How are you, dear?"

"Good." Murray swallowed. "Nice to be back."

"Everyone here is happy to see you again."

Murray arranged his face into a smile. "Thank you."

Brenda held Murray in an unblinking gaze. "Would you like to come to my office?"

Murray nodded slowly. Brenda motioned that he should follow. They exited the warehouse together and moved down a narrow hallway toward the cluster of corporate offices. Murray spotted a brunette he thought might be a finance intern but didn't make eye contact with her. He entered Brenda's office, and the intern disappeared. Murray looked across stacks of supply chain management books and framed certificates of operational excellence. Brenda settled into her chair and indicated Murray should do the same. She folded her hands in her lap. "Well then, how are you holding up?"

"I'm okay."

"I see." Brenda paused. "How can you say that?"

"I don't know."

"You've experienced an enormous tragedy."

"I mean, what else can you do?"

"Your father said exactly the same thing."

Murray nodded.

"I met your mother a few times," said Brenda. "I could sense that she was smart—a really remarkable woman. It was abundantly clear that she loved her children deeply."

Murray focused on the desk in front of him.

"And what I'm trying to say is that I'm just so sorry for your loss." She held the room silent. "If there's anything you need, anything at all, you just let me know."

Murray nodded.

"You have a job here as long as you want it."

"I a—"

"I know it's not the most glamorous work, but you'll be developing a strong foundation of business fundamentals. There's plenty of places to move around here—both laterally and upward."

"Like where?"

"Well, supervisor positions within the distribution centre, for one. We also have a customer service team. You could get experience answering phones and then progress from there. Plenty of work if you want it."

Murray swallowed and nodded. "I appreciate that."

Brenda took in a heavy breath. Her expression disintegrated, and she began to sob. "I just can't imagine what you and your father must be going through."

"Oh."

"It must be so hard."

"Is there anything else?"

Brenda shook her head. Murray rubbed his palms on his thighs. "Can I go back to work now?"

"Yes, of course." Brenda wiped tears off her cheeks and waved him away. "If you need anything, you know where to find me."

Murray stood up and exited the office. He caught sight of the finance intern again and smiled. She did the same and then looked away—Murray felt the beginnings of an erection. He reentered the warehouse, and the blister on his big toe popped. Murray ran a finger along the edge of a cardboard box. Blood trickled out the thin slice of skin. He scanned his surroundings. His coworkers looked beaten down: skinny frames and shitty clothes, sunken eyes, and sweet old ladies who never escaped minimum-wage work. Today, like many days the last several years, he felt as though he had never woken up.

Without warning, thoughts of Don Jr. and April Buchanan pummelled him. Murray saw his older brother and mother bloodied and deformed, trapped inside a twisted mess of steel on the Taconic State Parkway. The noise was most disturbing. Not the cooling of the Buick's mangled engine or the gurgling of spilled fuel, not Murray's mother calling out to God and pleading to be saved, not the panicked commotion as a bystander called 911.

It was the spine-tingling screams of Don Jr., an elite physical presence and unstoppable athletic star, crying at the pain chorusing through his nervous system. Murray's throat tightened. He pulled slow breaths in through his nose and stared forward. The intensity dulled. He tried to focus. There was work to do. Within the hour, he was delirious with boredom.

***

Byron looked out his dormitory window at the occasional set of orange headlights snaking along the Audubon Parkway. His room was dark, and he had the back of his chair tilted so its front two legs were off the ground and the tops of his thighs pushed up against his desk. A phone was to his ear, through which he spoke to Lesley Chang.

"My mom is excited about the election."

"I know a lot of people are."

"Like, really excited."

"Uh-huh?"

"I mean, Hillary or Obama as the Democratic nominee? She's beyond thrilled."

"It's an exciting time."

"The way she talks, you'd think *she* was running for president."

"And what do you think about it?" said Byron.

"It's great. Feels like the right thing at the right time."

"I don't disagree."

"But?"

"But nothing. I just don't really care."

"You're an abstainer."

"I guess I am," said Byron. "I'm abstaining from the responsibility of giving a shit."

"So you're not planning to vote?"

"Probably not."

"Can I convince you otherwise?"

"Nah."

"Come on."

"Can we talk about something else?"

"Like what?"

"Anything other than politics?"

"We're talking about a woman or a black man in the White House." Lesley's voice rose. "Think about the enormity of that!"

"I hear you, but I can't be bothered to inform myself, and it's irresponsible to vote without knowing the issues."

"You're no fun."

"Sometimes that's true."

"So what do you have going on that you're so busy?"

"School."

"Then how is school?"

"Good. Like, the paintings are coming together. The work keeps improving and getting better. At least I think it does."

"Fantastic!"

"And I'm always trying to broaden my horizons—I've started playing around with video collage and soundscapes. Whatever I can do to scratch the creative itch."

"That's exciting."

"I guess." Byron stared into the darkness. "And the deeper you go, the more you can't help thinking about the future. Like, what happens after I get out of here?"

"What does happen?"

"I need to think about what I'm doing next. Like, making something of myself. A name. Money. At least enough to live on. The way I see it, you need a body of work, and you use that body of work to create buzz, t—"

"How do you create buzz?"

"You get recognized by the community as someone whose work is worth consuming: industry publications, mainstream media, a nod from an established name, word of mouth between gallery owners and collectors..."

"And?"

"Then you use that buzz to mount a show and sell the work, then you get more buzz, more showings, more buzz, more showings, and hell, maybe a lucrative commission or two."

"You make it sound easy."

"Now I think the key with all of that is scarcity. Once you have the buzz, you make access to yourself and your work difficult. I'm told that people love hearing 'no.'"

"But not so much that people forget about you."

"Bingo. It's a fine line that should be carefully walked."

Lesley chuckled. "So what if you died before you became prolific?"

"I like where your head is, but I need to be somebody before I can die young."

"I wonder..."

"What?"

"Do you think you could fake your own death and parlay that into a career boost?"

"I like that a lot."

"Not bad, right?"

"How does that play out?"

"Well," said Lesley. "You take the work to a dealer and tell them you're interested in selling. They'll turn you down because you're nobody, then you fake your death in a public way—like feign falling off a bridge during rush hour or something. It would need to be public so word got back to the dealer."

"Of course."

"You'd also need representation set up ahead of time. Someone easily contactable to handle the sale of the work on your behalf. You'll be dead, after all—as far as the public knows."

"How do you fake falling off a bridge?"

"Mmm. Not sure. Maybe a fake drowning is easier?"

"This might be ill-conceived."

"Well, think about it."

Byron rubbed his face. "Let's hope it doesn't come to that. But I'm not above struggle. Like, I'll work a terrible job to support myself if I need to. Shitty work is important to the experience of finding the thing within yourself to share with the world. Living in a bad apartment and cooking a can of soup on a hot plate is fine by me."

"I think that's inspiring."

"Really?"

"What if you give it a real go and you still come up short?"

"I keep trying."

"And the people we went to high school with g—"

"Fuck 'em."

"They get houses, they get cars, they build retirement nest eggs."

"Why the fuck should I care about a retirement nest egg? What's the point? So I can sit around waiting to die? I need to keep moving. That's how I stay alive. Kandinsky didn't even start painting until he was thirty. Think about that! I've got my whole life ahead of me, and I need to keep going. I can't let up. I'm working until I die."

"What about burnout?" said Lesley.

"What about it?"

"Do you worry about it?"

"No. Do you?"

"Sometimes."

"Like when?"

"I'm applying to Stanford for graduate school. I've been talking to a professor there—a brilliant woman. It sounds like she's willing to take me on."

"And you're saying you worry about burning out?"

"Not sure, exactly. I'm confident in my abilities, and I'm handling MIT just fine. But still. The uncertainty. There are currently unanswered questions, and being out there is extremely high stakes." Lesley paused. "Oh!"

"What?"

"Shoot."

"What?"

"I meant to ask you."

"Yes?"

"Did you hear about Murray Buchanan's brother?"

"Sure. Don." Byron breathed out slowly through his mouth. "The car accident with his mom. It was awful."

"So tragic."

"Have you talked to anyone back home about it?"

"No," said Lesley. "You?"

"Same."

"It's terrible for everyone involved, really."

"I know."

"And it hits so close to home when you know someone affected by something like that."

"Uh-huh." Byron spoke slowly. "What did you think of Murray?"

"Well."

"Yes?"

"He was...confident and opinionated."

"Yeah."

"What did you think of him?"

"The same," said Byron. "If I'm being honest, he was kind of a bully. At least he was at Woodbury."

"He definitely was, but the whole thing is still awful. He must have had a tough year."

Byron titled his neck back. The room was quiet. He could not see the ceiling through the darkness. "It makes me sad, you know? That someone could just, like, disappear forever. What a fucking letdown."

CHAPTER 17

JUNE 2009

T HE DRESSER IN FRONT of me is flimsy with brass pull handles and an enormous flat top on which I keep a laptop computer and collection of old classical mechanics textbooks. An oval mirror rests between two arms that wind vertically. A dowel—connected at the mirror's narrowest point—allows the mirror to tilt forward and back.

I run my hand through my hair, which is thin and flat, like it always is. I square my face to the mirror and hold a neutral expression. I smile. My cheeks lift and the skin around my mouth wrinkles. I return my face to an even configuration. My skin flattens.

My mother sits on the polyester couch in the living room. She wears a three-quarter-length red dress and a large sun hat she has not bothered to take off. Presently, we will walk together to my convocation ceremony.

"You had a neat space here," says my mother.

I lean out my bedroom door. "It was time to be off campus."

"And is Jerry coming today?"

"Of course. He's graduating too."

"I'd love to meet him."

"We could do that, maybe."

"I can't remember the last time I saw you in a dress."

"That would be high school prom."

"Of course."

I make a noise of affirmation. A blue dress partially concealed within a dry-cleaning bag is draped across my desk. I put on underwear then let the dress drop down over my head and come to a rest on my shoulders. I lean into the living room. "How is work?"

"I love the dress, dear."

"Thank you."

"And I love you in the dress."

"Are you still at the hospital?"

"You're my dependent, dear. I wouldn't leave the hospital without telling you."

"I'm an adult, and I'm getting an enormous grant from Stanford this fall."

"And I'm so freaking proud of you."

"So the hospital is…"

My mom lets out a long sigh and rubs her face. "Stressful. The insurance companies are mad at me, the patients are mad at me, the doctors are mad at me."

"What about the nurses?"

"I think they're also mad at me."

"But that's part of the job, right? Hospital administration is inherently stressful, isn't it?"

My mother closes her eyes. "You go ahead and stay in your ivory tower just as long as you want."

I nod and say nothing.

"Are you wearing makeup?"

"I put on some blush."

"What about mascara?"

"Never liked it."

"I'll help you, dear."

"Doesn't matter. It's a waste of time."

The couch makes a squeaking noise as my mother rises. She moves toward the bedroom. "Sometimes you just need to wear mascara."

"I don't see the point."

"There are times to be stubborn and there are times to relent."

"I don't like relenting."

"Sit down, dear." My mother puts her hands on my shoulders and pushes me into a sitting position. Her skin smells floral. She reaches into her purse. I hear the removing of a mascara brush from its tube. "Hold still."

I stay silent and straighten my back. My mother's hand steadies my cheek. "You're going to look beautiful." She pauses. "Not that you're not already, and not that beauty should supersede anything you've accomplished academically. All I'm saying is a little mascara goes a long way."

I raise my chin and feel a slight tugging as the brush runs along my upper eyelashes.

"Has Dad called you yet?"

"Your father? No. Why would he?"

"He said he was going to."

My mother moves to my lower eyelashes. "He did?"

"He's in town on business. He said he's coming to the ceremony."

I feel a sharp tug on my eyelid. "He did?"

"He said he was going to call you."

"He hasn't."

"I think he's bringing someone."

"Is that so?"

"Well, maybe. He said he had a friend he might bring."

My mother twists the tube of mascara shut and chuckles quietly.

"How do my lashes look?"

"Wonderful."

"Really?"

"You look beautiful, dear."

I stand and flatten my dress against my stomach. We leave the apartment and walk east in the midmorning heat toward Killian Court. My mother's strides are long and deliberate. Sweat is quick to form around the edge of my neck and small of my back. I try in vain to stop my dress from contacting moist flesh. My mother clears her throat. "Tell me more about your father."

I shrug. "He's in Boston for a conference, and he said he wanted to come to the convocation."

"He called you?"

"Yes, we spoke on the phone the other day."

"And he's bringing someone?"

"That's what he said."

"Is she at the conference too?"

"Not sure."

"That's an interesting decision on your father's part."

"And for the record, he didn't explicitly mention who the friend was—could be an old pal from San Francisco for all I know."

"Hmm. How often do you talk to him?"

"Maybe once a month. We chat about school stuff and career stuff."

My mother nods, and we slide into silence as campus comes into view. Killian Court is a maze of metal crowd barriers and temporary grandstands. Balloons and signs welcome graduates from the class of 2008 and their guests. Bodies in slacks and summer jackets mill around. A haggard-looking woman with a clipboard asks me my last name then directs me to a classroom inside the Maclaurin Buildings. My mother hugs me and disappears into the crowd.

I walk into a windowless room and am asked my name by a second clipboard-carrying woman. She hands me long black robes and tells me how to walk and where to sit during the commencement ceremony. I nod and slide into a chair. To my right is a tall, muscular man with long blond hair I recognize from Physics of Energy and Introduction to Special Relativity but whose name I never bothered to learn. The room is air-conditioned. My body begins to cool.

The woman with the clipboard has positioned herself against a side wall and glances down to her wrist at regular intervals. She snaps to attention. I watch her poke her head out the door then quickly gesture for everyone to stand up. "Follow me, please. We're heading out now. Let's go."

The room rises in unison, and the woman leads us through the beige halls of Maclaurin Building 3. Our footsteps echo, creating a percussive pastiche of sound. We exit back into the heat of the day. The lawn of Killian Court is packed to capacity. I feel the eyes of two thousand people on me and scan the crowd as I shuffle forward. I manage to spot my mother off the left side of the stage. My father is nearby. He whispers into the ear of a slim woman I have never met. I take my seat.

The ceremony's graduates number several hundred. Guest speakers offer congratulations to the new alumni and advice for future career successes. At the request of the Master of Ceremonies, an ancient woman in long purple and yellow robes, ushers direct rows of students toward a cordoned holding pen off stage left. I watch the ancient woman adjust her bifocals and smile broadly as she calls the name Mary Abato. A round-faced girl I vaguely recognize walks across the stage and receives a cylindrical cardboard tube then has a cream-coloured hood placed around her shoulders. Mary blushes. She takes a moment to steady her balance and steps carefully down a set of wooden steps. Jack Ableson follows. Then Sarah Ackman. Then Brian Anderson.

My row rises. I stand and move forward as the line in front of me winds its way behind a long black curtain, shuffling a few inches ahead with the speaking of each name. I catch a glimpse of Jerry, still seated, before I disappear. The lighting is poor, and I approximate my foot movements as I slowly ascend steps up to stage-height. I see light between a gap in the curtain. Clarence Chaffin steps onto the stage to loose applause. I stay still and wait. I hear the amplified noise of lips separating and then "Lesley Chang" echoes across the lawn. I move quickly onto the stage and look out over the assembled audience. Jerry is smiling. I see my parents clapping. The slim woman whose name I do not know has her hand on my father's leg. I am given a cardboard cylinder, and a long hood is draped over my shoulders. I walk down the wooden stairs and back to my seat. My face stretches into an uncontrolled smile. This fall Jerry and I head west.

***

Murray's bedroom was tucked into the far end of the Buchanans' main-floor hallway. Baseball equipment and free weights took up much of the available floor space. Murray slouched in late Saturday evening light, Xbox controller in hand and finger joints moving with rapid precision. His father stood at the room's threshold.

"The basement needs to be cleaned tomorrow."

Murray exhaled and kept his tone noncommittal. "Sure."

"These things don't get done without someone to do them."

"We could hire someone."

"What time should I wake you?"

Murray was silent.

"How about 8:00 a.m.?"

"Not 8:00 a.m."

"How about 9:00 a.m.?"

Murray blinked and held his eyes shut for a long moment. "Sure."

"There's work to be done in the garden too. You know where the ladder and the pruner are?"

"The shed?"

"That's right." Don Sr. took in a breath and paused. "And we're out of milk. There's money on the chest of drawers."

"Sure."

"Thank you."

Murray sensed his father's lingering presence. "You want me to go now?"

"The store closes soon."

He groaned without opening his mouth.

"Thank you."

Murray raised himself to a standing position and shuffled toward the front hall. He slipped on shoes and moved to the garage, settling inside the red Ford Fiesta that had once belonged to his mother, then Don Jr., and was now his own. The interior was musty and the odometer read almost thirty thousand miles, put on largely from travel to baseball tournaments of varying sizes and levels of prestige across the northeast, and later, trips by Don Jr. to and from Vanderbilt. Murray inserted his key into the ignition and turned his wrist counterclockwise. The Fiesta's engine sputtered. He adjusted the rearview mirror, pulled the transmission into reverse, and backed out the driveway.

The Stop & Shop parking lot sprawled under an orange-hued sky. Murray exited his car and walked slowly past a shopping cart corral and through a double set of sliding glass doors. The store's air-conditioning raised hairs on his arms, and he shivered involuntarily as quiet pop music wafted from unseen speakers. Murray crossed in front of the checkout tills and turned left down the frozen food aisle. A jowly man stocking TV dinners pivoted as Murray approached—his face registered recognition. Murray knew the man as Jack Polito, a smoker acquaintance of Evan Friedman's and others on the baseball team. Jack nodded and offered a first bump. Murray obliged.

"How's it going, Buchanan?"

Murray shrugged.

"What are you up to?"

"Working. Got a warehouse gig right now."

Jack nodded. "Not in school?"

"Not right now. Did some JC, but it wasn't for me."

"That's cool." Jack pushed a stack of frozen lasagnas toward the rear of the freezer. "You still playing any ball?"

"Not really."

"Right on."

"What about you?"

Jack stretched his arms above his head. "Working for one more year to save money then going to college for policing. You can make decent money if you get in with the right division."

"Sounds like a good plan."

Jack tilted his head, and his expression turned serious. "You should consider it if you need better work. I have some buddies you can talk to."

"Nah." Murray shrugged and took a step toward the back of the store. "Just getting milk."

"Let me know if anything changes."

"Will do."

"Money is money."

"I hear that."

"Oh." Jack picked up a bag of frozen peas. "I'm really sorry about everything with Don and your mom."

"Yeah," said Murray. "Thanks."

"How are you holding up?"

Murray shrugged. "There are good days and bad days."

"The guys loved Don."

"I've heard that a lot."

"The whole thing is god-awful."

"I know."

Jack let a bag of frozen peas drop into the freezer. "Stay in touch, all right?"

Murray nodded and said he would. The pair exchanged fist bumps again. Murray moved toward the aisle's rearmost corner and opened the dairy cooler door. He cradled a one-gallon milk jug in each hand and approached a dumpy cashier with a round face who was no older than twenty-five but gave off a resigned tepidness, as though to move outside of whatever life she was living, wherever and with whomever she was living it, was impossible. Murray watched the woman ring up his milk with slow hands. Her face assumed a tired smile as she asked whether he wanted plastic or paper, then nodded in acknowledgement as Murray said neither were necessary. He paid and watched the woman twist her torso to make change. Her face registered the slightest expression of chronic pain. She was young enough, Murray thought, that her life could still be radically shaken up should her present supermarket employment not satisfy her to the extent she yearned to be satisfied.

A thin line of colour along the bottom of the sky was all that remained of the day's light as Murray moved through the parking lot and entered his car. He drove east on Hwy 17M and cut north on Averill Avenue, arriving at Monroe-Woodbury High School and coming to a slow stop near the football field. The evening air was quiet. He crossed over the manicured ground. The wire backstop and wooden bleachers of the baseball diamond materialized in pieces through the darkness. The present physical space had dominated his imagination for years, from Don Jr.'s transcendent on-field performances, to three seasons of his own unsuccessful varsity team tryouts, to a final redemptive year when he made the team and performed well, though not at the level necessary to receive attention outside the small community of fanatical New York high school baseball fans.

Murray spotted movement inside the visiting team's dugout. He squinted. Two figures of indeterminate age were engaged in a heavy make-out session, one sitting and the other standing with back bent forward. Murray detoured around the far side of the school. He eyed the dark classrooms and was hit by a wave of complete irrelevance. His tenure at Monroe-Woodbury was closed and inextricably sealed. The future seemed hopeless. He had nothing.

Murray returned to the car feeling as though he had swallowed lead. He accelerated out of the parking lot and turned onto NY17 heading west, exiting at the 208 and driving south before swinging onto a winding side road, the name of which he did not know. Streetlights were bright and infrequent. Murray drove until his surroundings were unfamiliar.

The car's low engine hum was soothing and methodical. Houses built upon lawns that were prim and green, even in darkness, floated through Murray's peripheral vision. He thought of Irwin Bullwright and his putrid efforts on the baseball diamond, now irrelevant as he wrapped up a finance degree that would assuredly produce gainful and lucrative employment upon graduation. He thought of class wienie Lesley Chang attending MIT and how he had academically matched her right up until their junior year of high school before everything changed. He thought of noted weirdo Byron Somerfield quietly escaping Woodbury to study art in Buffalo, waiting for talent that might or might not materialize. He thought of Evan Friedman earning the class's sole Division I baseball scholarship to the University of Evansville, and how in the third grade he could easily throw double Evan's distance, and it was only thanks to a freakish growth spurt between freshman and sophomore year that he had managed to get the attention of a decent sports school.

Inferiority poked and prodded. Murray worried he would never move beyond Polymer Imports' warehouse. Money like the kind his father made was outside the realm of possibility. On the off chance he managed to find good work, he did not know how he would rise from bed every morning and take meaning and purpose from whatever it was he did. He wondered how he would earn enough money to buy a house, or to make himself attractive to a woman, or to support a child, or to retire and live through his declining years. Baseball, and the promise of Major League prestige and pay, had been his opportunity for success as he defined it. Delusional. Fucking delusional.

Murray drove half an hour south, then west, then north. He cruised unfamiliar roads for two hours before an intersection, once passed with his mother en route to an away game in Monticello, reoriented him. He flipped the Fiesta's blinker and took Highway 32 east. His mind was worn and dulled. He turned left on Dunderberg, then left again on Woodward. Murray slowed as his house came into view. It was dark, like every other house on the street.

***

A good loft in New York City is a place like nowhere else. Sophisticated. A vessel for creative genius. Bookshelves crammed with Wolfe, Hemingway, and Pynchon. Original wood flooring. Complex canvases, vulnerable and alive with human emotion. Exposed brick. Old radiators. A personal refuge inside the greatest city in the world. Incomparable.

Frances Zaiontz's hair was pinned in a frizzy bundle on top of her head. She wore thick-rimmed bifocals and a loose blouse that fell over old carpenter jeans. Her voice was light and musical. Her physical movements were delicate. "It's so exciting to see an old student find success." She spoke slowly and deliberately. "Everyone at the academy is extraordinarily proud of you."

Byron pursed his lips as he paced Frances's apartment. "I'm nervous, of course—to have people see my work in that way."

"An artist's first show is special."

"It's just that the stakes are so high."

"Don't let that bother you. Aldens is a fantastic space. You will have many supporters."

"I appreciate your help with everything—those write-ups in *Cine* and *NuArt* were wonderful."

"People are impressed. Pulling together a show is no easy task."

"You'll be coming?"

Frances put her hands together, her fingers extended straight up. "I give you my word."

"It's important to me that you be there."

"Could you stop pacing for just a moment?" Her smile flickered. "You're making me nervous."

Byron froze in midstride.

Frances spoke softly. "Please don't forget to enjoy the evening. This is a big achievement."

"Of course it's a big achievement!" said Byron. "A show in New York City could launch my career. If all goes well, this could be a gateway to everything I've ever wanted!"

"You're not alone in those feelings of desire."

Byron started pacing again. "Like your apartment, for example. It's extraordinary. It's exactly how I want to live!"

"The life I've built required extreme sacrifice and exceptional luck."

"I'll sacrifice whatever is needed."

"But unfortunately, luck cannot be controlled."

"Are you saying your success was a fluke?"

"I'm saying any great artist has a closet full of terrible work that should never see the light of day."

"Probably not every great artist." Byron's steps slowed. "The work I'm showing is all I've got. The canvases. The projections. The soundscapes. This is my life. It's everything."

Frances smiled warmly. "You'll do great things, I promise." She spread her arms open. "And it means so much that you came to see me. The show will be a smash."

Byron nodded. He stepped forward and took Frances into a loose hug. "See you tonight."

Alden Projects Gallery was housed in a small storefront tucked into the radically southeast corner of Manhattan. It, like much of the city's cultural richness, existed within the ground floor of a brick walk-up building and appeared unassuming to those not explicitly seeking it out. Byron had coordinated the gallery's rental via an elderly Slovak woman with whom he communicated exclusively by telephone voicemails. The arrangement gave him free rein over the space for twenty-four hours and stipulated he was to have the premises vacated and clean by 8:00 a.m. the following morning. No trace of his work could remain.

Byron stood on Orchard Street. A pharmacy and discount men's clothing store book-ended either side of the gallery. His show, dubbed *B. Somerfield Opening: One Night Only*, featured works ranging in size from a 1'x1' canvas to an oblong piece that stretched the height of the room. The art had been driven from Woodbury that morning by way of a rented pickup truck, necessitating two trips along the Palisades Interstate and liberal amounts of cardboard wrapping and industrial blankets. A projector he borrowed from Frances ran digital loops shot discreetly in his old SUNY Buffalo studio space the previous year. Rented speakers played ambient recordings done at his parents' house with a Tascam four-track. It was at the specific request of Byron that neither James nor Joy Somerfield attend the show, sparing him the undue stress public family appearances had a habit of presenting. Everything was happening.

Byron unlocked Alden's front door. A dozen paintings leaned in neat rows against the papered front window. The gallery's interior was militantly pristine. Track lights ran lengthwise along the ceiling, creating hotspots of white light on the walls and floor. The air tingled with the smell of new paint—untapped creativity and limitless potential pulsed. This, the sharing of art with an audience, was the creative process's denouement. Byron's body shivered with anticipatory excitement.

Revenue of $1300 would need to be generated to cover the cost of alcohol, hors d'oeuvres, servers, gallery space, and equipment rentals. Byron would accept payment via cash, check, and credit card, and hoped to unload the entirety of his inventory that evening when fevered excitement would be at its apex. The task of pricing work had proved unexpectedly tedious and sent Byron into fits of insecurity over both the quality of his painting and the long-term implications of a career spent creating original art. It was his mother who provided levelheadedness on the matter, explaining that Byron must consider labour hours and material costs, then set prices to pay himself an honest living wage. With that, Byron had set a wall-sized still-life at $1600, a series of three metropolis cityscapes at $600 each, four upstate New York landscapes at $500 each, and four portraits lifted from obscure 1960s Time magazine advertisements at $200 each, the copyright ramifications of which were unclear at best. The evening's take would set the benchmark against which all future Somerfield exhibitions would be measured.

Byron lifted a canvas vaguely reminiscent of Edward Hopper's late career work and took measurements. He marked and rubbed the drywall with ethanol, then pressed a gallery-approved adhesive hook against the freshly sterilized spot. It was with meticulous care that Byron repeated this process for each canvas and its corresponding place of hanging around the entirety of the room. He then placed Frances's projector on a waist-high cabinet and pointed it at a clear space on the gallery's rear wall. A laptop held digitized files of his supporting media. He squinted at the screen and pressed play. The projector hummed and a fuzzy 4:3 image of a studio appeared. Byron dimmed the light and adjusted the projector's lens—the image came into sharp focus. He wired a pair of 2,000-watt Harbinger speakers through a receiver and into a laptop. He opened his digitized sound loop. Distorted ambient groans rumbled across the room.

Byron returned to the adhesive hooks and applied finger pressure—they held strong. He hung his dozen canvases and stepped to the room's centre. He raised the dimmer switch, and the projected video blended into the wall. He lowered the light, and the canvases sank into murky darkness. He raised the light slightly. The canvases remained dark, and the video looked flat. "Well, fuck," said Byron. "That sucks."

The time was 5:00 p.m. The caterers were late. Byron paced amongst Alden's back room. His call to the catering company yielded a chatty woman with a Midwestern drawl who explained the staff had been delayed by a malfunctioning walk-in freezer and were presently fighting their way through midtown traffic. She apologized profusely for the inconvenience and offered assurance that the caterers would arrive within the half-hour.

Byron exited the office and reentered the minimalist sheen of Alden's showroom. His canvases were carefully positioned so that the centre of each hung at the same latitude along the gallery wall. His output was a mixed bag hybrid of American realist and abstract expressionism, more playful than the likes of John French Sloan or William Glackens, but also tighter and more disciplined than Jackson Pollock or, God forbid, Willem de Kooning. He took in a moment of fleeting fulfillment at the evolution and demonstrated growth in the half-decade since first taking serious interest in the visual arts. In this moment, his canvases were just so. His work hung in New York City.

Slamming doors and hurried feet indicated the caterers' arrival. It was 5:40 p.m. A man in his early twenties with a muscular frame and disarmingly symmetrical face burst through the front door. A similarly aged and aesthetically jaw-dropping woman followed. Both blurted apologies and began unloading covered plates of salmon puffs, fresh rolls, crostini, mozzarella sticks, pakoras, black olives, and bite-sized spanakopita from the double-parked panel van.

The pair worked with remarkable speed, their faces locked in tight focus as they arranged finger foods onto platters and lined wine glasses along a makeshift bar. The man explained his plans to walk amongst gallery guests with a rotating selection of hors d'oeuvres while the woman worked the bar, smiling for tips and keeping a watchful eye out for overindulgers. They were operational at one minute to 6:00 p.m. Byron wore a freshly pressed black turtleneck and blinding white Nikes. He crossed the room and flipped the door's deadbolt. *B. Somerfield: One Night Only* was open for business.

Road traffic lurched and shuttered down Orchard Street. Byron stood on Alden's stoop as pedestrians moved quickly along the sidewalk. He watched a man in his forties approach a hotdog vendor. The proprietor, a short, stubbly man, was one of hundreds in Manhattan. His presence as a purveyor of buns and meat was a civic institution, with even the most uptight gourmand or symphony-goer stopping—at least in moments of weakness—for a street meat pick-me-up. New York was a living, breathing, tangible, beautiful thing. This was everything he wanted.

It was shortly after 11:00 p.m. when Byron decided not a single soul in the whole goddamn city was coming. Frances was a no-show. The readers of *Cine* and *NuArt* were nonexistent. His only human companionship was the caterers, their presence guaranteed by financial incentive and thus doubly sad. Byron heard approaching footsteps and turned. The male caterer nodded to him. "When are you, uh, expecting people?"

Byron spread his arms. "This is it, I'm afraid."

"Oh." The caterer paused. "And all this stuff is for sale?"

"The paintings? Yes, that's all for sale."

"Any interest?"

"You see anyone come through the door?"

"Yeah." The caterer shrugged. "Sometimes these things just don't take. New York City can be a bitch."

"I don't know what else I can do."

The caterer popped an olive into his mouth. "You let it go and you keep working."

"I wasn't ready for this."

"You're an artist. You better get used to being kicked around."

Byron closed one eye and grimaced. "Don't know if I can."

"Dwelling on failures will destroy you."

"Yeah." Byron's chin dipped. "I'm feeling pretty destroyed."

"You, me, and everyone else, brother. We're all in it together."

Byron nodded limply.

The caterer coughed. "Say, is it alright if we duck out early? This show's spent, and I have an after-hours gig in Brooklyn. Big industry thing. Lots of people going to be there."

"Oh." Tears formed on the sides of Byron's eyes. "Sure." His voice quivered. "Whatever you like."

CHAPTER 18

OCTOBER 2009

T HE APARTMENT WAS LOCATED on the top floor of a three-story walk-up in Brooklyn's Crown Heights neighbourhood. There were two other units like it off the cramped landing and nine in the building altogether. Byron had done several passes over the floor with a steam cleaner after moving in last month, producing buckets of soupy grey water but doing little to affect the smell of feline fur and cigarettes caked into the deepest depths of the carpet's fibres. Monthly rent was a miraculous $625. He lived paycheque to paycheque in the greatest city in the world.

Byron removed his cargo shorts and sweaty white t-shirt. He stood in the centre of his apartment's only room—entirely naked—and bent down to touch the floor. His calves and hamstrings stretched. He held the position and took meditative breaths, then rose back to his full height and pulled on basketball shorts. Tension exited Byron's body as he sank into his acrylic loveseat. The moments after returning home from a shift were some of the calmest and most relaxing of his day-to-day existence. To sit at home alone after standing from 5:00 p.m. through 1:00 a.m. with only a half-hour break taken in the back of a ghastly-hot Park Slope kitchen was full-body bliss. His hourly wage was the legal minimum. Tips were meagre once they trickled down from server through cook, host, and busboy to Byron, the dishwasher.

His mind buzzed with remnants of the night's activity. There came a point in every shift, usually just past the evening's halfway mark, when time slowed to a horrendous standstill and dishes piled insurmountably, bringing harsh words from management and fear that one might pass out from exhaustion. Somewhere past this point the rush died down, like it always did, and the end was in sight. Byron loved the measurable productivity of these moments and knowing that life would soon be his own again.

Pink Floyd's *Ummagumma* played through a small stereo system set up in the kitchen. Byron reached for a notebook and hovered a pen over a fresh page. His hands were raw from constant wetting, drying, and exposure to soap. He closed his eyes. The recorded sounds were ethereal. Byron pressed his pen down. He would create something large and expansive that captured the fears and anxieties of modern humanity trapped in its condition, longing for a meaning and legacy that would outlive its physical being. A play, perhaps. He would say everything that everyone had ever wanted said without falling into bloat or indulgence. He would be broad and expansive, and also precise and specific. There would be moments of humour, but the piece's tone would lean toward the serious and sincere, moving its audience to tears from deep and profound personal revelation.

Byron held his pen still and focused on the page. Ideas swirled. He craved a cigarette—a new habit from the restaurant—but pushed the urge aside, taking great heed in the way serious smokers' skin turned leathery and teeth stained dark yellow. Mostly, he liked smoking as an accessory to his desired look: a physical elegance à la James Dean mixed with the brooding intellectualism of Arthur Miller or Samuel Beckett. He liked the ritual of lifting the cigarette from its package and raising it to his mouth, then striking a match and cupping his hand around the flame so it stayed lit. He loved that first puff of smoke entering his body, the way his head spun and lungs burned, and that feeling of nimbly ashing into whatever receptacle was available, then butting out after the last pull.

As a compromise, Byron stood up and fixed himself a scotch. He returned to the loveseat, posture hard, and wrote. The words came quickly: rapid-fire stream of consciousness that captured the emotion and the feeling of the all-important here and now. Some sessions brought sinking disappointment and the certain knowledge that the writing was banal, purposeless, and trite. Tonight, his words were strong and bold. Veritable fire. Engaging, compelling, and above all else, honest. He had never felt like this before, not even with painting.

Theatre held a certain magic that made Byron's body tingle. He craved the immediacy of the art form and the unity between audience, performer, and unseen crew. The grandeur of large-scale performing spaces was astonishing—the shittiness of hole-in-the-wall alternative venues was romantic. The theatre was a ritual space in which important work had been performed for hundreds of years. It was art unto itself, long before the still image, the cinema, and the electric guitar.

Mounting a show presented several practical concerns. To save money, Byron would set the piece in a single location. He wanted the play to take place somewhere quiet, but also conversation-inducing, where characters could talk with one another and work off the physical environment: a train station, airport lounge, or music store, perhaps. A competent stage tech would need to be found to oversee the audio and lighting elements of the production, as would a venue amenable to putting on such a performance, neither of which would be hard to find in Brooklyn, providing that adequate funding was secured. Casting would be most crucial to the play's success and the trickiest to pull off. Byron could not quite articulate what separated skilled actors from the untalented and considered the profession full of fickle, insecure beings. The desire to perform lines in a room full of people was something he did not understand. The constant narcissism and need for validation was a turnoff, albeit necessary if the play was to move forward.

The sounds from the stereo had become more unusual now. Snorting. Grunting. Outdoor ambience. They were, in effect, noises, operating under the guise of artistic merit. Byron stopped writing and poked at his notebook. The costs of mounting a production, even at its most modest, would be more money than he could front. He wondered if a feasible business plan could be produced to attract investors and how big his audience draw in a frenetic city of eight million would be.

It was past 3:00 a.m. when a heavy wave of exhaustion washed over Byron's body. His pen kept moving out of habit. He thought *fuck it* and lit a cigarette. The sound of the match-head igniting was exhilarating. He breathed in sweet smoky air then wrote and wrote. His head drooped. He opened his eyes to crackling warmth. The sight of fire was horrifying. He came to properly and saw the cigarette on his lap, half-smoked, its tip glowing orange above his notebook, which was presently on fire. He bolted to his feet and rushed through the bathroom door. He felt heat on his hands—his notebook crackled and burned black. He lifted the toilet lid and dropped the flaming pages into the water. The embers hissed. The smell was repulsive. The night's work was already forgotten.

***

My daily coffee habit started innocuously at MIT as a means to cram the entirety of Statistical Physics II into my retrievable consciousness. Since then it has grown steadily. I yawn and sip from a mug bought on clearance at the Walmart off El Camino. My brain is groggy. The brew is strong and sends shivers across my nervous system.

I lean against the kitchen counter of my Palo Alto apartment. My mother's voice comes through the phone pushed up against my ear. "It's been so warm here. No sign of fall at all. Not even at night. Might as well be the middle of July."

"Mmm."

"How's the weather out there?"

"No complaints."

"Warm?"

"Do we have to talk about weather?"

"What's wrong with talking about the weather?"

"Isn't it just mindless small talk?"

"Mastering small talk is a valuable life skill, dear. Besides, it's important I have something to say to my daughter, no matter how busy I am."

I look out my kitchen window toward the parking lot. "Uh, the weather is fine: overcast and a little rainy."

"And your new place?"

"Small. Furnished it cheaply. The important thing is I have somewhere quiet to work."

"Sounds nice."

"Just as long as it stays quiet."

"Don't forget to have some fun, dear."

"It just needs to be quiet."

"How did the Mazda do?"

"Great. I was hoping to pull fifteen-hour days but couldn't swing it—averaged about twelve. That's the legal limit for truckers. I looked it up."

"How long were you on the road?"

"About four days." I pause. "And you know what? I kind of loved it. The Midwest is great. Town after town after town."

"I think the Midwest is a wonderful place to pass through."

"Don't be elitist, Mom."

"All I'm saying is the best and brightest spend at least a little time on a coast."

"Interesting you say that, because Stanford students are the most focused I've ever seen."

"You mean more than MIT?"

"Maybe it's the Master's thing. The intensity in my program is off the charts."

"How are you fitting in?"

"Okay, I think. People keep to themselves. We're all focused on our work."

"And Jerry?"

"He's fine."

"What does his company do again?"

"Something about a platform for global e-commerce transactions. Like PayPal but different."

"Are they profitable?"

"Not sure. You'd have to ask him."

"Can you put him on?"

"Forget it. How's Daryl?"

"Oh, he's fine."

"Still no plans to get married?"

My mother snorts and clears her throat. "Not sure what the point of that would be."

"Do you love him?"

"Please. We get along great and support each other."

"But not love?"

"I love him, but I also love other things. Working at the hospital, for example."

"You really love that?"

"Well, I love the idea of it." There's rustling on my mother's end of the phone. "You should ask your father why he hasn't gotten remarried. His girlfriend seems like the type."

"I g—"

"And I'm not saying that in a negative way. It's just an observation."

"We both know he's really focused on his career."

"No shit." My mother pauses. "Tell me more about Stanford."

"It's early. Just coursework and TAing for now. I've met with my thesis supervisor a few times."

"That's right. And he's a—"

"She. Isabel Kaminsky. An astrophysicist."

"You get along with her?"

"I do. She's an extraordinarily smart woman."

"Well, that figures. You're also an extraordinarily smart woman."

"Maybe, but I have some ground to make up." I look at my laptop. "I need to get going. There's a lot happening today. Give my best to Daryl."

"I will. I love you."

"Love you too."

I hang up and squint at a half-written briefing to Professor Kaminsky, detailing an incident during a quiz last week when I caught an undergraduate seminar student reading formulas off a piece of paper concealed within a pen cap. I issued an automatic zero—as mandated by departmental policy—and the student went ballistic. The matter is now escalating through the academic appeals process, creating an enormous pain in the ass for Professor Kaminsky and requiring rigorous documentation of all related events by me. We have a meeting with the academic affairs board scheduled next week.

I am told that freak-outs like this in Stanford STEM are common. Stakes are high. Hours are long. Work, sometimes, does not go as planned. A whiz kid in my year got poached by Silicon Valley halfway through September. Professor Kaminsky says there will be others. She reminds us weekly that formal higher education has irrefutable value. She says there is plenty of time to become corporate shills later.

I hear movement from my bed and look up. "Morning, Jerry."

Jerry Fujimoto grunts and moves his jaw from side to side. "Do you ever sleep?"

"Of course I do."

"I never see you sleep."

"That's because you're already asleep."

Jerry sits up in bed. "What are you doing?"

"Emailing my prof."

"About the cheating undergrad?"

"That's right."

"What's going to happen to her?"

"Not sure. Kaminsky is a tough lady to get a hold of." I pick at a freckle on my arm. "Apparently she had a kid last year."

"Apparently?"

"She's always got these enormous bags under her eyes and really pale skin. The senior students say she's been wrecked since coming back from maternity leave. She got a call from her husband last week while I was in her office. From what I could hear, the kid had shit itself so badly that Kaminsky needed to go out and buy it new clothes because every onesie they owned was soiled beyond repair."

"So you're saying motherhood is not for you?"

"No fucking way. Professor Kaminsky is a world-renowned astrophysicist. She shouldn't have to worry about shit like that."

"Literal shit like that."

"And when she answered the phone, I watched this horrible pained expression come over her face. She looked so fucking defeated. In that moment, I think she'd have traded it all in if she could."

"For?"

"Whatever she could get—probably anything without the kid and the husband."

Jerry let out a low whistle. "And nothing about that is appealing?"

I shrug. "No time. I need to stay focused on work if I want to get ahead."

Jerry nods. "My mom says people in their fifties without kids are all fucked up—nihilistic and bitter, with no purpose."

"Maybe your mom's just saying that because she wants grandchildren."

"Maybe."

"And saying that kids create purpose seems like a cop-out, don't you think? The world doesn't need more children. How about my purpose being a life-changing breakthrough in thermal dynamics? Or flame physics? Or anything that's not a dirty diaper? Sounds a heck of a lot better to me."

"I know," says Jerry. He rubs his face. "I need to go to the office today."

"You're always at the office."

"I'm behind."

"You're always behind."

"That's because it's impossible to catch up."

"What are you working on?"

Jerry leans his head back and groans. "It's a long story."

"Continue."

"And it's complicated."

"I can handle it."

"We have a demo due to investors in two weeks. No one else seems worried, but it's seriously stressing me out."

"That sucks."

"No shit. My resting heart rate is way up, and I'm having recurring dreams about looping structures. I don't know what I'm going to do."

"Your boss is working you too hard."

"Stanford is working *you* too hard."

"Not me. I've got everything under control."

Jerry shrugs and rolls over. I look across his shirtless frame. His pectorals are pointed and soft. Doughy skin bunches up against his midriff. I feel warmth course through me. He looks magnificent because he knows me like no one else in this whole fucking world.

CHAPTER 19

JUNE 2010

G REGORY FERGUSON WAS A man of twenty-eight with soft features and skin that seemed to radiate light. He stood in the foyer of Byron's apartment wearing a human-sized block of Antron fleece cheddar cheese. He nudged the door closed with a backward thrust of his buttocks.

Byron sat cross-legged on the bed. "How was work?"

"You know, it was really great." Gregory's voice was light and melodious. He kicked off a pair of running shoes and let a duffle bag fall to the floor.

"Where were you today?"

"Started at Grand Central, then up and down the fifties, then Times Square, then Houston and Broadway for evening rush hour."

"You must be tired."

Gregory shrugged. "People were nice—coupons and free cheese go a long way if you find the right crowd." He smiled. "Best part is I got a call about a job on my way over here."

"The toothpaste commercial?"

"That's booked and shooting next Tuesday. This is even better."

"What?"

Gregory turned his torso toward Byron, then counterrotated his left arm and swung his head forward. The block of cheese loosened and rose up over his face. He repeated the motion three more times until his body was free. "A gig this summer—sounds like it could be really big for me."

"Television?"

Gregory stood in nylon shorts and a t-shirt yellowed from perspiration. "Theatre. This experiential marketing stuff is fine, but I'm ready to take my career to the next level."

"That's amazing news."

"Three-month contract and good pay. It's a no-brainer."

"Broadway?"

Gregory shook his head.

"Off-Broadway?"

Gregory continued to shake his head.

"Off-off-Broadway?"

"Nope."

"So what is it?"

"Florida."

Byron's back stiffened. "Really?"

"One of those Disney cruises, you know? I'll get room, board, health insurance, free travel."

"I thought you didn't like travelling. Didn't you say it made you anxious? Didn't you say it detracts from your acting work?"

Gregory shrugged. "It's free, so I'm going to enjoy it. I'll still be based out of New York, of course, but professional theatre is an opportunity I can't turn down. I'm going to sublet my lease and see what happens."

Byron readjusted his sitting position and stared intently. "This is something you're interested in doing?"

"It's a chance to hone my craft like never before. We rehearse on shore for a month, then run two shows a day, six days a week, for the whole summer. This is the real deal." Gregory pointed to the bathroom door past the kitchen. "Do you mind if I shower?"

Byron gestured that he did not.

Gregory pulled off his shorts and t-shirt, revealing a skinny frame cut from cigarettes and Diet Coke. He was, as he explained to Byron shortly after their meeting at a Columbus Circle deli counter two months prior, a Lee Strasberg devotee, believing that any serious actor needed Strasberg's tenet of personal experience informing character experience to unlock one's true creative potential. Attempting a career in acting without Strasberg was, according to Gregory, a fool's errand.

Byron picked at lint in his navel. "So, can I come see you on stage?"

"I guess." Gregory shrugged. "Florida is a long way from New York."

"Watching you perform is exciting. It's a vulnerable thing, you know, sharing art with someone you care about."

Gregory nodded.

"Like when I showed you my paintings, and you said you loved them, even though I wasn't so sure."

Gregory continued to nod. "I remember that."

"Same with my recordings."

"I remember those too."

"Say…"

"Yes?"

"Out of curiosity…"

"Uh-huh?"

"Do you ever think about finding work that's a little more conventional?"

"From time to time. You'd be naive not to consider it."

"You think so?"

"But my career is on the up. I've got some heat, you know?"

"It sounds like you do. A bit, anyways."

"As long as I'm moving up, and as long as I'm having fun, I'm in!"

"I've been thinking about disposable income. Like, what it would mean to have it."

"Uh-huh."

"The flexibility that money would allow. Taking time off, investing in tools, hiring a publicist."

"Money can help success along, no doubt."

"And it doesn't mean I can't still be great. Wallace Stevens was an insurance executive *and* a great poet."

Gregory turned and entered the washroom. "Who's that?"

"He wrote 'The Auroras of Autumn.'"

"Never heard of it."

"I mean, Henri Rousseau was a fucking tax collector."

"The philosopher?"

"No, that's Jean-Jacques Rousseau. Henri Rousseau was a painter."

Gregory shut the washroom door. "Got it."

Byron remained on his bed. His creativity had stagnated since the two began seeing each other, and now his days consisted of rising, washing dishes at El Pollito Mexicano in Park Slope, then rendezvousing with Gregory whenever their schedules allowed. The sex was powerful and frequent, though not particularly pleasurable. The moments following orgasm were crushingly lonely and left Byron ambivalent on matters of human attraction.

Pipes rattled inside the walls of the apartment. Byron listened intently as water flowed from the washroom's showerhead. He liked the idea of another human comfortable and at ease within his personal space. He heard the subtle change in water rhythm as Gregory shifted body position and the hollow echo of a shampoo bottle being knocked over, then sliding skin against a frictionless surface as Gregory slipped and nearly lost his balance. Byron sat in silence until the sounds of water ceased and the bathroom door lock clicked open. Gregory emerged wet and with a small towel clinging to his hips. He looked stunning.

"The thing about professional acting is that it's a grind day in and day out. You're doing a job in exchange for pay—it's an important thing to remember," said Gregory.

Byron nodded. "Like, you're saying your relationship to the art shifts once it becomes a job?"

"Money changes the game. You're a professional amongst other professionals, and there's a corporate entity expecting excellence." Gregory paused and pointed a finger at Byron. "You want to know what greatness means? It's the ability to do the work when you feel like shit. If you can fake a performance and not let the audience know how you really feel, then you're cut out for the big-time." Gregory let the towel drop to the floor so that he was completely naked. "What do you think about that?"

"It makes sense to me," said Byron.

"I think that mindset could go a long way to improving your output."

"What do you mean?"

"Don't take this the wrong way, but your influences are all over the place." Byron snorted. "If you want to be a professional, you need to find your niche, then become so seasoned, you excel on your worst day."

Byron nodded slowly. "Sometimes my mind goes in so many different directions, and I get ahead of myself." He paused. "It's an intense desire that I can't shake. If I'm doing something, I'm doing it all the way. Then when it's done, I don't know what to do with it. Sometimes I feel like I'm flapping in the breeze."

"You need to rein that in if you have any hope of being a commercial success."

"I don't know that I can ever be that focused."

Gregory approached the bed and stood over Byron. He bent down and they kissed. Byron stripped. The mattress bounced and squeaked as Byron lay face-down while being thrust into. Gregory finished and disappeared into the bathroom. Byron heard the tinkle of urination and the toilet flushing. Gregory reemerged and picked up fresh underwear from his duffel bag. His scrotum hung comically behind pimpled ass cheeks.

"I have a question," said Byron.

"Uh-huh."

"Have you ever been with a woman?"

Gregory stood up and turned to face Byron. "Never."

"Have you ever thought about it?"

"Never been interested."

"And when you're with a man you care about, you can feel it? Like you're fully and completely invested in their happiness?"

"Sure, I guess."

"Because I'm not so sure I know what that's like."

"Don't be a fucking drama queen."

"I don't think I've ever quite felt it."

Byron began to dress. "Maybe you haven't looked hard enough."

"Did you hear about that woman who married the Eiffel Tower?"

"I have no idea what you're talking about."

"Like, there are people who form emotional connections with physical objects—great works of architecture and that sort of thing."

"That's fucked up."

"But is it really? Maybe we're just not being open-minded enough."

"I'm as open-minded as they come, and that's fucked up."

Byron put up his hands. "All I'm saying is I'd like to know more."

"Maybe you just need to lower your standards. Don't think too hard and just let it happen."

"Maybe."

Gregory bent down and kissed Byron again. "My schedule is really busy the next few weeks. I'm not going to have much free time until the fall."

Byron nodded.

"You understand if I bring a few things over here while my place is taken over?"

"I guess so."

"I just don't want a stranger going through my stuff."

"Right."

"It doesn't make sense to spend all that money on a storage locker if you're going to be here." Gregory pulled on new shorts and a t-shirt. "I'll be by next week with a few boxes—won't be much."

Byron nodded. Gregory picked up his bundle of Antron fleece cheese, the edges of which bulged, necessitating a two-armed bear hug then deftly lifting the duffle bag and twisting the front door doorknob open with his elbow. "The thing to remember, Byron, is to follow your dreams."

"I know."

"I really mean it. Follow your deepest desires with unrelenting commitment. Anything else is unacceptable." Gregory grinned. "I'll come over with some stuff next week. We can still fuck if you want."

***

The gas burner clicked three times and ignited, sending a ring of blue flames dancing around the stove's front right element. Murray dumped chopped onions and garlic into a saucepan, then ground beef, then a jar of tomato sauce. He brought water to a boil and added linguine. The range hood rattled and shook overhead as red sauce bubbled.

Murray exited the kitchen. His stocking feet slipped slightly on the transition from tile to living room hardwood. Don Sr.'s voice boomed from the upstairs office through a door that was ajar. Murray heard his father's words project slowly and methodically, like they normally did, though with a subtle excitement that was unusual. At times, he sounded downright gleeful.

Donald Buchanan Sr. had spent much of the last week holed up in his office. When he did emerge, he was heavily occupied with printed sales figures and dense legal contracts. Murray overheard loud phone conversations with lawyers, real estate agents, the bank, and a business partner. This was the liveliest Don Sr. had been since the accident.

Murray climbed the stairs to his father's office. He knocked on the open door and entered without waiting for a reply. "Dinner's ready."

Don Sr. sat at his desk, back arched forward, and nodded without looking up. The space was fanatically clean. Murray returned to the kitchen and shut off the stove and range hood. The whooshing of the intake fan subsided. Murray began to eat. His father arrived presently and sat down with a plate across from his son. He spoke sharply. "How's the warehouse?"

"Fine."

"You know I put my name on the line to get you in there?"

"I know."

"I've been acquainted with Brenda Trinh for a long time. She worked for me in the nineties."

"She mentioned that."

Don Sr. crossed his arms. "She says the warehouse can be a rough environment—apparently they've had trouble attracting quality staff."

Murray nodded.

"From what I understand, they've had to lower their standards considerably. Apparently a few criminal reference checks have been waived because of the need for a quick hire."

"Really?"

"That's confidential."

"Did she say who?"

"It's no matter. What do you think of your colleagues?"

"They work hard." Murray paused. "Maybe if the warehouse paid more, Brenda could hire better staff."

Don Sr. nodded silently.

"I mean fifty cents above minimum wage? Come on."

"Our world is built on inequality, Murray."

"Doesn't mean it's right."

"I'm not suggesting we have a debate. I'm explaining to you how it is." Murray's father stirred his pasta. "Do you see yourself at Polymer Imports long-term?"

"Hope not."

"They provide stable hours."

"I know."

"Mind you, to exist in that warehouse is to exist in a small pond—an extremely small pond. There comes a point in every one's career when they reach their ceiling. I don't believe you're there yet. You still have more to offer."

"I hope so."

"You have a skill set that will take you far: intelligence, charisma, and confidence."

"Maybe."

Don Sr. laid his utensils on the table. "I've just finalized the terms of a deal."

"What kind of deal?"

"A partner and I are making a purchase."

"Of what?"

"It's not official yet, so this is told in confidence. Papers will be signed next week, and we're expecting the transfer of ownership to take effect early next year." Don Sr. paused. "We have a motivated seller, and the price is right."

"What are you buying?"

"A radio station."

Murray's head tilted. "Really?"

"Sure."

"Which one?"

"106.5 FM WPDH in Poughkeepsie."

"Huh."

"Exciting, isn't it?"

"Can I ask why?"

"The balance sheet is surprisingly strong."

"Really?"

"You know I did some good business from radio media in the nineties?"

"Because radio's dead as far as I'm concerned—no offence."

"The seller was motivated."

"Are they in financial crisis?"

"I suspect they're close."

"And you think you're going to make money?"

"Eventually, yes. The station has been stagnating for some time—understandable given the current market conditions. We believe we've created a viable turnaround plan." Don Sr. squared his gaze on Murray. "There may be an opportunity for you, in the short term, should you be interested."

"What kind of opportunity?"

"I was thinking on-air, if you wanted. As a favour. I remember your brother saying you were a real hit in high school."

"What...you mean doing the morning announcements?"

"From what I understand."

"Is this a favour for me or a favour for you?"

Don Sr. waved his hand. "Everything will become clearer once the deal closes. They're targeting a male forty-five-to-fifty-four demographic—mix of rock music and sports talk. It could be right up your alley."

"I guess."

"And broadcast work is all about communication under pressure. You can be a great accountant or a great programmer, but you're going to limit yourself if you can't articulate your knowledge when it matters. Some time on-air at a reputable station will be a great primer for a career in sales, if you ask me."

"Maybe."

"I believe you'd do well in sales."

"Yeah," said Murray. "Maybe."

Don Sr. pointed with his utensil toward his plate. "This is tasty."

"It was easy."

"Your mother, bless her, was not a gifted cook."

Murray's expression stiffened, and he said nothing.

"We're going to be just fine."

"I hope so," said Murray.

"Everything will be okay in the end."

***

I squint at my laptop and feel my upper body tilt forward. My nose is an inch from the screen. A tingling spreads across my face.

My apartment has remained unchanged since I moved in the previous year. Sometimes I notice odd smells that cannot be accounted for. Once I was certain an animal had died between two sections of drywall, and I was about to call the landlord to see about an extraction when the man in the unit next to mine knocked on the door and explained his toilet was wretchedly backed up, so if I could please bear with him, it would be appreciated. That remains the only time we've spoken.

Earning an advanced degree from Stanford is a quiet and solitary undertaking. Gone are the daily built-in human interactions of high school and undergrad, even if it was something I mostly chose to avoid. In retrospect, the constant presence of human bodies was comforting in a way I did not appreciate. Now I go days without seeing another soul. So far, my work is proceeding according to plan. I have received A's in all classes and a glowing sign-off on my thesis topic from Professor Kaminsky: broadly speaking, a practical examination of low-temperature flames and their effects on pollutants and emissions during turbine combustion. The information being crammed into my brain is more detailed and specific than anything I encountered at MIT—hair-splitting differences only the most committed physics weenie would care about, but which must be reviewed with absolute certainty to ensure my output's integrity.

My mind spins and whirs. I have been grinding nonstop for several hours. I lean back and rub my eyelids. Jerry has gotten wrapped up in the hustle of Silicon Valley and regularly pulls fourteen hours without a break. He says it's best if we continue to live apart, at least for now, because work is just so crazy and he needs to commit himself to his career. His employer is on the brink of an IPO and in a horrid crunch to deliver to market. He's stressed in a way I have never seen him before, but also smug about the tremendous pressure being placed upon him. Once, he purposely left his phone screen unlocked for me to see his biweekly pay deposit. I told him he owed me dinner.

I lean back in my chair and scroll through the day's news. San Francisco 49ers. Elon Musk. President Obama. Healthcare reform. I pause and my thoughts drift to my mother. I type "Woodbury" into the search bar. The page loads slowly. I scan headlines and a story catches my eye: *Teacher Arrested In Child Pornography Bust*. I move my cursor over the link and click. The window goes blank, freezes, then appears fully loaded. Breath escapes my lungs, and I feel like I have been punched in the solar plexus. A picture of Mr. Marcotte stares back at me.

I read the article twice. From what I can glean, an unidentified female student came forward with accusations of sexual assault. A second accuser followed. Mr. Marcotte was placed on leave, and when police investigated, they discovered he was already under surveillance by their cyber crimes unit for alleged massive dealings in kiddie porn. He was arrested and charged shortly thereafter. Attempts by the media to reach him were unsuccessful. His lawyer would not comment at this time.

The room starts to get smaller. I feel panic pulsing from all directions. I push my chair back and stand up from my desk, walking past the kitchen and opening the window overlooking the parking lot. I extend my neck forward and stare three floors down to the ground. Outside air flows over my face. I hear birds and combustion engines. I take soothing breaths and try to process my thoughts. My balance falls out of calibration. I feel my weight shifting and my feet rising. I open my eyes. Gravity works against me, and my body falls forward. The asphalt parking lot fills my view. I grab frantically and latch onto the inside frame of the window.

My heart pounds. I right my balance, then move into the kitchen and sit cross-legged on the floor. I take slow breaths, and my body shakes. In the news photo, Mr. Marcotte was clean-shaven, with floppy hair. He looked unchanged from when I last saw him five years before. Sometimes at Monroe-Woodbury, I would fantasize about dating him. He was interesting and funny. He was also abundantly more mature than any of the boys at Woodbury and never once acted inappropriately toward me. Had he made an advance, I do not know how I would have responded.

I let my mind wander and consider what it all could mean. Inappropriate comments. Salacious correspondences. Touching. Alcohol. Sex. Rape. Pedophilia. Time warps and I lose track of what's going on.

Later, my phone rings. I look down and see that Byron Somerfield is calling. I raise the phone to my ear. "Hello?"

There is a slow exhale. "Hi, Lesley."

"How are you?"

"Okay."

"How is Stanford?"

"Uh, exhausting, but I knew that going in."

"And, like, Jerry's good?"

"He's working lots, but he's good."

"That's good to hear." Byron paused. "You keep up with Woodbury at all?"

"I do when something like this happens."

"Right."

"Uh-huh."

"So you saw the Marcotte news?"

"Uh-huh."

"My mom just called me. She says it's the talk of Woodbury. Apparently it was bad."

"No kidding."

"Like, one of the worst collections the police have ever seen."

"Right." I take long breaths and stay silent.

"It's crazy."

"That's a lot to process."

"You were close to him, weren't you?"

"I was."

"Like, really close, right?"

"You could say that."

"Because it sounds like this all stemmed from some sort of contact with a student."

"Uh-huh."

"So."

"What?"

"Did he eve—"

"No."

"There was never anything inappropriate?"

"I mean, never anything like that." I rub my hand over my face and speak slowly. "From my perspective, he was a great teacher."

"I know."

"When I was sixteen, there was no one else like him. He was the most exciting thing going." I pause. "I think he changed my life in a way. He inspired me to keep pushing forward and to be tenacious. He gave me the confidence to apply to MIT."

"So, like, are you saying there's some good in him, or are you saying he's a manipulative fucker?"

"Both, maybe. Probably the latter. It's difficult to wrap my mind around."

"He seemed to really like being a teacher."

"Makes sense, given his interests—alleged interests."

"Yeah."

"I guess he's an awful person who managed to inspire a vulnerable teenager half his age..." My voice trails off.

"I guess so," says Byron.

There is a long silence. "Do you go back to Woodbury often?"

"Try to get up there to see my folks," said Byron. "You?"

"Haven't been back in a while," I say. "Sometimes I miss it."

"I know what you mean."

"Sometimes. Sometimes I miss it a lot."

CHAPTER 20

JULY 2010

Byron sat cross-legged on the floor of his apartment and fiddled with the tape deck of a JVC camcorder. The smell of stale cigarettes was strong and permeated from all directions. His phone rested on a couch cushion near his head, into which Byron spoke. "What's up, Dad?"

"Where are you?" said James Somerfield.

"My apartment."

"How are you liking Crown Heights?"

"I got mugged on the way home from work last week."

"Are you serious?"

"Some guy told me to give him my money. He got my night's tips."

"Did he have a gun?"

"He pulled out a knife," said Byron. "And said he had a gun."

"What a loser."

"Me, or the guy who robbed me?"

"Who would do that?"

"Think of it as a tax I pay to live in an affordable part of New York."

"Are you going to tell your mother?"

"I wouldn't worry about that."

"Unbelievable."

Byron pushed the camcorder's tape deck closed. "Uh-huh."

"And how's work?"

"You know. It's kitchen work. Hot. Your body hurts after every shift." Byron paused. "But, like, you get into a meditative rhythm with the hose and the valve and the spray of water against the dishes. It's almost musical. On. Off. On. Off."

"I can barely hear you."

"I'm on speaker right now." Byron leaned his head toward the couch. "Is that any better?"

"A bit. What are you doing?"

"Working on something."

Byron heard shuffling on his father's end of the line. "Working on what?"

"Playing with some settings on a camcorder."

"For what?"

"Something I'm putting together."

"Is this new?"

"I'm trying out some video art stuff."

"Oh." Byron's father sounded annoyed. "Why?"

"Dunno. The whole medium is a bit questionable, if you ask me." Byron smirked. "But I want in."

"What do you know about video art?"

"I know what people think is good. Have you seen some of this stuff? The classics?"

"I've seen it."

"Like, how the hell did Sadie Benning ever get famous? That's the right place and right time with the help of an influential parent who himself probably got famous by being in the right place at the right time. And that's nothing against Sadie Benning. I'm just saying."

"Then why are you bothering?"

"Because why not? I've got this camera and I might as well use it." Byron paused. "I have this idea, that, like, if the audio mix is done right, if it sounds like you know what you're doing, the image on the screen can be anything you goddamn want and the audience will accept it."

"Okay..."

"Ideally I'd be hanging 16mm film strips and cutting on a Steenbeck. You know, the shooting constraints and discipline required would yield interesting results. But it's just not feasible with my resources. JVC camcorder it is."

"Sounds interesting."

"It does?"

"We're similar in a lot of ways, you and I."

"We are?"

"You're working away, you're adapting, and you're resilient."

"I am?"

"Uh-huh."

"And you?"

"Well, I wanted to tell you something."

"What's that?"

James Somerfield paused dramatically. "I'm moving forward with Dunkin' Donuts."

"You are?"

"That's the reason I called."

"Really?"

"Uh-huh."

"Wow…"

"It's exciting. Isn't it? It's all coming together."

"I guess so. What does Mom think?"

"She's coming around to the idea."

"I'm happy to hear that."

"I'll be working out of a Middletown location, learning all areas of the customer-facing business. Cash. Coffee prep. Food prep. Facilities. Ordering. Bookkeeping."

"Sounds complicated."

"It's huge for me. I couldn't be happier. I'm here where I need to be, and I'm doing it."

"That's great."

"This is an enormous step."

Byron held the camcorder's eyepiece up to his face and squinted. "Then I'm happy it worked out."

"That's right. The Somerfield men are making their way! I'm proud of us. Of *us*. Both of us!"

CHAPTER 21

MAY 2011

MURRAY SAT WITH HIS back erect against the Lincoln Continental's pristine leather interior. His father navigated late afternoon traffic, pushing along streets dotted with crooked white-siding houses and pockets of delicate trees. Car exhaust hung low in the sky, clinging to the tops of roofs and casting the surroundings in a bland haze. A leather-bound zippered portfolio sat on Murray's lap.

"This is the best thing for you right now, don't you think?"

"It's an interesting opportunity." Murray kept his gaze forward.

"I went through a lot to arrange this."

"I appreciate your help."

"To clarify, I spent a lot to arrange this."

"I will do my best."

"I'm confident this will be a good investment. You can be damn sure I wouldn't have put the money down otherwise."

Murray nodded. "Thank you."

"The station offers some unorthodox revenue opportunities."

"Oh. I thought you meant I was the good investment."

Don Sr. paused. "Yes. That too."

Murray lifted the portfolio from his lap—a high school graduation gift that sat unused for a half-decade until uncovered the previous evening during the final round of edits to his newly minted CV. He extracted a pair of stapled pages and took in the clean formatting and beautiful kerning of the black ink. A Clinton-era station wagon braked suddenly. Murray's father cursed and brought the Lincoln to a halting full stop. Murray's weight pushed up against the seatbelt and his hands moved automatically forward, crumpling the CV against the dashboard. His heart pounded uncomfortably. Don Sr. said nothing.

106.5 FM WPDH's offices stood well back from the road in a nondescript industrial low-rise. A chain link fence surrounded much of the property, with small breaks in the perimeter allowing access to a sizeable parking lot in one corner of which a half-dozen cars were clustered. Murray's father steered the Lincoln toward the station's front entrance, popping the transmission into neutral and rolling to a stop beside a rusted Chevelle. "I'm meeting the contractor about some building matters—we won't be long." He turned to Murray. "Good luck."

"Thanks." Murray unbuckled his seatbelt and tucked the portfolio up into his armpit. He watched his father light a cigarette and take an aggressive drag. A new habit since the accident.

The lobby was small and poorly lit. Identical potted plants flanked a front desk holding an old tube computer monitor and piled high with promotional pamphlets for the grand opening of an Albuquerque supper club two Saturdays previous. Murray eased himself into a black sectional couch and picked up the current issue of *Electric Radio*. He thumbed through its pages, focusing in on excerpts as they interested him though never finishing an article.

A beady-eyed man pushed open a glass door cut out of the lobby's extreme right wall. He wore suit pants and expensive Italian shoes with a light green sweater that was oddly informal. The man flashed a great wide smile. "Name's Kip. It's an absolute pleasure to make your acquaintance." He spoke with a light English accent.

Murray grasped his hand. It was meaty and large when compared to the rest of his body. "Nice to meet you."

"Will your father be joining us?" Kip looked past Murray expectantly.

"No. He's meeting the real estate agent—something about property stuff, I think."

"No trouble at all." Kip held his arms out, as if to convey Murray's father had absolute autonomy to do whatever he pleased. "Do you want to come meet some of the team?"

"Sure."

"Extraordinary!" Kip spun 180 degrees and dashed back toward the glass door. Murray followed, entering a room significantly darker than the lobby. Two men, one balding and wearing a sports coat and sunglasses, the other painfully skinny with a thin nose and wispy blond hair, stared back at him from across a table. Kip pointed to the rodent-like man. "That's Mac, resident tech wizard. He keeps everything operating smoothly and sounding radio-crisp."

Mac nodded. "Amazing to meet you, man. It's really great that you're here and all."

Kip pointed to Mac's left. "That there is Rowdy Ron Johnson, morning host for twenty-five years and local living legend. He wanted to meet you personally."

Rowdy Ron tilted his head, though he did not smile or take off his sunglasses. Mac leaned back in his chair. His gaze passed between Murray and Kip. "So, uh, what exactly is it you're doing here?"

Murray's arm twitched. His thoughts went to the leather-bound portfolio and three remaining copies of his CV, sculpted by an associate of his father to fluff up spotty employment and education history into an impressive story of self-guided learning and vague entrepreneurial ventures. He brought the folder out from under his arm.

Kip's smile flickered almost imperceptibly. "He's here about the late-night time slot, remember?" He spoke each word carefully.

"Oh, that's right," said Mac. "You're the rich guy's kid."

Kip's eyes bulged, and his accent became noticeably more pronounced. "Murray's father has decided to invest in the station. As it happens, we believe Murray will make a fantastic addition to the on-air team."

Murray had the portfolio unzipped now and extracted three stapled packets. He passed a copy to Kip and noticed—with total certainty—a typo in the opening paragraph's penultimate sentence, the word "through" staring hideously back at him with a missed "o" between the letters "r" and "u" rendering the sentence useless. Murray was furious, especially since the paragraph was the last to be reworked by his father's associate, and Murray had gazed into the late glow of his monitor, scanning the document time after time but still let an idiotic and potentially crippling error make it to print.

"May I see?" said Mac. He extended a hand forward at a sloth-like pace.

Murray forced his face into a polite smile and surrendered a CV. Mac acknowledged the transfer with a deep nod and began to read as Kip swept his arm over the table and invited Murray to take a seat. Murray obliged, positioning himself across the table from the three men. Mac had the papers flat on the table and was going through the text line by line. He circled the typo in bright red ink. Murray felt ill.

"So," said Kip. He bobbed up and down in his chair. "What do you think of the place?"

Murray exhaled. He did a full scan of the room. Promotional posters for 1970s-themed rock countdowns and live-to-air boat shows were positioned prominently among head-shots of past and present radio hosts, for most of whom the sarcastic phrase "face for radio" aptly applied. Beyond this, and observable through a thick window, was the sta-tion's live studio. A woman sat hunched over a microphone, her shoulders and back tight in concentration and an enormous set of headphones covering both ears. Beside her was a bona fide little person sitting on an extra high chair and wearing a matching pair of broadcast-standard cans.

"Drive time is beginning," said Kip. He leaned back and linked his fingers, resting them gently on top of the belly protruding from under his knit sweater. "Let's get started then, shall we?"

Murray nodded. Mac turned the page on his CV. Ron remained still.

"Normally there'd be a hiring manager present," said Kip. "Unfortunately, they're being phased out as nonessential. It's a challenging cost-cutting measure but very much a reality of our industry. The Internet has thrown a rather large wrench into our business model." He shook his head and paused. "Your father came to us as an angel investor. He went over the books, met our key personnel, and decided this was the sort of organization he wanted to be involved with." He looked to the ceiling. "We all know the glory days are gone, but radio still holds a special power that no other medium can match. There's something your father sees in the station." He spread his hands and leaned forward. "Does he have a background in broadcasting?"

"Kind of."

"Tell me more."

"He made some media investments in the nineties—I'm unclear on the details. He was mostly involved on the business end of things."

"Is he a fan of rock music?"

"Not particularly."

"Does he play any instruments himself?"

Murray shook his head.

"What about sports?"

"He likes baseball—used to at least."

"But now?"

"Less so now."

"I see." Kip shifted his buttocks in his chair. "The station is indeed struggling. The sum of money he put in—enough to become majority owner—is considerable. Tell me, what is it that your father does now for a living?"

"It's tough to say, really."

"Why is that?"

"Because I don't have a clear idea myself."

"What field is he in?"

"He was a lawyer. Now he's a consultant, I think. And an investor."

"So h—"

"Consults and invests."

"I see." Kip moved his interlocked fingers to the table. "As I alluded to earlier, an overnight spot has recently opened up."

"That was my dad's idea, wasn't it?"

Kip fixed Murray with a long stare. He opened his mouth, closed it, and opened it again. "There's no shortage of interns dying for on-air gigs. I can't recommend radio as a viable career these days, but still..." Kip waved his hands. "To be frank, your father's acquisition of the station has everything to do with your hiring. That is, your likely hiring."

Murray nodded. He looked to the live room. The little person had his face pressed up into a mic, gesturing with short, powerful chops of his hands as he spoke.

"The overnight slot has its own set of unique challenges," said Kip. "You should consider yourself a caretaker for the airwaves: talking around ads, playing a little music, taking calls, anything to avoid dead air."

"And people really call the station?"

"They do."

"Why are you making that face?"

"It's prudent to remember that you'll be working the midnight to 5:00 a.m. broadcast. Assume all callers are at least moderately deranged."

"I think that makes sense."

"Good. Now, Mac here will be working the overnight with you. He's a real pro. A true master of his craft."

Mac nodded and made no effort to conceal his enjoyment of the praise being directed at him.

Kip leaned back so that the front legs of his chair lifted from the floor. His interlocked fingers went back to his belly. His tone became more casual. "Did you know I went to school down in Boston?"

Murray squinted. "Why would I know that?"

"Granted, I didn't go to *that* school in Boston, but the experience was still revelatory. I moved out to London after graduation and got a gig with a little station out there—you ever heard of the BBC?" He grinned and his voice dropped. "My magnum opus is a postbreakdown interview with Syd Barrett. The broadcast got blocked at the last minute—something about his signed release lacking criteria for proper consent. I was court-ordered to surrender all copies of the interview." He lowered his voice further so that he was now speaking at whisper-level. "I've still got an analog copy back at the house. Fuck the courts." He leaned back and his voice resumed its regular volume. "Any questions?"

Murray shook his head.

Kip smirked. "Do you know who Syd Barrett is?"

"H—"

"Don't answer that! You're going to make me feel old." Kip rubbed his hands together. "So what do you think?"

"Well." Murray paused. "I believe I can do, uh, really great things here. I'm excited."

"And why do you think that is?" Rowdy Ron turned his head to face Murray. "Why can you do great things?" His voice was commanding and powerful—an absolute God-given radio talent.

"Well, uh, radio is just talking, isn't it?" said Murray. "I can talk."

Kip's gaze flashed nervously to Ron. Mac's mouth was open, thrilled at Murray's lack of respect for established radio hierarchy. Ron exhaled out his nostrils and began to laugh. It was a deep, full-body laugh that caused his chest and limbs to heave and shake. "Hey! The kid's got a point—we're just talking."

Ron slammed his hand down hard on the table. Kip looked worried. Ron extended a single finger and pointed over Murray's head. Murray turned. A clock hung on the wall between a picture of Janis Joplin and a drugged-out Keith Richards. "About time for that production meeting, isn't it? We need to talk tomorrow's show."

Kip looked up at the clock and frowned. "A little early yet."

"I don't believe there's much more to do here."

"Well, sure, we can get started if you like."

"I'd like that very much."

Mac put two fingers to his temple and saluted Murray. "A pleasure to meet you."

Kip stood up and gestured for Murray to do the same. He moved around to the other side of the table and put a hand on his shoulder. "Thanks for coming in."

"Oh, is that it?"

"We'll start two weeks from today at 10:00 p.m. sharp. How does that sound?"

"Oh, I guess that will be fine."

"I'll walk you out to the lobby." Kip maintained a wide grin that stretched his lips and teeth back to the point of being disconcerting.

Murray watched Mac take a long swig from a cup of black coffee. Rowdy Ron was still. The woman and the little person in the live booth were gesturing wildly now and speaking into the microphones with such vigour and conviction that Murray swore he could see bits of spittle flying from their respective mouths.

Kip guided Murray through the glass door and back out into the lobby—the afternoon daylight shone through the windows and stung his eyes. Kip turned and leaned closer to Murray. His smile had changed from professional enthusiasm to something more severe and intimidating. "While I have you here, there's just one more thing."

"What's that?"

"Your father's interest in the station—his purchase of the majority stake—that wouldn't have anything to do with our rather unusual real estate arrangement, would it?"

"What arrangement?"

"That would be the station's ownership of this entire complex, totalling an acre and a half of land, in what, over the next twenty years could become a lucrative centre of urban revitalization."

"Oh, I don't know anything about that."

"Because there is considerable concern that outside investment puts the future at risk. We here are entirely committed to the station. I got a look at the sales document and there's a period of time—eighteen months to be precise—where your father is barred from forcing the ownership to divest. Beyond that, it's anyone's guess."

Murray shook his head. "That's not any of my business."

Kip gestured to the front door. "Well then, we've got a lot of work that needs attending to." He shook Murray's hand again. Murray tucked his leather-bound file folder under his arm and exited the lobby.

Chapter 22

June 2011

Gentle music wafted through the supermarket's artificially cooled air. Byron clutched a vacuum-sealed tub of dark roast coffee grounds. He watched the cashier's hands move rapidly as she scanned through a grocery order with tuna cans and horizontal cereal boxes piled three and four high. A distantly familiar voice sounded behind him. Byron turned, his mouth morphing into a hesitant half-smile. "Wow."

A short man in slacks and sports coat grinned and extended a hand forward. "It's an absolute pleasure to see you."

"Phil Paxton from UB," said Byron.

"That's right."

"It's been a few years."

"Sure has."

"How are you?"

"Couldn't be better." Phil's gaze flickered over Byron's head. "Are you working on something?"

"What do you mean?"

"Well, the video camera."

Byron pointed at the RCA camcorder, resting on a folded towel and attached to his head with a yellow winch strap. "Oh, this? It's a project I'm in the middle of."

"Still doing the art thing?"

"Putting in the effort." Byron inhaled deeply. "I see you're wearing a wedding ring."

"Since last fall."

"Shit."

"It's an exciting time."

"Then congratulations."

"What is it exactly that you're working on?"

Byron repositioned the coffee grounds under his arm. "Been on a real experimental film tear lately: Deren, Brakhage, Buñuel…"

"Right." Phil nodded. "So what's the concept with this one?"

"Shooting some pick-ups right now. Not quite in a position to say yet, but soon."

"Sure. I get it."

"Yeah." Byron eyed Phil's sports coat. "What are you doing now?"

"Business development for an HVAC company."

"So like…"

"We mainly do commercial systems. Malls, convention centres, arenas…"

"Sounds complicated."

"It can be. We let the engineers worry about the technical stuff."

"How long have you been doing that?"

"I got a job almost straight out of UB—right around the time we lost touch. That was four years ago, and I've been with the company ever since."

"Really?"

"Uh-huh. There's real money in sales if you know how to sell."

"And you know how to sell?"

"I learned quickly."

"How?"

"Find the decision-makers and tell them they can't go on without you." Phil shrugged. "My wife and I have a one-year-old on a waitlist for Montessori preschool—we're on Long Island. Life becomes expensive."

"Fuck. I'm sorry."

"What?"

"You used to say you never wanted children because it would ruin everything that was good about your life. You said that, right?"

Phil tilted his head. "Did I say that?"

"Any time we got loaded in the studio. You wouldn't shut up. The crying, and the shitting, and the money, and the lifetime of commitment—you wanted none of it."

Phil put his hand to his temple. "Oh yeah, I guess you're right."

"And you were doing all those crazy paintings—the analogous colour ones on the canvases that were too big to fit through regular-sized doorways."

"Uh-huh."

"And people were displaying them outside, and they'd get rained on and vandalized, and it turned into this whole complicated social experiment, right?"

Phil shrugged. "Yeah, I was doing that for a while."

"And it got heat. Like, you were a big deal for a little bit there."

"I was a big deal regionally for maybe one semester."

"I wanted to be you so badly. In a way my whole life trajectory stems from that stuff."

"Really?"

Byron nodded vigorously. "Uh-huh. Times were tough there in Buffalo for a bit, but you gave me the energy and the drive to keep pushing through."

Phil frowned. "I did?"

"Yes."

"I see." Phil was silent for a long moment. "Did someone commission this new project?"

Byron shook his head.

"Did you get grant money?"

"Not a chance. There's no funding for something like this. My work isn't designed to be commercially successful. I've come to terms with that."

"So this is a passion project?"

"Yep. Painting and music and writing are great, but there's something about the film medium—the freedom." Byron shuffled forward and placed his coffee tub on the checkout counter.

"A man of many mediums."

"Trying to be."

"And what are you doing for money?"

Byron shrugged. "Working in a kitchen. It's honest. I've thought about getting into an office gig, but for now I like the flexibility of the restaurant business."

"Which restaurant?"

"A taco spot around here. El Pollito."

"What kind of heating and cooling do they have?"

"I could not tell you."

"Too bad. Do you feel like lunch?"

"Oh, no," said Byron. "I couldn't."

"Why not?"

"I've got a lot to do today."

"Because I'm almost done here." Phil leaned toward Byron and raised his eyebrows. "This location has a competitor's system—I'm scouting a conversion."

"I really shouldn't. But thank you."

"No problem." Phil paused. "Where are you going?"

"My apartment. I've got a lot of editing to do."

"You're cutting?"

"That's right." He pointed to the camera on his head. "Need to make this into something compelling."

"Does it always end up compelling?"

"In one way or another, yes."

"That's terrific."

Byron shrugged. The cashier scanned the coffee tub and smiled, causing the silver stud piercing in her chin to wiggle. Byron reached into his pocket and paid with loose change. He tucked the coffee tub under his arm and exited the store with Phil. "Listen, I really do have a lot of work to do."

"Are you walking?"

"Yes."

"I'll come with."

"Oh. Okay."

Phil removed a cigarette from his pocket and brought it to his mouth. He hunched his shoulders against the breeze and sparked a lighter.

"You're still doing that?"

Phil nodded. "A lot less than I used to."

"What about that other shit?"

"No, no. That's done now."

"Cold turkey?"

"It tapered off after I met my wife." Phil dipped his chin toward the cigarette between his middle and index finger. "This shit is sticking with me."

"Even with your kid?"

"I haven't quite decided yet."

"You were the mule for the whole art department back in Buffalo."

"I know."

"So what happened?"

Phil took a long slow drag. "Dunno. There was no one around once I started working. I just sort of stopped."

Byron nodded. "For a little while I really thought it was helping my creative energies, you know? Like I needed to be a mess to be successful. Those days are mostly gone now."

"Mostly?"

"Booze sometimes." Byron shrugged. "Do you like your work?"

"Of course. I don't have the creative outlet I used to, but I'm more productive now."

"Productive how?"

"Back when I was a painter, I spent so much time just sitting around and thinking."

"But you were prolific."

"Maybe. That was mostly bullshit, though—the art stuff I was doing was easy. I just got lucky that people thought it was interesting." Phil took another drag. "My desires were changing. I wanted to fall in love and be a great dad."

"Really?"

"Yes."

"That doesn't sound like you at all."

Phil shrugged.

"But anyone can have a kid, and the world is overpopulated. Those canvases you did were the coolest things going!"

"I mostly look back at them and cringe."

"Why?"

"They were so...arbitrary."

"But executed with confidence! That's what made them so amazing."

"Maybe you're on to something."

"Of course I'm on to something."

"Too late now."

"It's never too late."

Phil snorted. "It's too late."

"So what happened to those paintings?"

"They're mostly sold. My mom still has a few. She couldn't give them away now if she tried."

Byron held his hands out in front of him. "I think you've got a legacy dipped in mystique. I would do anything to have your artistic output, even if it was short-lived. Anything."

"Why would you say that?"

"Because you finished your work, and it was original and it was great. I want to have a record of my life after I die—like you do. I don't want to be forgotten."

"Listen, I made more money my first six months in sales than I ever made painting."

"So you just work now?"

Phil shrugged. "Raising my kid is fun. I watch television sometimes."

"What do you watch?"

"Whatever's on."

Byron shook his head. "Watching crummy TV only magnifies my own failures. Like, why did those idiots make it and I still haven't?"

"Everyone has failures."

"I have a lot of failures. Sometimes I think I only have failures."

"What are you talking about?"

"It's b—"

A ringing sounded from Phil's back pocket. He reached with his cigarette-wielding hand and pulled out a phone. "I'm listening, Byron. Keep talking."

"I said it's been four years, and I've never done anything that anyone has given a shit about. My apartment is full of notebooks and music gear and paintings and HDV tapes—none of it is appreciated."

"Uh-huh."

"All I want is one little piece of greatness, you know? I just want to be acknowledged as competent."

Phil held his phone out in front of him and squinted. "There's no doubt in my mind that you will get your moment. Maybe this camera-on-your-head thing will be your break." His mouth dropped, and he went bug-eyed. The cigarette fell to the sidewalk. "I'm sorry. There's an emergency with work."

"What kind of emergency?"

"I have to go, but I'm going to call you."

"You don't have my number."

"You can call me then."

"I don't have your number."

Phil shrugged. "No time." He took off running, his pants stretched against his legs and jacket bunched awkwardly above his shoulders. He disappeared behind a UPS truck. Byron stood in the street with his tub of dark roast coffee grounds. He was alone again.

Chapter 23

October 2011

Jerry and I are in my apartment together. The stove's left rear burner is on, and I have a pot going with onions, carrots, celery, chicken, garlic, pepper, parsley, and thyme. I am not interested in cooking, but Jerry says chicken soup is his favourite. I am giving it a try. The smell, he says, reminds him of the good parts of childhood.

I stir carefully and eye him. "How am I doing?"

"Well, it smells like you're doing a great job."

"Is that really true?"

"There's nothing like the smell of good soup cooking. It drove our family cat bonkers."

"Mmm, I hope it lives up to your expectations."

"My expectations are extremely reasonable."

"It's important that they remain reasonable."

"They will." Jerry smirks. "Did I tell you a recruiter contacted me today?"

"I don't think you did."

"He called me at the office."

"That's bold, isn't it?"

"He was extremely aggressive. I didn't like him, per se, but I respected his hustle."

"Who was he hiring for?"

"Wouldn't say. They want to make sure you don't go behind their backs and contact the hiring manager directly. I've been getting a lot of calls lately."

I smile. "That's because competent computer nerds are in demand."

"I'm more than competent."

"I know you are."

"There's a lot of money in tech—a lot."

"That's good if you like money."

"It's weird, though."

"What?"

"Everything moves so quickly. It's like…the product currently being delivered is almost irrelevant. It's all about what's next."

"This is why some people stay in school forever."

"And we talk about our users like they're gods. User this, user that. As if what we're doing is some sort of intrinsic good. I don't think most of our customers even realize they're our customers. We're just more anonymous tech. More. More. More."

"So then quit."

"Speaking of more, I got another promotion."

"Have you seen your company's financials?"

"No."

"Are they generating revenue?"

"Some. But it's doubtful that there's any profit at the end of it. The model is we get bought and let another company worry about making money."

"What do your parents think?"

"They're damn thrilled. I send them screenshots of my bank account every month."

"Really?"

"Yes. But I'm not after their approval."

"Are you sure about that?"

"Positive."

"Do they ask you for money?"

"No. But I'd give it to them if they did."

"Your family must think you're a real asshole."

Jerry shrugs. "A job is a job. If I'm going to work, it might as well be for the money."

"Does anyone say that you're selling out?"

"Selling out what? This is my career. Forget selling out. I'm making money. Fuck everybody else." Jerry points at me. "Your time will come too, just wait."

"I need to get through Stanford before I can even start to think about selling out."

"Not true! You have a physics degree from MIT. You could sell out right now if you wanted to."

"Are you sure about that?"

"Positive. There'll be plenty of opportunities whenever you choose to take the plunge." Jerry grinned and shook his head.

"What are you smiling at?"

"It won't interest you."

"Try me."

"It really won't."

"Come on."

"Well, since you asked, some of the guys at work were discussing ayahuasca."

"Oh, boy."

"Don't give me that. We're talking about the health benefits of psychedelics, as documented by serious scientific study. This shit should be right up your alley."

"I'm just cooking soup here."

"I wasn't quite clued into the culture of this stuff. Everyone knows about Steve Jobs and LSD and all that. But there can be real positive career ramifications if you're tripping in the right circles."

"You mean like some drugged-out networking event."

"Not quite like that."

"Who'd you hear that from?"

"Tech guys who know what they're talking about." Jerry paused. "These are intelligent people with a curiosity for life."

"People you work with?"

"Sure. Software engineers grinding fourteen-hour days minimum. Sharp individuals."

"Do you think people exaggerate their working hours? Like, are you really at work, being productive, for fourteen hours a day?"

"I swear to you I am. And the same goes for the majority of my colleagues. When we talk about psychedelics, we're talking about substances that have been consumed safely for hundreds of years. When used properly, the effect can be serious spiritual revelation about one's purpose on Earth. These are massive existential matters that need addressing—you should know that better than anyone else. Why not explore it?"

"Then why is ayahuasca illegal?"

Jerry rolled his eyes. "Trust me. We all know government is extremely conservative with this sort of thing. Give it some time."

I chuckle and turn back to the stove. The soup's surface has begun bubbling, causing little bits of chicken grease to pool and collect in loose circles. "This is going to be good, I hope."

"Of course it will be," says Jerry. "You're doing great."

***

Murray sat alone in the live room of 106.5 FM WPDH. A Shure microphone hung at mouth height supported by a desk-bolted metallic extension arm. Glowing monitors displayed audio levels, a muted live news television broadcast, and an audio log of upcoming songs, sweepers, and commercial spots. He stared through soundproof glass as Mac worked the soundboard. Bodily clicks and creaks were extra-pronounced.

The "on air" sign was dark now but would soon illuminate, and Murray's voice would broadcast across the greater Newburgh area via the station's 1,000-watt signal. He watched Mac turn his body sideways and take a swig from a bottle of something. Murray placed headphones over his ears. The inside of his mouth made wet smacking noises.

Flashy synthesizers kicked in, and the "on air" sign lit up. A prerecorded voice introduced "Overnights with Murray Buchanan." Mac squinted at his monitor as low-end rumble shook the studio speakers. Murray leaned toward the microphone and took in a breath. He did his best impression of a seasoned radio host. "Welcome to 106.5 FM WPDH. You are listening to Murray Buchanan, joining you on a quiet Tuesday night in beautiful Newburgh, New York." Murray paused and the tail end of the show opening faded into sonic oblivion. He was alone. "Coming up, we've got songs from Zeppelin, The Eagles, Heart, AC/DC, uh, The Beatles, The Stones, and many more. Plus, we talk some NBA, NFL, and Major League Baseball." Murray glanced at the countdown clock on his monitor: five seconds of airtime remained. He took a measured pause. "Let's kick things off with Boston and their 1977 hit 'Peace of Mind.'"

Vocal harmonies filled Murray's ears, and he let his weight fall to the back of the chair. A producer had been sitting in on the show's first month of broadcast. Tonight was Murray's first shift unsupervised. He stared ahead. After Boston, "Ramble On" by Led Zeppelin would play, then a sweeper advertising the station, then three minutes of paid advertisements after which time Murray would be on mic for ninety seconds. He flexed his triceps.

The station paid him minimum wage for five hours of broadcast time Monday through Friday. He arrived an hour before his shift to review playlists and confirm copy for the eight to ten sponsored ads he read each show. Some days Rowdy Ron would show up early and bully him with long-winded stories from radio's heyday. Murray had no health insurance and no paid vacation—Mac did not fare any better. Somehow, it was all still better than the warehouse.

Murray listened in silence to Robert Plant's screeching vocals, then to ads for a furniture liquidator, personal injury law firm, mortgage broker, and two different real estate agents. He watched the live countdown clock on his monitor. The "on air" light lit up, and Murray leaned toward the mic. He swallowed and opened his mouth. "Welcome back to the program. My name is Murray Buchanan. We are right smack in the middle of the ALCS, and it is a good day to be a Yankees fan. Tonight, with the series on the line, we witnessed an absolute beat-down of the Tigers 10 to 1. An evisceration. Our boys showed yet again why they're the greatest franchise in baseball and, with all due respect to the Dallas Cowboys, the greatest professional sports team in the USA."

Murray took in a breath and squinted at typed notes on his monitor. He felt removed from his body, like he was watching himself from the corner of the room. "Uh, A.J. Burnett has been struggling lately, and questions are being asked about his role on the team. Tonight, he comes out and pitches five and two-thirds innings in an elimination game. Four hits. One earned run. Three strikeouts. We'll take that thank you very much, Mr. Burnett."

Murray scrolled through the box score. He leaned closer to the mic and lowered his voice. Mac tweaked the levels. "The game is close through seven innings. In the eighth we explode." Murray leaned back and returned to his usual volume. Mac adjusted accordingly. "Al Alburquerque replaces Phil Coke on the mound. He balks, and A-Rod scores. Can you believe it? A score on a balk. In a closeout game. In front of a home crowd in Detroit. Are you kidding me? That's undisciplined baseball, and I love it." Murray took another pause. "What happened next? Uh, Teixeira scores. Alburquerque gets yanked and Schlereth comes in. He throws a wild pitch and Montero scores. Then Martin scores, then Gardner scores, and Schlereth gets yanked. The game was decided by that enormous inning."

Murray glanced at the countdown clock. "The series wraps up Thursday night back at Yankee Stadium. The forecast is a clear night, and it's going to be a doozy of a matchup. I love this game!" He paused. "We're taking calls after Neil Young."

Murray watched the "on air" light go dark. He looked at the thin strip of parking lot visible from the studio window. Light rain was falling. He thought of his brother, and time warped. His face began to spasm.

"You okay?"

Murray jolted to attention. "What's that?"

Mac's amplified voice filled the room. "I said are you okay?"

"Of course."

"You missed your cue. We had five seconds of dead air."

"Fuc—"

"It's fine. I pushed some Floyd forward, and you've got three callers waiting in the queue. No one will notice. We just need to make up the time after the next commercial break."

"Shit. I'm sorry."

Mac shrugged. "No skin off my back. Are you sure you're okay? You looked like you were going to cry and stuff."

"I'm fine."

"Cause you were doing decently with a producer here. First night on your own and you fuck something up—it's real out of character."

"Just nervous, I guess."

Mac got out of his chair and slid open the door to the live room. He held out a bottle. "Whisky. You want? For all the great work you've done."

Murray shook his head. "Nah."

"We've got the whole show to get through—don't want your nerves fucking things up again. Take a swig to celebrate your good work, would you?"

"Sure..."

"Down the hatch. I'm not telling anyone."

Murray obliged. The whisky was harsh and burned his esophagus. He coughed.

"Attaboy. Lots more where that came from."

Mac returned to his post. He placed headphones over his ears. "We're back, and we're taking calls." He looked to his monitor. "We've got Gary up the road in Hyde Park. Gary, how are you tonight?"

"Doing real good. How are you, Murray?"

"I'm great. Thank you for asking. What do you have to say about the Yankees, Gary?"

"Joe Girardi is the difference for me; '09 is his second year managing the team, and he wins a World Series. The guy is a gamer."

"Not to mention thre—"

"Three World Series championships as a player with the Yankees."

"A solid catcher," said Murray. "Great leadership. A glue guy."

"I feel real good about him running the show."

"So let me ask you something, Gary. Would you rather have a stud manager and a team of scrubs, or a bunch of all-stars and a ham sandwich on the bench?"

Gary snorted. "I'll take the sandwich and the all-stars, but this year's Yankees can have it both ways. You need to keep the players accountable. Girardi does that for me."

"Agreed. And that's some great talk there. Now we have Patton on the line. Patton, what do you have to say?"

The station hung in silence. "Hello, Patton? Uh, you've got three seconds. Two. One. Goodbye, Patton. On the line now we have Marshall. Marshall, welcome to the program this evening."

"The world is ending and you should know it better than anyone."

Murray tilted his head. "Okay..."

"Do you hear me?"

"Uh, because the Tigers are perennial playoff contenders?"

"You're a fucking fraud."

"This is a live program, and my tech guy just bleeped you. One more strike and you're out."

"You're a fraud and a failure."

"Hanging up now on our friend Marshall."

"You. Murray Buchanan. From Woodbury. Son of Donald Buchanan Sr. and April Buchanan, rest in peace. Brother of Donald Buchanan Jr., rest in peac—"

Murray cut off the call. "Let's all say goodbye to Marshall." He sat still and felt his pulse rise. He took deep breaths as a life insurance advertisement started playing through his headphones. "What the fuck was that?"

"I hate when people do that," said Mac.

"That happens?"

"Sometimes."

"Why? Who does that? How does he know who I am?"

"Welcome to radio."

"You didn't screen him out?"

"He seemed normal. Fuck that idiot."

"Well then I'm not going to let it bother me."

"Don't let it bother you."

Murray nodded and continued taking slow breaths. The commercial block ended and Blue Öyster Cult led into Guns N' Roses, then Sly and the Family Stone, then Rush, then another commercial break. Murray watched the countdown timer. He moved toward his mic and squinted at the monitor again. "Welcome back, folks. We are into Week 5 action in the NFL. My New York Giants are coming off a big win against the Cardinals. Eli Manning throws for 321 yards and two touchdowns—162 of those yards were to the mighty Hakeem Nicks."

Murray paused. "Up this week we've got the Seattle Seahawks. Quarterback Tarvaris Jackson is no Eli Manning, but let's be real, Eli Manning is no Tom Brady. What concerns me is a man by the name of Marshawn Lynch. It's a big concern. Is the value of individual running backs diminishing in today's game? Probably. But Lynch might just be an exception. He's quick. He's durable. He takes a beating and still moves the ball forward. Coach Tom Coughlin will need to find a way to contain Lynch. The defensive line must elevate its game. The linebackers must elevate their games. Plug the holes. Be strong. Be quick. Watch your tape and do your homework." He paused and chuckled. "Now listen to this one by The Guess Who."

Murray lifted the headphones from his ears. He rose from his chair and slid open the door to the board operator room. "That one felt good."

Mac nodded. "That was all right."

"It's weird. I don't know if I know what I'm saying when I say it. But when I say it, and it sounds right, I think I know it."

"Whatever you say."

"Any more whiskey?"

Mac shrugged. "Of course."

Murray lifted the bottle to his mouth and drank. He coughed. His body felt warm.

"How do the levels sound?"

"Fine."

"You're happy with them?"

"Of course. They're always bang-on."

"Good." Mac glanced toward the lobby. "How is the station doing for your dad?"

"No idea." Murray shrugged. "He doesn't say much about it."

"The ship has sailed on radio. Whatever this was, it's over." Mac looked around the room. "I heard a rumour your dad wants the building to develop the property—turn it into condominiums or some shit and then sell the broadcast license to whoever will buy it."

"He hasn't said anything to me about that."

"The people here are good people. I consider myself real lucky to have this gig."

"I know about that."

"Most places won't look at me." Mac paused. "Spent some time in jail a few years back, and it's fucked me ever since."

"Really?"

"Uh-huh."

"Uh, you're not going to kill me, are you?"

"For a totally nonviolent crime. I got out after a month. The station manager here took me on when no one else would."

"And now you're drinking on the job?"

"Fuck it. So are you." Mac smirked. "You're on in ten seconds."

Murray swore and sprinted back to the live room. He flung himself into his chair. "Welcome back to the program. My name is Murray Buchanan. If this were normal circumstances, the NBA preseason would be underway and we'd be getting our first look at the rookie class." He took in an enormous gulp of air. "This year, we're dealing with an indefinite lockout situation. Could the whole season go unplayed? Could the Larry O'Brien trophy go unclaimed? Major League Baseball has no champion for the '94 season. I'm no hockey fan, but sources tell me the NHL lost '04-'05 to a labour stoppage. Why not the NBA too?" Murray took a pause. "Last year James Dolan signed Amar'e Stoudemire to a five-year, $100 million contract. Amar'e will be forfeiting $250,000 for every cancelled regular season game. Think about that next time you collect your paycheque!"

Murray looked forward. Mac was pouring a line of white powder onto his desk and moving it around with a credit card. "Uh, the NBA owners are skilled businessmen, most of them. Unfortunately, our guy in New York has earned himself a bad rap. Bringing Amar'e to Manhattan could turn the tide on Dolan's legacy, provided Stoudemire stays healthy and continues to perform." Murray traced his finger along the monitor. "We need a deep playoff run. The last time the Knicks won a championship was 1973. The people of New York deserve another." He took in a breath. "Listen now to Jefferson Airplane."

Mac leaned over the desk and snorted a line of powder. He stood up again and reentered the board room. He gestured to the table. "You want?"

Murray shook his head.

"You sure?"

Murray paused. "Is it good?"

"Real fucking good."

Murray shook his head. "No, thanks. But I'll have some more of that whiskey."

"Please. What's mine is yours."

Murray took another drink. Then another. Then another. He returned to the live room, and Mac did another line. Time blurred. The rest of the show was a chaotic mix of classic rock, sports talk, and ham horns. Murray sat hunched over the mic until darkness waned and faint morning light came through the studio window. He felt his mind returning and drifted into quiet melancholy.

Headlights lit up the thin strip of parking lot. The beams became firmer and more precise. A sedan pulled into Murray's field of view and stopped in the space adjacent to the station's front door. Murray watched Rowdy Ron slump into the studio, pour himself coffee, and slide open the door to the live room.

"Morning, boy."

"Morning."

"Always be early. That's my advice if you want to stick around this business."

Murray nodded.

"How was the show?"

"Good."

"Just good?"

"I think I might have something here."

Rowdy Ron produced an enormous hacking laugh. "This place is a dump." He put his weight on the desk. "No one was listening. Not a damn soul."

***

The Park Slope sidewalk off 5th Avenue was dark and free of food traffic. Byron stood, shoulder leaning on the iron gate covering the kitchen entrance to El Pollito Mexicano, and took a drag from a cigarette. His skin felt soapy and hot. An apron clung to his hips. He nodded to a slim line cook with a pronounced lisp, standing nearby and also holding a cigarette. "There's nothing quite like a post-rush smoke."

The line cook spit on the ground. "Been a disaster today. Enchilada special. Veg prep was a nightmare."

"Like, it's such a victory once you make it through that biggest pile of dishes."

"My right hand feels like a claw."

"A tower of dishes. Worked through. Done. It's a beautiful thing if you're in the right headspace."

"Kitchen was short-staffed too. Bullshit if you ask me. Tonight was about survival."

"Then we had another successful night of survival."

"You're a good dishwasher," said the line cook. "I can tell. You give a shit."

"I don't think that's true."

"You bring an intensity to the job. You're focused."

"My body is sore just about every shift. I've been thinking about moving on. You know, maybe some sort of temp job. In an office. Something where I can sit down."

The line cook leaned back and blew smoke into the air. "Grass is always greener on the other side. We get free food here. That's not nothing."

"I've been having a lot of dreams lately. Like, my mind's on fire."

"I'm bored already."

"I had one the other night where I was sitting in an office and all my coworkers had paper bags over their heads. You know, with little eyeholes cut out so they could see. What the hell do you think that means?"

"Were you also wearing a paper bag?"

"No, but I think I wanted to. Like, I felt left out."

"That means you're a square. Or you aspire to become one."

"Then my boss called me into the boardroom for a client negotiation. He ended up sucking the dick of their senior director while everyone else took pictures with their phones. What do you make of that?"

The line cook snorted. "That's some fucked mix between *Office Space* and *Eyes Wide Shut.*"

"It's weird, like, that I have that in my subconscious."

"Could be your future if you leave this place."

"Maybe I've outgrown it here."

"You could try to move up. See if the kitchen needs help. They know you're reliable, and there's always turnover. Think about it. Get yourself a nice little pay increase."

Byron's pocket vibrated. He pulled out his phone and held it in front of his face. "That's my mom."

The line cook butted out his cigarette and moved past Byron. "I'm going back in."

Byron put his phone to his ear. "Hi, Mom."

"How are you?"

"You know, no complaints. No real complaints."

"What are you doing?"

"I'm working. On a break right now."

"At the taco place?"

"That's right."

"Good."

"Uh-huh."

"How's the apartment?"

"Small. Smelly. But I like it."

"Were you planning on coming by Woodbury any time soon?"

"Wasn't planning on it, but I also wasn't explicitly not planning it."

"It would be nice to see you."

"I can try to find some time."

"Good."

"Why?"

"Because there have been some changes you should know about."

"You mean like redoing the bathroom?"

"Structural changes."

"To the bathroom?"

"The family."

"What does that mean?"

"We've decided to separate, your father and I."

Byron lowered his chin and remained silent.

"As a step in the formal divorce process."

"Uh-huh..."

"What do you think about that?"

Byron looked back into the kitchen. "I don't know."

"I understand it's a lot to digest."

"Like, you should do whatever makes you happy, I guess."

"It's for the best, for both of us."

"It sounded like things were good with Dad last time I talked to him."

"Is that so?"

"I think?"

"Your father has a way of stretching the truth."

"He was really excited about this Dunkin' Donuts thing he has going on—getting that franchise and building a solid source of income. You know, making a name for himself, even if it is just donuts and coffee."

"Your father is a con artist."

"I mean, we all kind of are, right?"

"An aspiring con artist. He's not a particularly good one."

"What do you mean?"

"He told you he bought a Dunkin' Donuts franchise?"

"Uh, I think so?"

"He's a goddamn liar."

"So then what is he doing?"

"That Dunkin' Donuts 'job' he got was a part-time assistant manager position."

Byron paused. "Are you sure about that?"

"Nothing near ownership."

"Really?"

"And guess what? He was let go last week for not following process."

"You're serious?"

"Of course I'm serious."

"Why would he lie to me like that?"

"He's a bum."

"I can't believe that."

"I'm sorry to put it on you, Byron. But it's true. He's a bum, and I'm done with him."

"So that's why you called?"

"Correct."

Byron dropped his cigarette on the sidewalk and crushed it with the ball of his foot. "What am I supposed to do with that?"

"You keep on living your life, dear. It's what we all do."

CHAPTER 24

DECEMBER 2011

THE LEATHER COUCH IN the Buchanans' living room was oversized and squishy—the family's most comfortable piece of furniture and a place where Murray had spent hours of his youth watching cartoons, and later, weekend Yankees games. Now, he would nap there when time allowed, with moments being chosen carefully due to the room's proximity to main hallway traffic. It was best to avoid his father whenever possible.

Murray saw only black. He felt familiar cushions against his side. His arms, legs, and buttocks occupied their usual grooves. His body was still, and he kept his eyes closed. Moments of stillness and calm after reentering conciseness were fleeting bliss.

A car door slammed outside. Murray heard muffled voices and footsteps approaching the house. He kept his eyes closed as a key slid into the lock and the front door opened. Murray heard his father speak and forced his eyes open.

Don Sr. entered the front hallway carrying paper grocery bags. Beside him was a slim brunette woman in her thirties named Angela—his girlfriend of several months. Angela removed her shoes and turned toward the living room, making Murray acutely aware of his ragged underwear and shirtless torso, softened from an unfocused workout schedule and a far cry from the eight abdominal bulges of his prime playing days.

Murray sat up and smiled. His pectorals and lower belly drooped. Angela held eye contact as she asked Murray how his day was going. Her tone was bubbly and sophisticated. Murray muttered that things were okay and looked at his father. Since the accident, interactions between the pair were largely administrative. April Buchanan had been the proverbial glue that held the family together.

Angela turned to Murray's father. "Are you ready to get dinner started?"

"Of course."

"Do you want to help with the vegetables?"

"I do." Don Sr. looked sideways at his son. "What?"

"What?"

"What was that expression you just made?"

Murray shrugged. "I've just never seen you cook before. Ever."

"I mostly do meal prep. Angela is in charge of the actual cooking, but I'm learning."

"You are?"

"Of course."

"Oh." Murray paused. "Why?"

"Because I can. It's something we're doing together."

Don Sr. followed Angela down the hallway and into the kitchen. Murray walked to his room and pulled on jeans, poking at the protruding pouch of flesh just above the top seam of his pants. Murray looked in the mirror. His hair was oily and shot up at odd angles. He went to the bathroom and stuck his head between faucet and sink, running warm water over his head and towelling his hair dry. He pulled on a t-shirt and approached the kitchen. He made eye contact with Angela.

"How are things going?"

Murray looked to the floor. "Good."

"Your dad says you're doing a great job at the station."

"I guess. Did he mention they're shutting it down next year and putting in a development? Condos and a gas station, apparently."

"He did mention that." Angela crossed her arms and smiled professionally. "Your father is excited about the investment."

"I know."

"I've listened to the show a few times."

Murray nodded.

"You're quite talented."

"Don't know about that."

"Do you have plans once the station closes?"

Murray shook his head. "Still figuring that out."

"Angela is a hiring manager," said Don Sr. "One of the best in the state."

"Your father is exaggerating."

"She's sensational, and she's happy to help you find work." Don Sr. turned to Angela. "I believe Murray is building a strong skill set for a sales career. Radio was never meant to be a forever job, but it's an excellent stepping stone."

"I have several clients looking to fill associate sales positions."

"Oh," said Murray. "There's a few different career directions I've been thinking about. I want to maybe, really, shake things up."

"Happy to help," said Angela. She turned to Don Sr. "Can you do the veg for me?"

"Absolutely." Don Sr. looked down at the counter and picked up a chef's knife. "Onions?"

"Chopped, please."

"Pepper?"

"Cut it in half, take out the seeds and stems, then dice it."

"Carrots?"

"Peeled and cut."

"Coriander?"

"Leave that for now."

"Mu—"

"Cilantro," said Murray.

"Pardon me?"

"You called it coriander." Murray pointed to the counter. "That leafy green plant is cilantro."

"No."

"It is."

Don Sr. shook his head. "That's coriander. I'm sure of it."

"You can be sure of something and still be wrong."

Don Sr. pointed the knife at Murray. "We'll have to agree to disagree, kiddo."

"Since when are you a vegetable authority?"

"I'm not. Since when are you?"

"I'm not, but I know that's cilantro."

"You're mistaken."

"I'm really not."

Don Sr. rolled his eyes and leaned toward Murray. "Why are you going to bat on this one?"

"Because I'm right."

Don Sr. laid the knife down on the chopping block. He spoke slowly. "I really don't like you talking back to me."

Murray stared. "I'm an adult."

"You are."

"But...?"

"Living rent-free in his father's house."

"We both know Grandpa gifted you the down payment when you didn't have any-thing," said Murray.

"Sure. And I worked my ass off to make something of myself."

"He also got you your first job."

"So what? I earned every opportunity that came my way."

"And for what?"

"I have a good life."

"Are you sure about that?" said Murray.

"I think so."

"Your wife and son are dead!"

"Excuse me?"

"All you've got is me and—sorry—but our relationship leaves a lot to be desired!"

Don Sr.'s face tightened, and he whipped a green pepper at his son's head. Murray ducked and caught it in his outstretched hand. He cocked his arm and fired it back toward Don Sr., hitting him square in the face. Don Sr. lunged at Murray.

"Stop it!" Angela grabbed at Don Sr.'s collar. "What the fuck are you doing?"

Murray pulled his father to the floor and pushed his forearm up against his neck.

"Don't do that! He's an old man!"

Don Sr. heaved and sent Murray flying off him. "No, I'm not!"

"Cut it the fuck out or I'm calling the police!" said Angela.

"Call the police! My house. My rules!"

Don Sr. lunged at Murray. Murray moved sideways, and his father crashed into the refrigerator.

"You're acting like children!" said Angela. "This is unbelievable!"

Don Sr. shook his head and faced his son. "Teaching the kid a lesson." He swung a fist wildly and missed.

"You idiots!" Angela held her phone to her ear. "I'm calling the police."

"You do whatever you have to do."

Angela ran out of the house as Murray and Don Sr. circled one another. Don Sr. faked a punch and kicked Murray in the kneecap. Murray cried out and braced himself against the counter, his finger sliding across the blade of the chef's knife. "Fuck me."

"Now you're bleeding, you idiot."

"Shut up."

Don Sr. shook his head. "What the hell happened to you?"

"Shut up."

"So much wasted potential."

"Would you shut up!"

"You're a goddamn failure!"

Murray snorted. "I bet you wish it was me who died instead of Don, don't you?"

"How could you say that?"

"Come on, old man. Answer the question."

"I won't."

"But what if you had to?"

"One of you was destined for the Major Leagues. One of you was not."

Murray clenched his teeth and grabbed the chef's knife.

"Are you a lunatic?"

Murray held his position.

"Put the knife down."

"Apologize for kicking me in the kneecap."

"Not happening."

"Apologize for saying you wish I was dead."

"I didn't say that."

Murray's grip on the knife tightened. Don Sr. froze, then bolted from the kitchen and locked himself in the main floor bathroom. Murray dropped the knife and chased after his father. He pounded on the door. "Let me in!"

"No."

"Open it!"

"Not until you calm down."

Murray smashed his shoulder into the door.

"Murray?"

"Open it now!"

"Murray?"

"Open up?"

"Murray?"

"What?

"Are you still holding the knife?"

Murray paused. "What does it matter?"

"Do you hear those sirens outside the house? The ones getting louder?"

"I do."

"You're going to want to make sure you're not holding the knife when the police come inside." Don Sr. paused. "Can you do that for me?"

Murray paused. "I dropped the knife."

"You did?"

"It's back in the kitchen."

"Good."

There was commotion down the main floor hallway as the front door opened and Angela reentered the house with two police officers. "Don?!"

"Yes?"

"Where's your father?"

Murray pointed to the bathroom door.

"Police are here, Don."

"This really wasn't necessary."

"Can you come out, please?"

"Didn't have to drag the authorities into this."

"Come here."

The bathroom door clicked and eased open. Don Sr. emerged.

"Kitchen table," said Angela. "Everyone sit."

Murray lowered himself into a chair. Angela positioned herself between father and son. Two police officers sat on the opposite side of the table. The older of the pair, a middle-aged woman with a stocky build, spoke. "My name is Officer Jenkins. We were called here to investigate an altercation in progress." She paused. "Can you tell me what happened?"

Don Sr. looked at the table. "Nothing, really."

"And your name is?"

"Donald Buchanan."

Officer Jenkins nodded and wrote in a notebook. "Age?"

"Fifty-three."

"We got a call about a fight between two men at this address."

"A personal conflict that got out of hand. It was blown out of proportion."

"Your spouse Angela thought enough of it to call the police." Officer Jenkins looked at Murray. "What's your name?"

Murray shook as he spoke. "Murray Buchanan."

"Age?"

"Twenty-five."

"Can you tell me what happened?"

Murray shook his head. "Just a difference of opinion."

"Was there a physical confrontation?"

"There was..."

"But?"

"I don't know."

"What does that mean?"

"We're a sports family. These things happen."

"You're telling me 'boys will be boys'?"

"Something like that."

"The kitchen looks like a bomb went off."

"It often does."

"Like this?"

Murray shook his head. "No. Not like this."

"Who lives at the house currently?"

"My dad and me."

"Anyone else?"

Murray shook his head.

Officer Jenkins's jaw tightened. "This address came up in our database." She exhaled through her nose. "The crash on Route 9. Was that your mother and brother?"

Murray nodded.

"I'm sorry to hear that."

"Thanks."

"How have you been coping?"

"My mother and my brother died, so not great."

"Have you gone to therapy?"

Murray shook his head.

Officer Jenkins looked to Don Sr. "Have you?"

"No."

"I suggest both of you look into that."

"Yes." Don Sr. spoke quietly. "We could."

Officer Jenkins turned back to Murray. "How do you like living with your father?"

"It's fine."

"And you, Don?" said Officer Jenkins. "How do you like your son living with you?"

"What do you want me to say? He's my son."

"I'd like to move out eventually," said Murray.

"Do you feel safe here?"

"I do."

"And do you, Donald?"

"I do."

"And what's stopping you from moving out?"

"I just need to sort out a better-paying job first." Murray's gaze shifted to the younger officer. He was blond, with a boyish face that could pass for that of a high school senior. Murray pointed a finger forward. "Do we know each other?"

The officer narrowed his eyes.

"We do!" said Murray. "Monroe-Woodbury class of '05. You were friends with Evan Friedman. I remember you pulling down a girl's pants in sophomore math. And there was a good stretch when you were smoking weed in the forest almost every lunch."

The man swallowed. "I'm reformed now."

"Because it wasn't all that long ago. You were a real asshole."

"I've matured enormously since then."

"That was like six years ago."

"Six years is a long time." The man crossed his arms. "And here we are."

"Do you like being a cop?"

"It got me out of my parents' house, that's for damn sure."

Officer Jenkins held out her hand. "Based on what I'm hearing, there's no need to proceed further at this time."

"I agree," said Don Sr.

"Please do your best to coexist with one another. Seek counselling. Call us if there are further problems."

Don Sr. nodded silently. Officer Jenkins stood up and wished everyone a good night. The blond officer followed, and the pair exited the house. There was silence. A pipe creaked in the basement.

"I'm going to go," said Angela.

"I'd like you to stay," said Don Sr.

"We can do dinner another time. Tonight sounds like it was long overdue."

"I'll call you tomorrow."

"Fine." Angela paused. "And you should know it's called coriander in Europe and cilantro in North America. You were both right. Idiots." She walked out of the house and slammed the door.

Don Sr. exhaled slowly. "Life is a complicated thing."

"I understand that," said Murray.

"Do you?"

"In a general sense, yes."

"And there comes a time when, in order to keep moving forward, you need to make compromises."

"Sure."

"As a parent, I worry that I've created a false sense of security for you—a living situation that doesn't reflect your reality."

"Okay."

"I'm going to start charging you rent."

"Are you serious?"

"Market rate."

"What if I don't pay?"

"I'll evict you."

"That can take months if I work the courts, can't it?"

"Just try me."

Murray nodded. "Right."

CHAPTER 25

FEBRUARY 2012

THE HOUSE IN MOUNTAIN View is owned by a Google software engineer named Abdel and typical for the area as I understand it—grey stucco bungalow with meticulous grass and tidy flowerbeds. The interior is modest, and the walls are mostly bare. Abdel has a pudgy frame and a bright purple collared shirt. He buzzes around making sure Solo cups are filled and music is playing.

There are a dozen or so people present inside the living room. We sit on a velour couch together, Jerry and I, which is also occupied by a burly redhead man who has not spoken since we arrived. The room is warm, and there are several conversations happening simultaneously. Jerry taps my knee and leans toward my ear. "What do you think of this place?"

"It's nice."

"Abdel bought it a few years back. Getting into the market here is a big step. He's done well for himself."

I nod.

"It's pricey."

"How much, do you think?"

"A bit over $1.75 million," says Jerry. "I looked it up."

"That's a lot of money for a little house."

"But it's in Silicon fucking Valley!"

"I know."

"I mean, you could always buy a place in Arkansas."

"But then you'd have to live in Arkansas."

"Exactly."

"Maybe I'll look into a house here one day," I say. "Or maybe not."

"Abdel works hard and has enormous technical talent. He also knows how to have a good time."

"Okay."

"He's celebrating a serious AI milestone—it's all under NDA, of course, but apparently it's a big deal."

"Impressive."

Jerry pauses. "He and I have been chatting about psychedelics."

I roll my eyes.

"Seriously."

"How did you meet this guy again?"

"A friend at work. And get this. Abdel's tripped with a guy who tripped with Steve Jobs back at Reed College. No joke—one of Apple's first employees."

"So you're saying the guy whose house we're in did drugs with a guy who did drugs with the founder of one of the most successful companies on the planet, back when they were in college?"

"Co-founder. Don't forget about Steve Wozniak and that other guy no one remembers. Still, it's pretty cool, right?"

"I'm not sure that it is."

"I love the balance he's struck." Jerry points to Abdel, deep in conversation with a skinny, bespectacled woman. "The man can explore crazy new intellectual vistas on serious LSD but also thrive in a demanding job. He's got spiritual fulfillment and career fulfillment. It's a beautiful thing."

"That's cool, I guess."

"You bet it is!"

"Right."

Jerry raises his hand and smiles past me. I turn and watch Abdel bound toward us. He extends a hand, which I shake. His grip is firm and eye contact spot-on. "Nice to meet you," says Abdel. "Jerry's told me about you."

"Good things, I hope?"

"Are we in the presence of a goddamn rocket scientist right now?"

"It depends how you define 'rocket' and how you define 'scientist.'"

Abdel claps. "She's a genius, and she's funny!" He leans closer to us. "I'm going up tonight, care to join?" He puts his hand into his pocket and produces a vial, pinched between thumb and index finger, which he holds up in front of his face.

"Not tripping?" says Jerry.

"Taking a break from the psychedelics and getting jacked up instead. Tonight is about living in the goddamn moment and celebrating being alive."

Jerry turns toward me and shrugs. "Eh?"

"Thanks, but I'll pass."

"No trouble at all!" Abdel grins and runs off into the kitchen.

I put my hand on Jerry's stomach. "I'm tired tonight."

"What do you mean?"

"Like I'm tired. I don't have much energy."

"Then why did you come out?"

"Because you wanted me to."

"If you were tired I would have just sai—"

"It's no trouble. You go do whatever you want. I'm fine to just relax. I can take a cab back to my place."

"But that's no fun for you."

"This is a change of scenery—anything to be out of my apartment."

"A—"

"Go have fun."

Jerry shrugs.

"Enjoy a few hours off, for God's sake. You earned it."

"Okay." Jerry stands up from the couch. "Do you want anything?"

I shake my head. "I'll get water from the kitchen."

"Are you sure?"

"I'm fine. Don't worry about me."

Jerry pats my head. I watch him amble over to Abdel and slap him on the back. The two start talking, and Abdel offers Jerry a Solo cup. They drink. The couch is comfortable, and I slide deeper into it. The burly redhead man near me tries to initiate a conversation, but I keep my answers monosyllabic. I feel sleepy and also great relief to be out of the apartment and thinking about something other than Stanford. I watch Jerry lean and tilt his head forward. I do a double-take as he snorts a line of fucking cocaine off the kitchen counter, then rubs his nose and looks pleased with himself. I stand up and cross the room. "What the hell was that?!"

"What?"

"You do that shit now?"

"What shit?"

"Give me a bit of credit, please."

"Not regularly."

"Well, you just did."

"I'm experimenting."

"You were talking about experimenting with psychedelics."

"And?"

"Coke is the opposite. People die from that stuff."

"So you're an expert?"

"No. Are you?"

"I'm not, but Abdel is, and tonight we're doing what he wants to do."

"Well, I'm shocked."

"I'm trying to relax. This is a night off, like you said."

"Right." I put my hands out. "You're right. Do whatever you want."

"We can talk about this later."

"Don't worry about it."

I turn away from Jerry and walk back toward the couch. The redhead looks at me strangely. "You new around here?"

I slump down into the cushions. "Huh?"

"Are you looking to score?"

"Excuse me?"

"Mind-expanding substances."

"No. Thank you."

"Because if you are, you know where to find me."

"Sure."

"Right on."

I scan the room. Jerry has disappeared. The redhead is still looking at me. I stand up and walk toward the kitchen sink. Bodies mill around me. I pull on the facet and pour water into a cup. I sip slowly and thoughtfully as I walk toward the bathroom. I push open the door and gasp. Jerry is bent over the sink, being thrust into by Abdel. Blood drains from my head. Jerry grunts, his face contorted into an expression of deep concentration. My mouth hangs open. "Are you fucking kidding me?"

Jerry's eyes go wide. Abdel stops thrusting, pulls up his pants, and walks past me out of the bathroom without saying a word. "What the fuck?" I say. "What is happening right now?"

"Uh."

"Well?"

"Uh."

"Aren't you going to try and explain?"

"I can explain."

"But you can't explain."

"I think I can."

"Go ahead."

Jerry shakes his head.

"You didn't even think to lock the door?"

"Uh."

"What?"

"I guess I let the moment get away from me."

"The moment?"

"Yeah."

"What are you talking about?"

"Well...what do you want to know?"

"Is this the first time you've done...this?"

"You're going to need to define 'this.'"

"Why didn't you tell me?"

"I don't know."

"Is that it?"

"I think so."

I tell Jerry to forget it and storm back into the living room. The burly redhead lowers his chin. "Everything okay?"

"Your offer still stand?"

"Always stands. Got a burner phone right here. Should be good for another few months or until things get too hot."

I say great and take the number, then leave the house and move west through the dark night. The streets are quiet and lonely. The walk back to my apartment takes ninety minutes. I climb the stairs alone. Everything is messy, and I am achingly lonely. I am crying and too wound up to work. I cannot concentrate on reading or watching a movie or listening to music. I am on my bed. Alone. Still crying and still existing.

***

Murray sat in his bedroom and stared at his computer screen, clicking between listings across several different job boards. Promising roles were sorted into marketing, sales, administration, finance, manual labour, and public service. He was averaging three applications a day to organizations across the state of New York. Today marked the end of his second week of aggressive searching.

The house's back door opened and closed. Murray heard his father cough and kick off his shoes. Don Sr.'s cigarette intake had increased since the police visit. There had been no mention of Angela in almost a month, and his general demeanour had softened slightly. Most nights now, they had meals together. The threat of paying rent had been stayed, at least for the time being. Once, his father even asked Murray how he was doing and had listened intently to his response.

Murray looked through a posting for an administrative assistant role with a real estate office. Baseball was done and buried forever. He wanted to move on from the past. It was only now, with time, that he could properly appreciate how completely the pursuit of athletic excellence had dominated his ambitions, and how truly mediocre his achievements had been.

Creaks sounded up the stairs as Don Sr. entered his office. He had been buried in 106.5 FM WPDH matters for weeks. Murray looked forward. The fog persisted now. Forever. A permanent brain reconfiguration by way of a fastball to the temple and rock to the back of the head that had normalized to the point where he was not sure what his mind had been and what it now was. His capacity was diminished, but he was stable in his reality, with an everlasting reminder of Don Jr. to boot.

Murray would push forward. He heard Don Sr. moving around his office. He thought of Mitt Romney running for president, Greek debt bailouts, and Whitney Houston dead in a hotel bathtub. Murray wanted nothing to do with the open-ended chaos of the world. He wanted to bury his day in calm and order. He wanted control. He was ready for a life. A proper life with a proper job. Wherever that job may be and whomever it may come from.

An email appeared in his inbox. Murray scanned the screen—a human resources coordinator from the Village of Nyack requesting time to speak about his application to a parking enforcement role that closed the previous week. Murray rubbed his chin and considered the matter. He felt excitement. He felt pride. He felt duty and meaning. Most of all, he felt the possibility of purpose. Maybe this was just what he needed to make everything all right.

Chapter 26

March 2012

I wake up unsure of the time or day of the week as I look around my apartment and rub my face. My mind is still groggy, and I sit up, feeling off-balance. Thoughts push their way through my head and struggle to arrange themselves into something coherent.

I have been sleep-deprived for a decade. Now I am tired in a different way—a full-body near-paralysis in which I can move if I focus my attention but where everything feels so damn heavy, I do not know if I can commit the energy to bother. The last few days are the first time since middle school I have slept without an alarm clock. I am considering the possibility that I have gone my whole conscious life without being present.

I move off my bed and onto the floor. I am foggy from the recent psychedelic experience, facilitated by the burly redhead I met in Mountain View. The awareness that expanded from my brain into the room has crept back onto itself and left me mentally exhausted. After dosing, the rise through the first forty-five minutes was bumpy, before escalating rapidly over the next hour through weirder and weirder headspaces. I levelled off just past the two-hour mark and settled into properly exploring my experience, with some modulation possible by focusing on different parts of my apartment or adjusting the interior light levels. This feeling held steady for five or six hours before I slowly regained coherence and attention span, allowing time to reflect on what had come to pass.

A knock echoes from my front door, and I nearly fall onto my backside. I peer through the peephole and see Jerry Fujimoto standing in the hallway. I now vaguely remember placing a call to him at an indeterminate time in the past. I grasp the doorknob, twist, and pull. Jerry stands on the threshold of the room, looking enormously confused. I realize I am mostly naked and put on sweatpants, then tell Jerry to come inside. He remains still.

"Are you okay?"

"Uh, not sure."

"Okay..."

"But I'm here."

"Are you sick?"

I shake my head slowly. "What time is it?"

"Just after 6:00 p.m."

"And what day?"

"Are you serious?"

"I'm always serious."

"It's Monday."

"Right. I've been disconnected for a few days."

"You've been ignoring my calls."

"Not intentionally."

"Are you sure about that? I've been worried about you."

"I'm trying something new."

"And what would that be?"

"Going wherever life takes me."

"Mmm." Jerry raises an eyebrow. "Where have you been so far?"

"Nowhere. Just here."

"Did you go into the lab today?"

"Not a chance."

"Did you tell your boss?"

"I told Dr. Kaminsky I was ill and would be back just as soon as I could be."

"What did she say?"

"She expressed concern. I told her I would be fine."

Jerry's shoulders hunch. "What are you doing now?"

"I'm relaxing fully and completely—starting to realize just how hard I was working. I've put aside all stress, and it's wonderful."

"So, you're just here?"

"I've been doing a lot of personal reflection the last few days. I've been a rule-follower for so long—totally fuelled by the approval of others. I feel like I'm finally starting to think."

"You were doing plenty of thinking back in Boston."

"I was existing within a predetermined framework."

"And excelling!"

"Sure, but it was on MIT's terms." I pause. "You know that psychedelics are on the cutting-edge of science, don't you?"

"Of course." Jerry pauses. "But I don't like hearing that from you."

"You're all about psychedelics!"

"Maybe, but I've never missed a day of work."

"I did acid on Saturday."

Jerry rubs his forehead. "And why did you do that?"

"What I've been reading says tha—"

"What have you been reading?"

"The literature. Research has come a long way since Timothy Leary and all that hippie stuff. Apparently, LSD ingestion can have significant positive effects on medium- and long-term mental health, regardless of the short-term trip."

"This is out of character, and it worries me."

"Well, here we are."

"Most people start with something a little softer."

"Screw it. Needed to shake things up. I went all in."

Jerry looks pained. "So then how was the short-term experience?"

"Exhilarating. Intense. Emotional. I became an audience member to my own life. It fundamentally changed the person I aspire to be."

"Uh-huh."

"I need to start working on accepting what is out of my control. I need to be more empathetic, work less, and stress less."

"How did you even figure out where to get LSD?"

"You, indirectly."

"What do you mean?"

"That redhead guy on the couch at the Mountain View house."

Jerry nods.

"You left me alone to go fuck Abdel. Remember that?"

"I do."

My gaze flickers to the floor. "All that stuff you were saying—I was interested even if I didn't like it. I've been having a hard time lately, and if there's a temporary way out, well, I'm interested in that."

Jerry shakes his head slowly.

"I bought five hits for a hundred bucks. Is that good?"

"You got ripped off."

"Fine by me. The guy came to the apartment and showed me how it all worked. He even stayed while I tripped."

"Did he do anything...weird?"

"No! He was a total gentleman." I shake my head. "I was looking down the barrel of infinity, and it was too much. This was a nice change."

"I'm worried about you."

"Forget about me. How are you?"

"I'm fine." Jerry scrunches up his face. "This really needs to be about you."

"Forget it."

"We need to talk about what's going on."

"How long have you been interested in guys?"

"I don't know, really."

"What do you mean?"

"I mean, I was such a social wreck for so many years, I couldn't put it all together until we got out to California."

"Are you serious?"

"I had an inkling, maybe, but I was underdeveloped as far as all of that stuff goes."

"And then?"

"It all just blew open. Like, all the way fucking open."

"Okay."

"And I'm not explicitly not interested in women—in you. It's just, well, you know, Kinsey Scale and all that. I guess I'm following my heart?"

"So you're telling me that you're interested in dating men, and what we had is unsustainable and cannot continue?"

Jerry keeps his eyes trained on the floor and nods.

"So that makes me a phase?"

"A close friend."

"Are you an Abdel exclusive?"

"No way."

I nod. "Any guy in particular you're interested in?"

"No. Just guys. Quite a lot of them at the moment. Occasionally several at the same time."

"Is that true?"

"Yes. But I'm still worried about you."

"Okay."

"Are you okay?"

"I'm happy for you."

Jerry shrugs and puts his hands in his pocket. He looks around the apartment and suggests I get into the shower while he tidies up. I oblige. Warm water falls over my body and hits the tile floor in an uneven rhythm. I try in vain to grasp the present. Live, exist, understand, and appreciate the ever-elusive motherfucking now. The shower is comfortable. My body is intact and my mind is sound, at least sort of. I have my health, here in this vanishing moment of peaceful content. I emerge from the bathroom. We decide to go for a walk.

The streets of Palo Alto are bland and impersonal. I say to Jerry how I have been going nonstop for twenty years and need a rest. Jerry says I should take a vacation somewhere. I say a vacation will not cut it, and I would just be stewing in anxiety and dread about my PhD. Jerry says it sounds like I am in the middle of a challenging situation, to which I tell him not to condescend to me. He says he suspects all sorts of people feel the same as me, and they are probably real close to the edge, white-knuckling it through and doing whatever they can to hang on. I tell Jerry that I feel sadness when something ends, even if I don't like it to begin with, and he tells me that this simmers just below the surface of everything we as living, breathing people do. I say I am not sure if I even want love, but still wonder if I am going to find another human to love me, and whom I will love back. We keep talking like this until we return to my building's lobby. Jerry hugs me and wishes me well. He says he must be going. I stand alone and feel awful despair.

CHAPTER 27

APRIL 2012

MURRAY SAT INSIDE THE lobby of a red brick county building and stared forward. He wore brown slacks, into which was tucked a white-collared shirt that billowed out at the back, and shoes that were dull but which he took care to make sure matched his belt. No one inside the building had acknowledged him. He was not worried. It was still fifteen minutes until his scheduled start time.

The offer of employment from the Village of Nyack Parking Authority included a salary of $38,000 per annum less applicable deductions, paid in arrears on a biweekly basis. Murray would also receive ten days of paid vacation a year prorated from his start date and automatic enrolment in group medical, dental, vision, drug, and pension plans. Now, more than any other time, stability was exactly what he craved.

A woman entered the lobby from behind a closed door. She smiled and introduced herself, then asked if he had had any trouble finding the place. Murray replied he had not. The woman led him through the closed door and down a long hallway, the ceiling of which was low and water-stained. They entered the office of Frank Rammo, Murray's new boss.

Frank appeared late middle-aged and had the approximate body composition of a walrus. He groaned as he rose up from behind his desk, then coughed into his elbow and extended a hand forward. "Welcome aboard. Happy to have you on the team."

"Happy to be here," said Murray. He shook Frank's hand. "Excited to get started."

Frank leaned forward and coughed again, holding a handkerchief to his mouth and heaving so aggressively that his desk rattled.

"Is everything alright?" said Murray.

"Sure hope so. Doc says I'm clinically depressed."

"Oh?"

Frank shrugged. "Thank God for heavy medication." He reached into his desk and handed Murray a stapled packet. "Just kidding. Here's your onboarding itinerary. Hope you like classroom work."

"Thanks."

Frank puffed out his chest, producing a loud popping sound from inside his abdominal cavity. "We have a good team. Most of the staff are a little older than you—looking forward to some young folks around here." He coughed. "How are you feeling?"

Murray stared. "No complaints."

"Good." Frank moved out from behind his desk and leaned on a cane. "Let's go then. Get the door, will you?"

"Sure thing."

Frank hobbled down the hallway. Murray followed. "How long have you worked here?"

"Thirty-nine years."

"Do you like it?"

Frank began coughing uncontrollably. He pointed toward the end of the hallway and spoke between heaves. "Take the next left. You want the second door on the right side."

"Are you okay?"

Frank waved him on wordlessly.

"Are you sure?"

"I'm okay, you're okay, and everybody else is okay." He held up his cane. "Enjoy your day."

Frank turned back toward his office. Murray moved down the hallway and knocked on the second door on the right. A voice told him to come in. Murray turned the doorknob and pushed. The room was small, with a laptop connected to an overhead projector and a cluster of a dozen desks, two of which were occupied. A spindly man stood at the front of the room and shook Murray's hand. He introduced himself as Brad then welcomed Murray to the parking authority and handed him a thick bound booklet. Murray settled beside a woman dressed all in black and behind a young man with a flat nose.

Brad looked at his watch and said they would get started in another five minutes. The woman dressed in black tapped Murray on the shoulder and asked how he was doing. Her intonation was zombie-like as she said she could not wait to get started and that a job in parking enforcement was the culmination of years of hard work. Murray turned to the front of the room. He sensed movement behind him and swivelled his head, coming face-to-face with the flat-nosed man who said that he had been homeschooled since kindergarten and that it would be nice to finally meet some friends. The noses of Murray and the man were a fraction of an inch apart. The man asked if they could be friends. Murray nodded.

Brad cleared his throat and requested everyone open their training material. The group moved through dense departmental policies on matters of legal and ethical workplace practices, dress code, hours of work, statutory holidays, overtime, unexpected absences, vacation, performance management, and accident reporting. At page thirty, he directed the class's attention to the overhead projector and nudged his computer, causing the screen to light up and reveal a low-resolution video clip of two horses fucking. Brad muttered to himself and minimized the video. Murray looked around the room. His peers made no acknowledgement.

The group broke for a recess at page fifty. Murray rubbed his eyes and stretched his forearms. Brad smiled solemnly and dipped his chin. "Congratulations. You're one step closer to becoming parking enforcement officers."

***

Sunlight glare on my computer screen makes serious concentration impossible for approximately half an hour each morning. The lab has invested in semitransparent blinds that usually remain pulled down and help to keep light at comfortable levels but do little to block out direct hits of sun to the cornea. My request for blackout curtains was categorically dismissed by Dr. Kaminsky on account of the perceived health benefits of natural light and the general weirdness of encasing oneself in manufactured illumination. I asked since when does anyone around here care about being weird? To which Dr. Kaminsky did not reply.

I reposition my monitor and lean to the left. My body obstructs the sun and minimizes glare. In front of me are pages of SAS code. I squint and scroll through three lines, then rotate my wrists twice, then scroll through another line. Little specks of dust on the monitor's surface are visible. I wonder where the lab's cleaning supplies have gotten to.

Something is not working as it should. I tap my keyboard's down arrow and move quickly through three more lines, praying to find a fat-fingered typo or obvious omission. I scroll and squint and read and count as I have been doing for days. The lines begin to disorient grotesquely. I shut my eyes and run my fingers over my eyelids, then wheel my chair closer to the screen. The numbers flicker, then shake, then invert briefly. I am lost.

I take slow breaths. The problem at hand relates to higher than expected emissions in a theoretical high thermal efficiency burner, the crux of which is mind-bendingly complex and nowhere close to resolution. I scroll through the screen again and feel as though I am pushing around unwanted food that will never be consumed.

A freckled labmate pokes her head over the cubicle wall and asks if everything is okay. I nod without looking at her and say that it is, even as I can feel little droplets of sweat on my cheeks and know that everything is not okay. The labmate says I am making weird noises and asks what's going on. I part my lips to reply and burst into tears. She pulls back. I step away from my desk and into the hallway, then duck into a storage closet where I stand amongst office furniture and computer monitors and question every fucking decision I have ever made. My heart races and my vision distorts. It is all crumbling, and every last thing is over. I am wasted potential that will never become successful enough to be forgotten. I am scared and do not know what to do if I fail.

I exit the closet, my face a mess of salty tears. It's all done with. I have never before left work in the middle of the day.

I walk along Bowdoin Street in a daze and step blindly into an intersection, then get honked at by a delivery truck as it swerves to my left. I fall into bed and lie still for twenty minutes. My heart beats uncomfortably fast. I do not think I have fallen asleep, though I cannot be sure. My sheets are wet from tears and sweat. I reach for my phone. I have two missed calls from Dr. Kaminsky and a text from my freckled labmate asking what is going on. I call my mother. There is no answer. I call Byron Somerfield. The same. I call my father, and he answers on the third ring. His voice is polished and soft.

"Hi, Dad."

"Lesley. How are you?"

"I've been better. How are you?"

"I'm at the hospital right now. It's a zoo."

"It's always a zoo."

"That comes with the job."

"Uh-huh."

"How is Stanford?"

"It's really hard."

"That was to be expected, wasn't it?"

My voice cracks. "Not like this."

"What's going on?"

"It's too much to get into."

"I have time for this."

"No, you don't."

"I do."

"Well," I say. "My thesis is a disaster."

"I'm sorry to hear that."

"Everything is a mess."

"I'm sorry to hear that too."

"I don't know what to do."

"A PhD will have its challenges—you know that."

"Not like this."

"What does your professor say?"

I begin to cry.

"Have you talked to your professor?"

"She doesn't care."

"Do you really think that's true?"

"She has other students. She has her own research. She has a kid. She doesn't care."

Distorted chatter is audible on my father's end of the line. "Well, how bad is it?"

"Bad. I don't think I can finish."

"What do you mean?"

"I mean the data isn't doing what I want it to do. I didn't spend enough time on the foundational structure. I was cocky, and I'm paying the fucking price."

"Can you retool it?"

"I don't have the mental energy. There's nothing left. I would need to start over. I just can't do it."

"I'm sorry to hear that."

"I don't know what I'm going to do."

"Talk to the registrar. It's in the school's interest to graduate PhDs—especially someone like you."

"What do you mean 'like me'?"

"Someone as smart as you. As gifted as you."

"Everyone is smart here. I'm nothing."

"You're extraordinary."

"How would you know?"

"Because I watched you grow up."

"You're not around me now."

"But I know what you're capable of."

"You haven't been around me for years. You're in no position to judge my intelligence."

"I—"

"How can you pretend to know what you're talking about? You were basically absent for half a decade, then you have the audacity to bring the woman who broke up your marriage to my graduation when you know Mom is going to be there, and you parade her around like she's part of the family? Give me a break."

"The woman at your graduation didn't break up my marriage."

"Well, some woman did!"

I hear my father breathe in through his nose. "She did not break up my marriage."

"Well, fuck."

"You're upset right now."

"Don't be condescending. You were a shitty parent."

"Are you sure about that?"

"Of course I am."

"I supported the family for a long time." My father's voice rises. "Your mother and I gave you every opportunity to succeed, which you did. I understand you're angry, and I understand you're frustrated." My father pauses. "I made mistakes, no doubt, but do not call me a shitty parent."

I let tears fall down my face in silence.

"Have you talked to your mother?"

"No."

"Do you want me to come visit?"

"No."

"Do you want to come up to Buffalo?"

"No." I say. "Don't bother, there's no point. I just need to figure this out." My voice shakes. "I'll figure something out."

Chapter 28

May 2012

Byron descended the uneven staircase to his apartment's lobby. His hours had been long and all-encompassing, and he had, as a matter of habit when such mad bursts of productivity occurred, barricaded himself indoors, subsisting on ventilated air and coffee so black it caused stiff tremors and involuntary mouth-wrenching. He extracted a sizeable bundle of envelopes and glossy fast food meal deal flyers from his unit's mailbox. His gaze passed across a thin white envelope with *Sundance Film Festival* stamped across its left corner. Byron felt a lightness in his gut. He brought his finger lengthwise through the envelope's sealed flap. The typed letter was short, printed on a single piece of paper, and stated the festival committee's decision to pass on his feature film submission, *Cynosure: Volume 1*.

Byron held his breath. A pained sensation started up deep in his abdominal cavity. He retreated up the staircase and back into his apartment. A slight ringing had taken over his auditory space. He push-pinned the paper to a cork board dominating the street-facing wall and considered the bevy of rejection letters staring back at him. The ringing grew louder and more acute.

Byron reflected on a recent dream, one that was remarkable in both its intensity and specificity. In the dream, frustrated by the lack of venue for *Cynosure: Volume 1*, a project that had dominated his time around the clock for months, Byron had sought out an audience of his own. He was not interested in alienating himself from his peers or hustling for ticket sales. He wanted control. In the dream, Byron had taken a trip to the pet store and bought hamsters.

He remembered vague nausea creeping forward as he sat on the subway, worsened by warm public transit air and the pervasive sensation of stranger's body sweat. He had exited, he figured, at DeKalb Avenue and walked into City Point Mall, where he had requested a dozen hamsters for immediate purchase from a dumpy man with a thin moustache.

The hamsters were uniformly gold and fluffy, with small pink noses and claws hidden by furry volume and poof. Byron took them back on the subway and into his apartment, depositing them in a wire cage facing his television screen. Byron had stood before his rodent audience and sucked in his breath. He perspired and then he had spoken. "Good afternoon and thank you for coming. I've been a working artist for several years now—today is the debut of my first feature film. *Cynosure: Volume 1* was designed to explore the acceptable limits of the filmmaking medium. Principal photography lasted eight weeks, during which time I wore an RCA camcorder strapped to my head twenty-four hours a day, necessitating precise hand-mirror-eye coordination, careful sponge bathing techniques, and a heavily modified sleep schedule. I firmly believe artistic constraints foster the best kinds of creativity. In this spirit, I forbade raw chronological frames from appearing adjacent to one another in the film's final cut. This proved challenging, to say the least, and I allowed myself several days of pick-up shooting during the editing process to help shape the narrative, if you can call it that. The results are disorienting and challenge the conventions of audience endurance. It was a one-person job and something I am extraordinarily proud of."

Byron had exhaled and started his film, causing bright sharp images to flash across the television screen, their context blended unintelligibly into a garble of visual noise. An occasional recognizable object or place had registered on the most basic level of consciousness, immediately disappearing back into the mess of headache-inducing hodgepodge. He had watched the entirety of the film, wincing at moments of creative uncertainty and indecision. Occasionally, something would pop perfectly, and he would feel a jolt of pride.

A horrid smell had filled the room as the credits rolled, and he brought the lights up. Even now, back in his present reality, Byron remembered the smell. Eleven hamsters had lay dead, having voided all gastrointestinal entry and exit points. An appalling quantity of excrement, urine, and vomit crowded the cage. The surviving hamster looked up at Byron. Its whiskers twitched and its eyes glistened. It turned to its closest deceased sibling and took an enormous bite out of its head. That was it. That was everything. The dream had ended.

Byron stood now—in the painful present—inside his apartment. *Cynosure: Volume 1* had officially been rejected from the two dozen festivals he had applied to. All of them. Every last goddamn one. He looked to the floor. A round bump protruded from his lower belly, a legacy of the horrific diet and prolonged periods of sitting brought on by the film's intensive year-long editing process. It was all over. Byron began to cry. His sobs were quiet at first, soon becoming louder and more distressed than any bodily function he had ever produced. Darkness and heavy self-loathing crept forward. His chest heaved and shook with such earnestness that he feared he might die. He felt confused and hopeless and unmotivated to care about or do anything. His heartbeat echoed in his chest. A strong itch developed on the right side of his neck. He itched but felt nothing. His art. His work. He wanted it all to be done.

***

The room at Stanford Medical Center's psychiatry clinic, where I've been staying the last thirty-six hours, is rectangular and beige-walled. There is a small glass window, also rectangular, over which are thin venetian blinds through which daylight peeks. The presence of a window, and a side table with hard edges, and a chair not bolted to anything, and especially the absence of physical restraints around my limbs, is promising.

I get regular visits from nurses. There is a call button on a wire wrapped around the arm of my bed, which I have not used yet but will if I need to. I am given three meals a day. I know hospital food has a reputation for being undesirable and can now confirm this with certainty.

There are a dozen or so other patients on the ward, some of whom I have chatted with casually in common areas. As far as I know, I am able to leave my room whenever I wish and move freely around my immediate surroundings, though I suspect in doing so I would be observed and be asked to return to my room should my behaviour be considered disruptive. I am, according to a nurse, unable to leave the ward boundary unless supervised.

I have met with a therapist, a young woman with an MA in psychology from the University of Missouri, to discuss tips for managing stress and anxiety. The concepts are not necessarily challenging but good to reinforce through discussion. The therapist said I should identify troubling thoughts as they enter my consciousness, let them flow through my mind, then exit without grasping onto them. Enter. Pass through. Do not engage.

I was also briefly visited by a psychiatrist, an older woman from up the coast who prescribed me Celexa once a day and Xanax for acute episodes. We talked about the value of both pharmaceuticals and therapy as part of an ongoing treatment plan, especially once I reenter the world, whenever, and in whatever capacity, that is.

The incident that landed me here happened two days ago. I had been alone in my apartment and was thinking about Jerry when it all clicked how broken our relationship had been and how the time we dated felt like a sham, and that, coupled with the potentially catastrophic structural challenges going on with my PhD, the last few years felt like a total, absolute, no-questions-asked flop. My field of vision had started to blur and swirl and get worse and worse, and there I was, looking at myself alone, having a serious academic failure on my hands and no real work experience with which to navigate the world outside of higher education.

I cannot confirm this to be true, but I remember hearing a pop just before it all happened. Like something blowing open inside my head. I felt my body moving independently from my brain. I felt disoriented, then I felt overwhelming fear. My mind blanked. My body ran out of my apartment and into the street.

Even when the ambulance came and I was horizontal, and then when I was in the hospital talking to nurses and the doctor, it still took several hours to pull myself back into the present. When they said I could use the phone, I called my mother first. The line was busy, and I really wanted to speak with someone, so I called my father and he picked up. I explained that my situation had gotten worse since the last time we spoke, but that I was managing considering the circumstances. He said he was getting on a plane that night. Later, I reached my mother, who also said she was getting on a plane. I told her not to. She objected, and I objected to her objection. We settled on twice-daily phone calls. I did not want to risk the chance, however unlikely, of my parents crossing paths and having a public spat.

Now, I am staring at the door to my room and can hear movement in the ward hallway. The door opens. My father enters. He looks tired. Wrung out. His body is tense. What remains of his hair along the sides of his mostly bald head is wiry and unkempt. His expression is serious. "How are you, Lesley?"

I open my mouth and pause. "Been better."

"Are you comfortable?"

I nod.

"It's important that you be comfortable."

"I am."

"And the care you've received?"

"Good."

"Are you sure?"

"I am."

"I'm happy to hear that."

"You didn't need to come, you know."

"You're my daughter."

I nod again. "Then thank you for coming."

My father pulls the room's chair close to my bed and sits down. "How are you feeling?"

"Good."

He leans forward and squints slightly.

"I'm not bedridden, you know."

"Then would you like to go for a walk?"

"It's fine. We can stay here for now."

"I'm glad that you feel good."

"It's been a weird two days."

"I don't doubt it."

"But there have been some good moments. Staying in the hospital away from all the stress and the problems—it's been a remarkable thing."

"You're wise to channel those good moments."

"I think I stopped believing in myself. That was really the difference. I can handle stress just fine if I believe what I'm doing is truly worthwhile. But when that falls apart, when I don't have the faith in what I'm doing, that becomes a problem." I pause. Tears start up out the sides of my eyes, and I wipe them away.

"Do you have a plan for continuing your treatment?"

I shake my head.

"What do you think about moving somewhere else?"

"What do you mean?"

"There are exceptional in-patient facilities," says my father. "You'd get extraordinary care and be able to take the time you need to get better."

"That sounds expensive. Really expensive."

"You can't worry about that."

"But I have to."

"You must focus on getting better."

"Who's going to pay for it?"

"There are arrangements that can be made. You have insurance through Stanford?"

"I do, but I don't know anything about it."

"That's a good start. After that, your mother and I will work something out. I will take care of it all, administratively speaking."

"I—"

"You owe yourself good health."

I nod and say nothing.

"You really do."

"I know."

"I'm glad that you do."

I shift my back against the hospital bed and pull the covers up around me. "How is Buffalo?"

"It's busy, but it's good."

"I didn't take you away from anything too important, did I?"

My father shakes his head. "I have a good team at the hospital. You're my daughter. I'm happy to be able to help. I'm trying to do better, you know?"

I nod. And sniffle. Then I begin to cry.

Chapter 29

June 2012

Murray Buchanan's gaze drifted across Lot # 1507 in Nyack, New York and over a four-lane road as cars sped past. A clump of high school kids stood behind a bus shelter, looking daft. Murray squirmed. The department-issued polyester shirt clung stubbornly to his fleshy back, limiting his range of motion and causing dark patches of sweat to spread quickly through the thick material.

Murray patrolled his route with precession, seeing that fines were levelled against those guilty of a bevy of offences including: parking on a bridge, viaduct, tunnel, or underpass, parking within fifty feet of a railroad crossing, parking in a bus stop, parking in a designated emergency, snow, or fire route, parking in a school zone, parking within fifteen feet of a fire hydrant, double-parking, etc. The violations ran like a ticker tape across his consciousness.

On this day, a bright red sedan sat firmly in one of the lot's two handicapped spots. Murray approached the vehicle. Neither the front dashboard nor sun visor contained a permit. He removed his handheld ticketer from his overstuffed utility belt and squinted at its glowing screen. His fingers moved smoothly as he keyed the violation. The ticketer's printer squeaked and whirled. Murray placed a yellow ticket between the car's windshield and wiper blade with an air of absolute duty.

Shouting could be heard in the distance. Murray looked up as an elderly woman hobbled toward him, her gait uneven and supported by a cane. "Hey!" Her voice was spry.

Murray moved toward the back of the lot. The high school kids eyed the woman closely.

"I'm talking to you. Is that a ticket?"

Murray puffed out his chest. "Yes, ma'am. You need a permit to park there."

The woman's features tightened, and she leaned forward so that Murray could smell her stale breath and see the depth of the wrinkles etched into her face. "How much?"

"It's $150. You have fourteen days to pay or state your intent to challeng—"

"I'm on a fixed income. Do you understand what that means?"

"I u—"

The woman made it entirely clear that $150 might not be a lot of money to everyone, but for any responsible, honest-working person, the sum of money for such a questionable offence was exorbitant.

"I'm sorry, ma'am. Once the ticket has been issued, there's nothing I can do."

"Tear the darn thing up!"

"Can't. It's in the database now. You'll need to formally appeal the charge."

The woman held Murray with a piercing stare. "You must have the most horrible, most thankless, most reprehensibly worthless job in the entire state. You're a useless leach."

A tingle ran down Murray's neck, and his heart rate quickened. He held his position. "I respectfully disagree."

The woman ripped the ticket from the windshield and squinted at her outstretched hand. "You've got some nerve."

"Have a good day, ma'am."

"Unbelievable."

Murray's face twitched, and he glanced down at his watch. Another hour and his shift would be finished. He stepped onto his ten-speed and merged into traffic. Murray pedalled north and looked over his shoulder—the high school kids advanced on the woman. He watched the largest boy grab her arm and riffle through her pockets. Murray swung around and cut back across the street. A bus honked and slammed on its brakes.

"Hey!" said Murray. "Stop it!"

The boy turned and considered Murray. His eyes radiated male bravado. "What?"

"What the hell are you doing?"

The ends of the boy's wispy moustache glistened in the late afternoon sunlight. He reached into his jacket and pulled out a switchblade. His hand shot forward. Murray tripped back and fell, smashing his tailbone on the sidewalk. The boy charged as the remaining kids scattered. Murray's heart pounded and stuttered. The boy lunged. Murray closed his eyes and swung his arms wildly, connecting with the boy square in the chest and sending him bouncing off the grass. The boy sprang back to his feet. He narrowed his eyes. Murray's whole body shook. The boy spat on the ground and walked away.

Murray was tachycardic. He took deep wheezing breaths and turned to the elderly woman. "Are you okay?"

"Of course I'm okay!"

"Do you know those kids?"

"Never seen them before in my life."

"I'm glad you're okay."

"I've had worse."

"Really?"

"Sure." The woman paused. "Now about that ticket. I was nearly robbed at knifepoint on town property. How are you going to make that right?"

Murray shook his head.

"Are you kidding me?"

"I'm sorry." Murray looked at the sidewalk. "There's still nothing I can do."

The woman yanked open her car door, hopped in, and drove away.

Murray rubbed his face. He felt a moistness in his underpants. His nostrils flared. He had nearly shit himself but would persevere. Murray knew his work was noble. He kept order.

***

Byron slouched in a tan club chair inside his Crown Heights apartment, the lower half of his backside parallel to the floor and his belly protruding out from the bottom of his t-shirt. He gazed at his television set, on which an episode of *Full House* about a Golden Retriever giving birth inside the Tanner house had just wrapped. Byron watched the end credits roll. The broadcast went to commercial. He stared at an overhead shot of a tidy domestic suburb then gasped audibly and sat straight up in his chair. His old lover dominated the screen.

Byron watched Gregory Ferguson—the Disney cruise actor—move smoothly through the frame in khakis and a polo shirt, a toddler resting on his hip and an objectively beautiful blonde woman to his left. Gregory loaded the child into a car seat, then drove off with the blonde through a busy cityscape. A car insurance logo faded onto the screen.

Byron's mind buzzed. He changed the channel to an episode of *Seinfeld* that climaxed with a madcap scene between Jerry and his barber set to Gioachino Rossini's *Barber of Seville*. The show went to break. Gregory's commercial played again. Byron felt his pulse rise. He counted over a dozen shots, three shooting setups, and two locations. Production values were pristine. Costs were surely enormous. All for an insurance commercial starring an out-of-the-closet gay man with no intention of settling down pretending to be a loving father and committed heterosexual spouse. The whole spectacle was a farce.

Byron fidgeted in his chair and channel-surfed. He settled on an episode of *Friends*, watching Chandler and Joey try to sell a piece of furniture out of their apartment, Monica on a date with Rachel's high school crush, and Phoebe obsess over a stray cat she thought was the spirit animal of her adoptive mother. The show ended, and Gregory's commercial played for a third time. Byron swore and hurled the remote at the television as hard as he could.

The phone rang. Byron jumped. He leaned off his chair and reached to the right. "Hello?"

"Hi, Byron."

"Lesley." Byron paused. "You sound tired."

"You could say that."

"What's going on?"

"Been better."

"What do you mean?"

"Been worse, but I've also been better."

"What are you talking about?"

"I've been institutionalized."

"Excuse me?"

"Well, sort of."

"Where are you right now?"

"Uh, I was on a psych ward for a bit."

"And now?"

"Somewhere nicer. It's a long story. Suffice to say I experienced what doctors call a mental health crisis."

Byron exhaled. "Like, shit. What happened?"

"It's tough to say exactly."

"What do you think happened?"

"Not sure."

"Can you take me through it?"

"Well, I was standing in my kitchen. Then I got hit with this wave of loneliness—nothing like I've experienced before. It was this horrible all-encompassing feeling of being completely by myself, with no way out."

"Then what happened?"

"I just felt so fucking awful."

"I don't know if I've ever heard you swear."

"Well, shit, I was alone, I was scared, and deep down I knew that no one else cared. Does that make me selfish?"

"Mmm, only in a healthy way."

"I see people around me that look totally comfortable with their reality." Lesley spoke slowly. "I just want to feel the contentment I perceive others feel."

"You're not alone there. What happened next?"

"I was in my apartment feeling awful. My brain was groggy. I'd been on a bit of a run the last little while."

"What do you mean by that?"

"Just, not sleeping. Self-medicating. That sort of thing."

"Self-medicating with what?"

"Oh, you know. The usual."

"The usual?"

"Yes."

"Okay...so what happened next?"

"Well, I was alone, and I guess my mind wasn't quite right. I started thinking about my thesis and how royally messed up it is, and how I can't start over, and how I'm coming face-to-face with the fact that I might not be as smart as I think I am."

"Everyone knows you're smart."

"Plus, I'm already twenty-five and the only man I've ever dated turned out to be mostly into guys."

"You mean sexually?"

"That's right."

"You mean Jerry?!"

"Uh-huh."

"Is that recent news?"

"It is."

"Like, shit. I'm sorry."

"It was awful."

"I bet."

"So let me ask you something," said Lesley.

"Uh-huh?"

"When you realized you were gay..."

"Yes?"

"What was that like?"

"Long overdue. Like, the world made a lot more sense once I put that piece of the puzzle together."

"Do you think Jerry knew when we started dating?"

"He probably didn't. Maybe. But he probably had an inkling at least."

"Which I confirmed?"

"Don't look at it like that."

"I've never had a functional relationship," said Lesley.

"You're telling me."

"It's weird."

"What's weird?"

"Well, I don't think I want a child."

"So far, so good," said Byron.

"But if I do, I want it to be before I'm thirty-five, and I want to make sure I'm compatible with the person I have the child with."

"Since when does any of that matter to you?"

"I'm still not sure that it does, but maybe I want to give it a try! That makes sense, right?"

"It does if it makes sense to you."

"What the heck does that mean? This is serious business. What if I stay like this and can't work? What am I going to do about that?"

"There's a whole lot of people in that exact same position."

"Well, they must have figured out a way to compartmentalize, because I was standing there in the kitchen, and it hit me all at once," said Lesley. "My brain started to spin and churn, and spin and churn faster, and then I got lightheaded and ran outside into traffic. The super of my building came out and tried to talk to me. I don't think I was making sense, and I must have looked like I was in trouble, because he asked me if I wanted an ambulance."

"Huh."

"I said I did."

"It sounds like you had, like, a panic attack."

"I did, I think. But it wouldn't let up. I thought I was going to die. It took me a full day and a full night to start regaining my faculties. The hospital confiscated my shoelaces!"

"Were you going to harm yourself?"

"I don't think so, but here I am."

"So, they held you?"

"I was placed on an involuntary hold."

"Oh God."

"My dad flew to California. I told him I wanted to stay out here, at least for the time being. He made arrangements to get me into private in-patient treatment."

"Where are you now?"

"San Jose. The facility is swanky. The cost—I can't imagine. Insurance is paying for some of it. My dad said he was going to work the rest out with my mom."

"What's it like?"

"Fine," said Lesley. "The staff is nice. The food is good. I have my own room. There's group therapy. There's individual therapy. It's interesting. I feel lucky—most people don't have this kind of support."

"Do you think you're getting better?"

"The staff says my case is promising because there were known external triggers that caused the episode. Right now I just feel so much relief. I'm not worrying about my students or that stupid thesis. My only job is to think about getting myself better. That's beautiful."

"It's good to hear."

"Yes." Lesley paused. "Question about Monroe-Woodbury for you."

"Sure."

"Do you ever think about the Marcotte thing?"

"Sure I do."

"Because I can't quite shake it. I've been talking with my therapist here about him quite a bit."

"You said he didn't do anything to you, right?"

"Right."

"And he really didn't?"

"He really didn't."

"That's good."

"But I worshipped the guy. For a time in my life he was my biggest male influence. He was so interesting and so cool. I had an enormous crush on him." Lesley took in a breath and spoke slowly. "If he had approached me, propositioned me or whatever, especially when I was a senior—I don't know what I would have done or how I would have reacted."

"Right..."

"Kids are vulnerable to charismatic adults."

"Of course they are."

"So now I'm thinking that if he's a monster, no man is excluded from potentially being a monster. My dad could be a monster, my gay ex-boyfriend could be a monster, you could be a monster."

"I don't think I'm a monster."

"I hope you keep it that way."

"Is Marcotte in jail right now?"

"Long sentence," said Lesley. "By the sounds of things he'll be there for at least a decade, even with good behaviour."

"Wow."

"He's a monster."

"Guess so."

"And I don't want to talk anymore about him today."

"Okay."

"How is life on the outside?"

Byron shrugged. "I'm living."

"Doing what?"

"Like, stuff."

"What sort of stuff?"

"Art, still. You know, trying to grow and evolve creatively. I've been doing some reading lately."

"And?"

"Well, I've gotten into this idea of large-scale performative pieces."

"Okay..."

"Remember when we were joking about faking my death for a career boast?"

"Sure."

"If I ever pulled that off, it would be an artistic achievement in and of itself."

"I think I follow."

"It's fascinating. Like, Marina Abramović is an absolute treasure. A singular voice and vision. Uncompromising. Extraordinary. I wish I could have even an ounce of what she has."

"She's the one who sat in the museum, right?"

"Among other things. I've got something big I'm working on right now."

"Sounds exciting."

"I sure hope so."

"Are you making money?"

"Not really."

"But some?"

"Not really at all."

"Still working at the taco place?"

"Still fucking there." Byron slid lower into his chair. "It's a real complicated thing, doing creative work. The failure involved is astonishing. I think work in the face of failure is important. I always want more, and I still want more. I don't know what more looks like, but I know that I want it. I'm doing the work of achieving what version of it I can."

"That's inspiring, but also kind of depressing."

"I don't want you thinking depressing thoughts right now."

"I appreciate that."

Byron paused. "But can you tell me what having a nervous breakdown is like?"

"Awful."

"No kidding."

"Terrible."

"I bet."

"The feeling of losing control is scary. When you're in that experience, you feel like you'll never escape it and never get better."

"That's horrible."

"But there are good people taking care of me. Sometimes you just need to sit in one place and hurt for a little bit."

"What are you doing when you leave?"

"Going back to Woodbury, I think. My mom retired and is way into local politics now. I'm going to help her run a campaign for trustee. After that, who knows."

"You should take your time before making any big decisions."

"Maybe," said Lesley. "I'll figure it out one day, this life."

Chapter 30

July 2012

My mother's voice crackles and distorts out the speaker of my old Mazda3, presently cruising eastbound on the UT-201 through downtown Salt Lake City.

"I can tell you're in the car," she says.

"I got a Bluetooth adapter."

"Some of the executives at the hospital use Bluetooth."

"Can you hear me clearly?"

"Kind of."

"This is the future, Mom. Happening now."

My mother pauses. "How are you feeling, dear?"

"Oh, I'm good."

"Just good?"

"I'm feeling a complicated series of things. But there's some good in there."

"Can you tell me more?"

"Maybe later," I pause. "How are you doing?"

"I'm doing really great."

"How's Daryl?"

"Funny you should ask."

"Oh?"

"We're no longer seeing each other."

"Oh."

"Yes."

"I'm sorry to hear that, I think?"

"These things happen," says my mom.

"Maybe it was for the best?"

"He broke it off."

"Really?"

"He said he didn't think I was sufficiently invested in the relationship."

"Was he right?"

My mother chuckles. "I still had no interest in marrying him, if that's what you mean. But he was nice to have around. I miss him."

"Seems like he wanted more."

"The urge to keep moving forward is an odd thing, isn't it? What about keeping something that's comfortable the same? Hell, how about allowing for a little regression from time to time?" My mother sighs. "We reached the natural end of the relationship's lifecycle, and that's just fine."

"I'm sorry."

"It's no matter, dear. Life is still exciting! Especially with the campaign coming up. I've had some dealings with Mayor Queenan. He knows I mean business."

"Good." I let my gaze drift across the horizon. Mountains draw slowly closer. The roads are quiet. I haven't hit traffic since Sacramento.

"You know, I think we often confuse career peaks for life peaks," says my mother. "It doesn't need to be that way. I've worked with some extraordinary people over the years. Intelligent. High-achieving. Egotistical. But I have more to offer."

"Sounds great, Mom."

"This is my fourth quarter, Lesley. There's still plenty of time on the clock, but this is where legacies are built."

"You know I'm terrible with sports analogies."

"I'm saying I have lots of experience, lots of connections, and for now, my body and mind are firing!"

"I love hearing that."

"Where are you now, dear?"

"Moving across Salt Lake City as we speak. After that it's eight hours through the mountains to Denver. Reception will be spotty."

"Be mindful of other drivers, please. The car accidents we'd see come through the ER—unbelievable."

"Of course." I pause. "There's something about driving east, you know? It's a whole lot less exciting than driving west."

"Don't say that."

"It does feel like a bit of a failure."

"I won't let you say you're a failure!"

"It's not that I'm a failure, exactly. The present circumstances just feel like I've missed something important."

"You've accomplished much!"

"Maybe, but I came out west planning to stay here forever. I was expecting a PhD and a cutting-edge job—now I'm headed back to Woodbury with neither."

"There are many good times still to be had. Trust me."

"Did you know that Utah invented the Pastrami Burger?"

"Mmm. I don't even know what that is."

"It's like a hamburger, but instead of ground beef you have pastrami."

"Interesting."

"Weird, isn't it?"

"Mmm."

"What?"

"You know, Lesley, it was difficult for me to hear that you were in the hospital."

"Only for a bit."

"This is something a mother never wants to hear about her child. Ever."

"I know, but you don't need to worry."

"But I do. And I will."

"I needed help and got it."

"It makes me wonder how I was as a parent—what I did well and what I could have done better."

"You were great, and I'm good. A little raw, but I feel good."

"And I hope you're able to protect your mental health. There will be challenges ahead, but you'll be great."

"I know there will be."

"I appreciate the support your father provided. He rose to the occasion."

I stay silent.

"He showed that he cared."

"Yeah."

"And that's a beautiful thing. We had a long talk on the phone after you were settled in San Jose. He's had his own challenges, you know? Patient care issues. A few lawsuits. This is stuff he all used to internalize. Maybe he still does, mostly. I don't know."

"Right."

"It was nice to talk to him."

"I'm getting close to the mountains, Mom."

"You need to go."

"I might lose reception."

"Focus on the road."

"I will."

"I love you, Lesley."

"I know."

"And?"

"I love you too."

CHAPTER 31

SEPTEMBER 2012

Byron's visits back to Woodbury were infrequent and usually brief. On this day, he drove his mother's Mercury Sable west on Highway 6 to see about a free bathtub via a Craigslist ad from a man named Luca. He turned south on Lakes Road, allowing quick glimpses of Walton Lake out the driver-side window. This time was different. Something big was happening.

Byron steered onto a forested residential side street and counted out house numbers, arriving at a dark wood colonial two-story with a wraparound porch and a dumpster in the driveway. He parked on the shoulder and exited the station wagon. Gravel crunched underfoot as Byron approached the house. He knocked on the front door, and a stocky man in a white t-shirt and jeans answered. He nodded. "You Byron?"

"That's right."

"Luca. Nice to meet you." He paused. "You want to see the bathtub?"

"Sure do. This is exciting."

"Just over there." Luca pointed to the garage at the left side of the house. He moved out the doorway and off the porch. "You're doing a reno?"

"An art project, actually."

Luca grunted and pulled on the garage door handle. The metal tracks groaned, and the door slid up to reveal a cluttered concrete space covered in dust. An oversized porcelain bathtub with clawed legs and an off-white finish stood in the corner. "There it is. You want it?"

"Amazing," said Byron. "This is perfect!"

"You got a truck?"

"It's magnificent."

"Sure is, but you got a truck to get it out of here?"

"Station wagon."

"Saw that, but you're not listening to me. Station wagon won't do the job."

"Seats fold down. I can manage."

"Whatever you say. I'm not liable if something gets fucked," said Luca. "Bring it up and we'll load it in."

Byron nodded and walked back to the Sable. He swung the steering wheel into a three-point turn, then twisted his neck and reversed slowly up the driveway.

Luca had his arms crossed. "You said you're some kind of artist?"

"That's right," said Byron.

"You do paintings?"

"All sorts of stuff. You ever heard of Marina Abramović?"

Luca shook his head.

"She does large-scale performative pieces. The best in the business. Some of the purest work I've ever seen."

"Right." Luca narrowed his eyes. "So that bathtub is yours if you can get it out of here. No charge."

"I have some rope in the trunk."

"You sure it's gonna hold?"

"Not my first time around the block, so to speak."

"Because the cops will pull you over if you're not careful."

"I'm not worried about that just yet."

"Whatever you say." Luca shrugged. "Go ahead and lift it on your end there."

Byron bent his back and wrapped his hands around the bathtub's legs, then shuffled with Luca toward the station wagon. Byron popped the latch. They tilted the bathtub ninety degrees and positioned its lip on the ledge of the trunk. They pushed forward.

"You got it?"

"Hold on," said Byron. "Leg is caught."

"You going to be able to handle this thing on your own?"

"Hold on," said Byron. He raised the leg up. "Push now."

The bathtub slid into the trunk and rode up against the backside of the front driver seat. Luca dropped his shoulder and rammed the tub's rear. "Still got a few inches out here. You going to be okay?"

"Sure thing," said Byron.

"You positive?"

"Yes, sir."

"Well then, all right." Luca held out a beefy hand. "Pleasure doing business with you."

"The pleasure is all mine."

Luca raised an eyebrow. He turned on his heel and walked back toward the house. Byron tied the latch of the trunk below the bumper and pulled the rope taut; the trunk stuck open a foot. He drove back past Walton Lake and along Highway 6, then exited into Woodbury and cruised the east end of town at a slow clip. Today was the first of the month. He had been monitoring potential sites for several days, and everything was coming together.

Byron pulled up to a red-brick house set against a sloping lawn of yellow brush. A familiar *For Rent* sign was stuck into the lawn just off the street, and a red Ford Fiesta was parked in the driveway. Byron felt a surge of excitement. He went to his mom's house and slept for several hours.

Byron returned to the red-brick house at midnight and parked on the side of the road. He popped the trunk and pulled. The tub hit the sidewalk with a deep clunk that reverberated across the quiet neighbourhood. Byron swore. He gripped its outer ridge and pulled in short bursts, dragging the tub into the backyard. Byron drove back to his mother's house. He slept late into the morning and awoke bursting with anticipatory adrenaline.

Byron returned to the red-brick house a final time. He crept around the east wall and unwound the garden hose, then squirted shampoo into the tub and opened the facet. The tub began to fill. Byron stripped naked. He stepped gingerly into the bathtub and started rubbing himself with soap bubbles. The water was chilly, and the light September breeze caused his skin to prickle and goose-bump. He had considered warming the water, but the resources at his disposal did not allow for it. This was just fine. After all, artistic constraint was essential to proper focus.

Byron continued to rub his naked body. His hair soaked up water and laid heavily on his shoulders. Occasionally, motorists slowed down and pointed. One even honked.

Why, thought Byron, was an action socially acceptable in one physical location like a bathroom and socially unacceptable in another physical location like a backyard? Why did nudity bring such enormous shame when we are all, at our purest, naked human beings? And why the fuck should one's actions be altered to conform to societal expectations, when those expectations were so damn malleable and this was our only living, breathing life—the one chance we all had to do something serious and important, but also joyful and fun? This was Byron's art. This was everything. His piece was called "Neighborhood Greeting"—his welcome to the new tenant.

Motorists continued to pass and stare. Byron counted over a hundred cars. His largest audience to date. The experience was exhilarating. He splashed water against his face and took it all in. A siren was audible in the distance. Byron dunked his head underwater and allowed himself a moment of uninterrupted quiet. The bathwater created a distortion of auditory space as his heart beat in slow, rhythmic pumps. He rose back into the outside air and saw a squad car parked on the side of the road. Byron jumped out of the bathtub and into a pair of sneakers. He made eye contact with a fit-looking police officer and took off running.

Byron worked his legs quickly. He moved past an elderly neighbour trimming a forsythia bush and hopped onto the sidewalk. His penis flapped against the inside of his thighs as the officer gave chase. Byron darted into a clump of trees. Twigs and branches ripped at his body. He moved back onto the sidewalk and turned his shoulder. The officer gained. Byron sped up, and his chest began to cramp. The officer lunged. Byron's legs disappeared from under him. He fell and hit the cement sidewalk. His hip and elbow ripped open. Blood poured. His body stung. The officer cuffed Byron and stuffed him into the cruiser. He sat naked, his back cold against the hard plastic seat. The piece was complete. He thought of the years spent working away at his craft, sacrificing finances, a proper social life, and potential romances. He thought of the boy he was, all those years ago, visiting the Guggenheim, and the man he had become. An artist. Currently naked in the back of a police cruiser, but an artist nonetheless. He knew that life was complex, and painful, and a real goddamn slog. The process, therefore, must be enjoyed with courage and grace, because being alive was all he had.

***

Murray crouched on the living room floor of his new rental among scattered cardboard boxes and discarded pieces of masking tape. First and last month's rent had been paid in full to a contractor associate of his father's, with plans to level the house and build an income duplex, pending municipal approval. The arrangement yielded a below-market rental rate away from his father's house for Murray and reasonable assurance that a trusted tenant would occupy the property until building could commence.

Murray's knees popped as he rose. He took long strides through the hallway and entered the kitchen. The sink was nestled into a peeling countertop. The refrigerator was bare.

The telephone rang, an aged rotary model left by an unknown party, shrill and rude in its manner of getting one's attention and paired with an archaic tape-style answering machine. Murray reached into the living room and lifted the phone's receiver. "Hello?"

"Good morning. I hope your day is off to a great start. Is this the homeowner I'm speaking with?" The voice was friendly and enthusiastic.

"No," said Murray. "I'm the new tenan—"

"Because today is your lucky day. I'm calling with a valuable opportunity to protect your property."

"It's not really my propert—"

"Does your landlord have insurance?"

"He mus—"

"Did you know that standard homeowner's insurance doesn't cover against many types of damage?" The voice was speaking quickly now. "For only dollars a month, you can secure your appliances against flooding, theft, wear and tear, and electrical malfunction."

"All the appliances here seem fine."

"Our policy covers refrigerators, washing machines, dryers, barbecues—heck the world could be ending, and we'd still be here for you."

"The appliances don't seem to have any issues."

"That's the beauty of insurance: it's there when you need it." The voice paused. "What's your name?"

"Murray Buchanan."

"What do you do for a living, Murray?"

"I work in parking enforcement."

"And you just moved in?"

"That's right."

"Well, you tell the homeowner to give me a call. It would mean a lot if you can do that for me, Murr—"

The line went dead. Murray laid the receiver in the cradle and lifted it back to his ear. There was no dial tone, only the vacant sound of quiet air. He pressed firmly on the switch hook several times with no effect. Murray scratched his scalp, just recently showing the earliest signs of thinning hair. He turned his gaze to the backyard, and his body tightened.

A large, bright white bathtub sat between a sickly spruce tree and a decomposing flower box. Murray slid open the back door and moved across the lawn. He ran his hand along the tub's gold-plated spout and ornate claw legs. It had not been present the previous day, and there was no proper way to account for its sudden appearance.

Murray was perplexed. He reentered the house and moved into the living room, then sunk into a chair and opened his parking enforcement employee handbook, brushing up on less-referenced material. Soon, he began nodding in and out of sleep and some time later returned to the kitchen, pulling a smudged metallic cooking pot from the cupboard and gazing at his distorted reflection as he turned on the faucet. Murray filled the pot with water and positioned it on a rear burner. Sirens could be heard in the distance. Murray looked to the backyard again. His pulse quickened. The large, bright white bathtub was full of soapy water. Inside crouched a long-haired man waist deep in suds, his scrawny arms contorting as he scrubbed the small of his back. The man was familiar, though unplaceable. Murray crossed the kitchen and opened the back door. He watched the man's eye bulge and a police officer run into the backyard, then the man vault onto the grass, dart across the yard and over a sagging chain link fence, then down the street, sopping wet and entirely without clothing, the police officer in quick pursuit. Murray saluted the officer and watched both men disappear. He rolled his sleeves past his elbows and dropped an arm into the water. He removed the drain plug. The water gurgled and flowed out onto the lawn.

Murray stood in silence. The bathtub's appearance, and the appearance of the mysterious man, was curious. He made a mental note to ask his father's associate if he could think of any reason for there to be a bathtub in the backyard, or a naked man, or a naked man in a bathtub.

Murray stared deeper. The bathtub was objectively beautiful, though its presence in a residential backyard was a sure bylaw violation. His mind hummed. The house would be torn down at an indeterminate point in the near future. The upstairs bathroom was barely functional. His father's associate had acknowledged as much apologetically. This tub—whatever its origin—was an obvious upgrade and tremendous opportunity for Murray to roll up his sleeves and channel some goddamn practicality. This was meaning. This was purpose. Its appearance was serendipitous. Perhaps it was a sign—possibly even divine direction. Murray thought briefly of his mother and Don Jr. It was all decided. He locked into tunnel vision.

Murray pulled at the tub and dragged it toward the back door. Little tufts of dirt and grass clung to its legs, slowing his progress and causing him to curse under his breath. He manoeuvred into the kitchen, withdrawing to the living room and returning with an armful of unpacked bed sheets to be layered between the floor and the tub's curved legs. Murray pushed toward the staircase.

The water in the kitchen had begun to boil, and the pot's lid clanged and spit little bits of piping hot spray around the stove. Murray reached the staircase and moved to the front of the bathtub. He dropped his hands behind him and grasped at the thin porcelain ridge, then lifted and moved forward. The lower legs hit the bottom stair. Murray rocked back and forth and jumped the legs to the next step, repeating the movement several times with growing proficiency and fatigue. He grimaced. Muscles untested since baseball weight-training a half-decade earlier sprang back into use.

The pot of water boiled furiously. Plumes of steam curled toward the ceiling, and a smoke detector began emitting shrill, unconscionable beeps. Murray grunted and abandoned the tub wedged diagonally between the stairway and the wall. The beeps were deafening and horrible. He shifted the pot onto an unused element and cleared the steam with wild waves of his hands. The piercing beeps persisted.

Murray returned to the stairwell as the telephone rang. He turned and dashed into the living room. "Hello?"

"Good morning! Is this the homeowner?"

"Can't talk now," said Murray.

"We've been having some connectivity issues this morning, but your call is important to us. Is there another time that is mo—"

The line went dead. Murray grunted and climbed back up the staircase, squeezing around the bathtub and clutching its ridge. He rocked the legs up another stair. Sweat dripped from his face as the smoke alarm cut out, leaving the house in a state of odd, buzzing silence. He exhaled. His body loosened.

Murray pulled higher. There was a loud knock at the door—the house's walls shook. He wedged the tub into the stairway for a second time and manoeuvred around its rigid frame. He descended several steps. Another knock, then a thud, and a sliding noise signalled immediate and irreversible trouble. Murray turned and braced himself as two hundred pounds of finely crafted porcelain slammed into his jaw.

He lay awkwardly pinned. Ringing vibrated the hallway. Murray kept still, disoriented. A loud crack from the mail slot focused his attention, and he craned his neck to see a laminated card settle onto the ground, partially upright, with the phrase *Mary Anthony for Town Trustee* printed in large lettering. The ringing became louder and more pronounced before quitting outright. A dull click and a beep sounded, then the mechanical noise of analog tape brought a friendly and enthusiastic voice floating in from the living room. He struggled, unable to free himself. Murray hoped the voice would call back.

THE END

About the Author

Conrad Smyth

Conrad Smyth is a Canadian writer. His work has been featured in *The Malahat Review*, *Torontoist*, and *The Feathertale Review*, among other publications. *Everything Started in the Bathtub* is his first novel.